Fantastic Four

NEW YORK'S FINEST

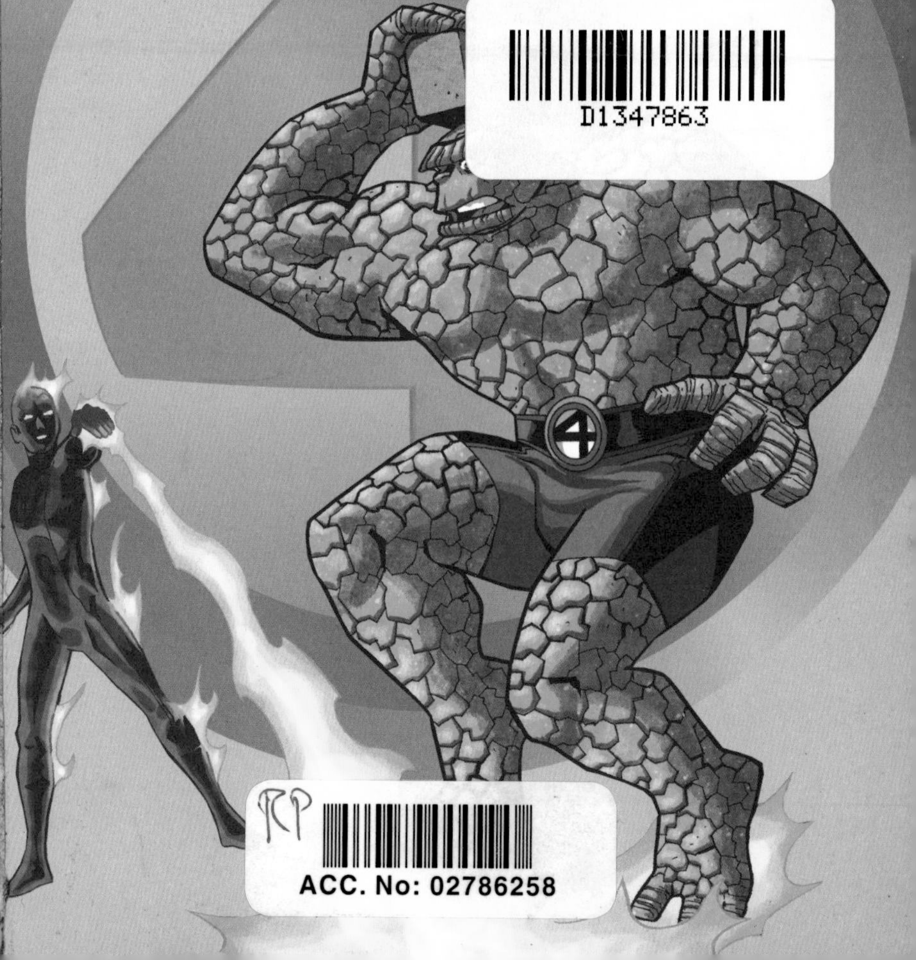

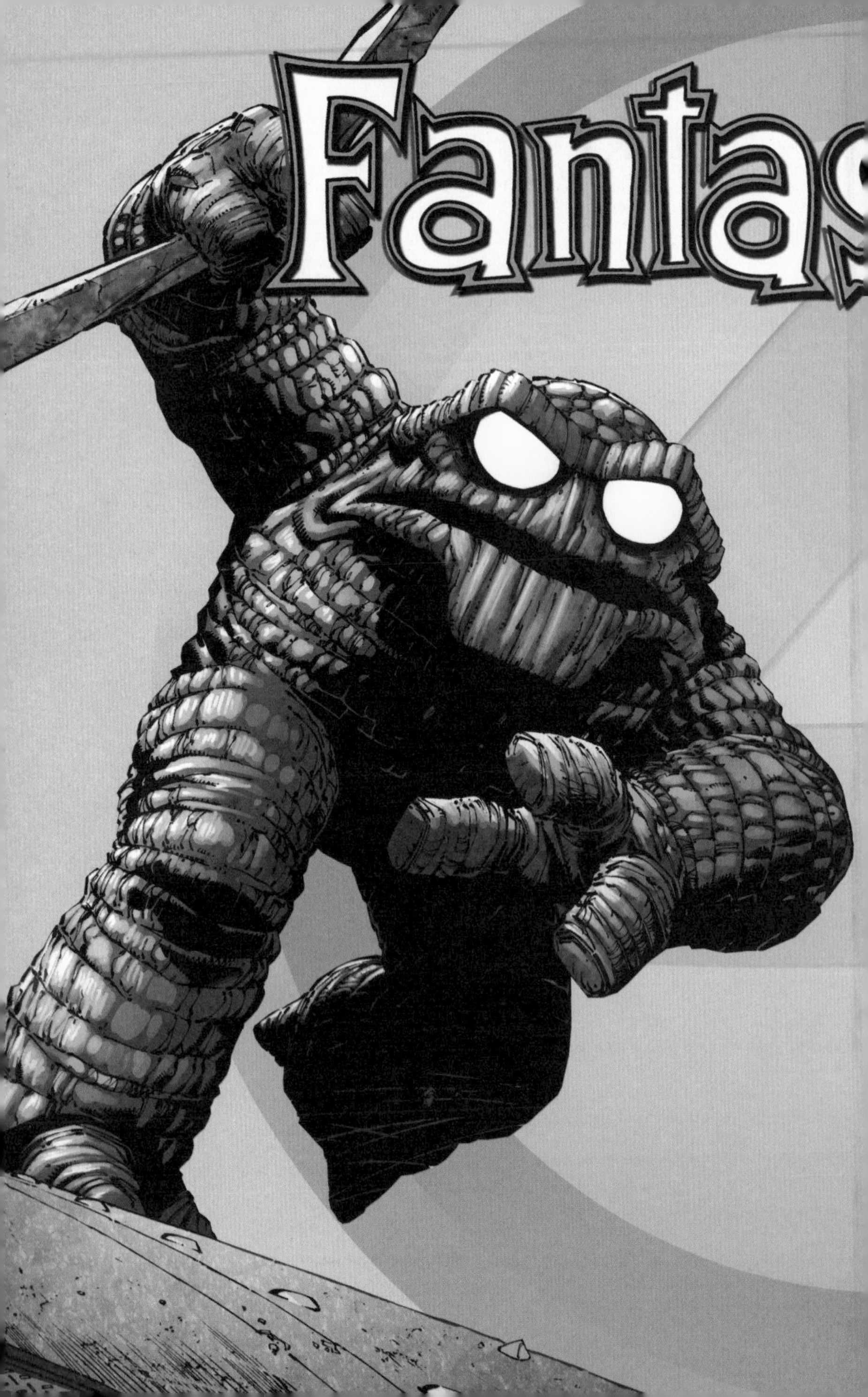
Fantas

tic Four

NEW YORK'S FINEST

Writer:
Paul Tobin
Pencilers:
David Hahn & David Nakayama
Inkers:
David Hahn, Kris Justice & Cory Hamscher

Colorists: **Guillem Mari & Wil Quintana**
Letterer: **Blambot's Nate Piekos**
Cover Art: **Tom Grummett, Graham Nolan,**
Dennis Calero, Terry Pallot & Brad Anderson
Consulting Editor: **Mark Paniccia**
Editor: **Nathan Cosby**
Special Thanks to MacKenzie Cadenhead

Collection Editor: **Jennifer Grünwald**
Editorial Assistant: **Alex Starbuck**
Assistant Editors: **Cory Levine & John Denning**
Editor, Special Projects: **Mark D. Beazley**
Senior Editor, Special Projects: **Jeff Youngquist**
Senior Vice President of Sales: **David Gabriel**
Vice President of Creative: **Tom Marvelli**

Editor in Chief: **Joe Quesada**
Publisher: **Dan Buckley**

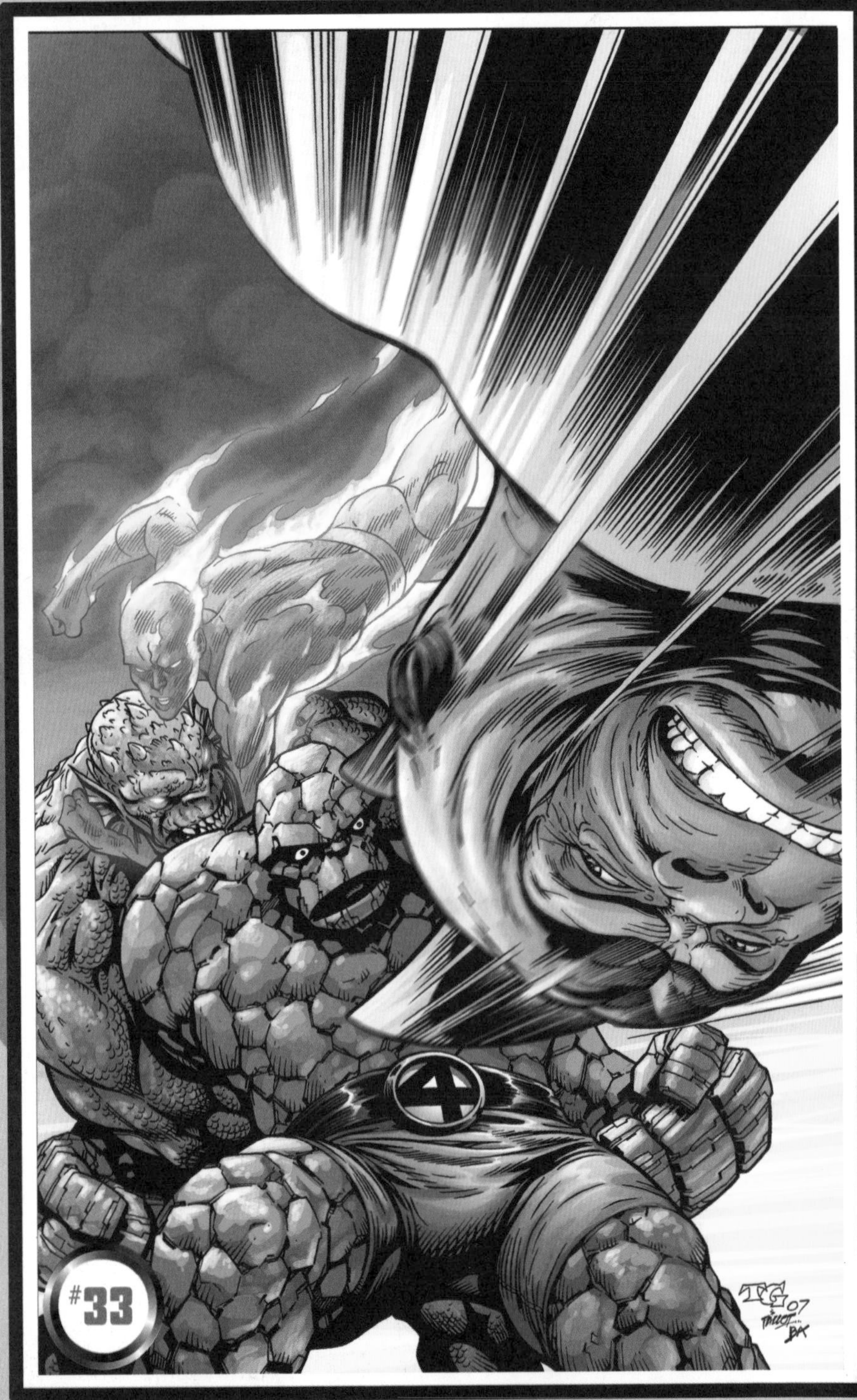
#33

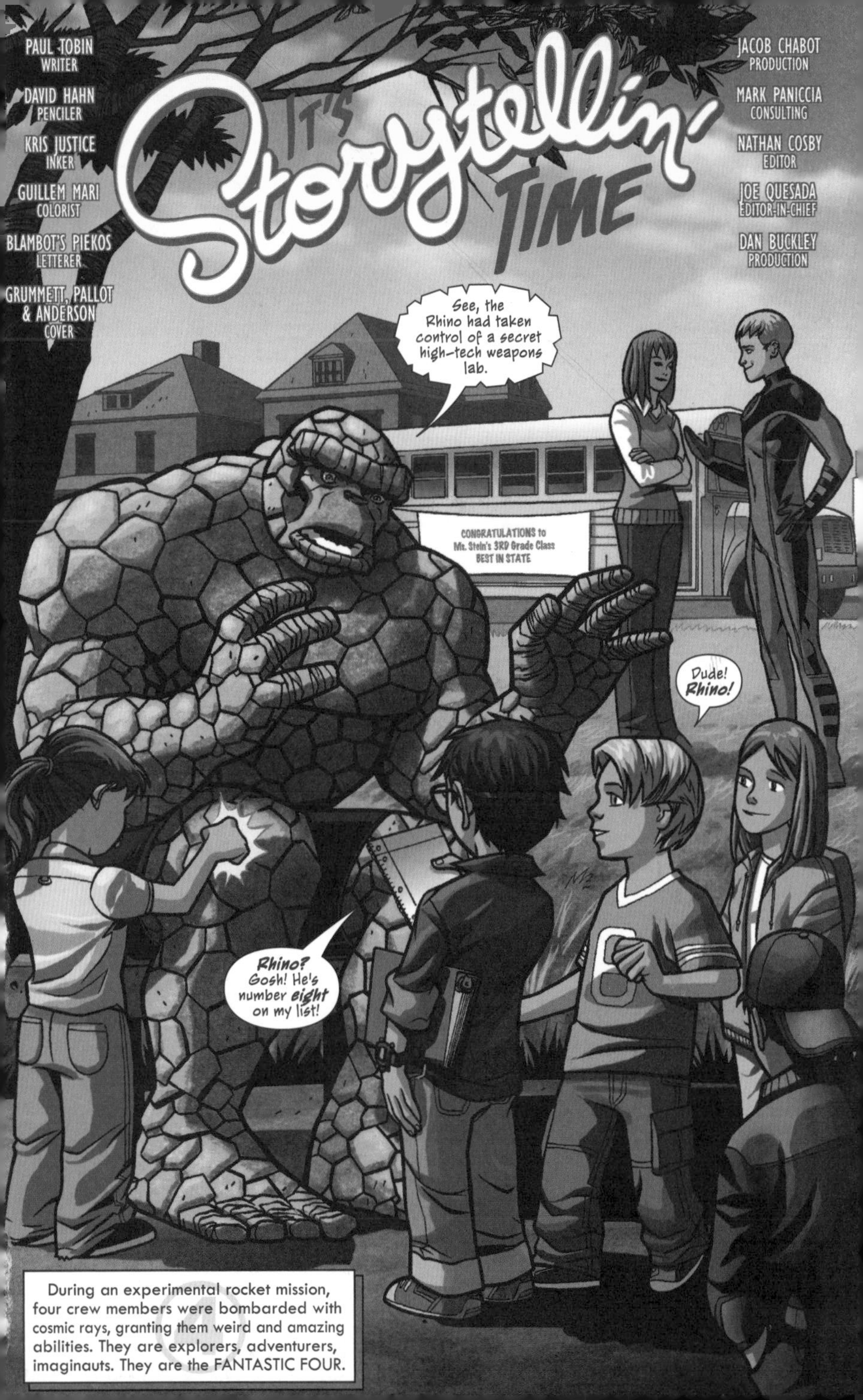
It's Storytellin' Time
PAUL TOBIN WRITER
DAVID HAHN PENCILER
KRIS JUSTICE INKER
GUILLEM MARI COLORIST
BLAMBOT'S PIEKOS LETTERER
GRUMMETT, PALLOT & ANDERSON COVER
JACOB CHABOT PRODUCTION
MARK PANICCIA CONSULTING
NATHAN COSBY EDITOR
JOE QUESADA EDITOR-IN-CHIEF
DAN BUCKLEY PRODUCTION
See, the Rhino had taken control of a secret high-tech weapons lab.
CONGRATULATIONS to Ms. Stein's 3RD Grade Class BEST IN STATE
Dude! Rhino!
Rhino? Gosh! He's number eight on my list!
During an experimental rocket mission, four crew members were bombarded with cosmic rays, granting them weird and amazing abilities. They are explorers, adventurers, imaginauts. They are the FANTASTIC FOUR.

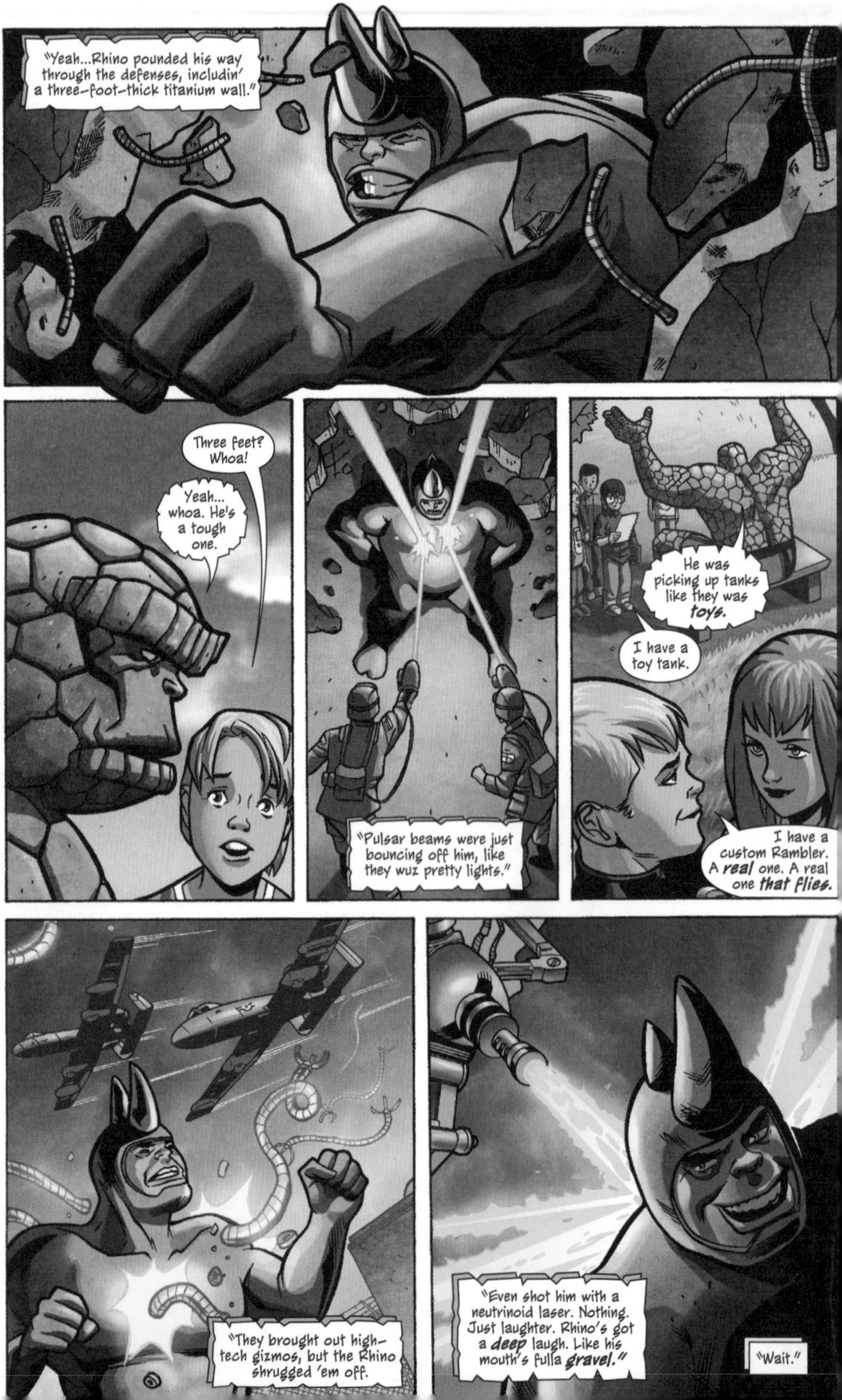
"Yeah...Rhino pounded his way through the defenses, includin' a three-foot-thick titanium wall."
Three feet? Whoa!
Yeah... whoa. He's a tough one.
"Pulsar beams were just bouncing off him, like they wuz pretty lights."
He was picking up tanks like they was *toys.*
I have a toy tank.
I have a custom Rambler. A *real* one. A real one *that flies.*
"They brought out high-tech gizmos, but the Rhino shrugged 'em off.
"Even shot him with a neutrinoid laser. Nothing. Just laughter. Rhino's got a *deep* laugh. Like his mouth's fulla *gravel.*"
"Wait."

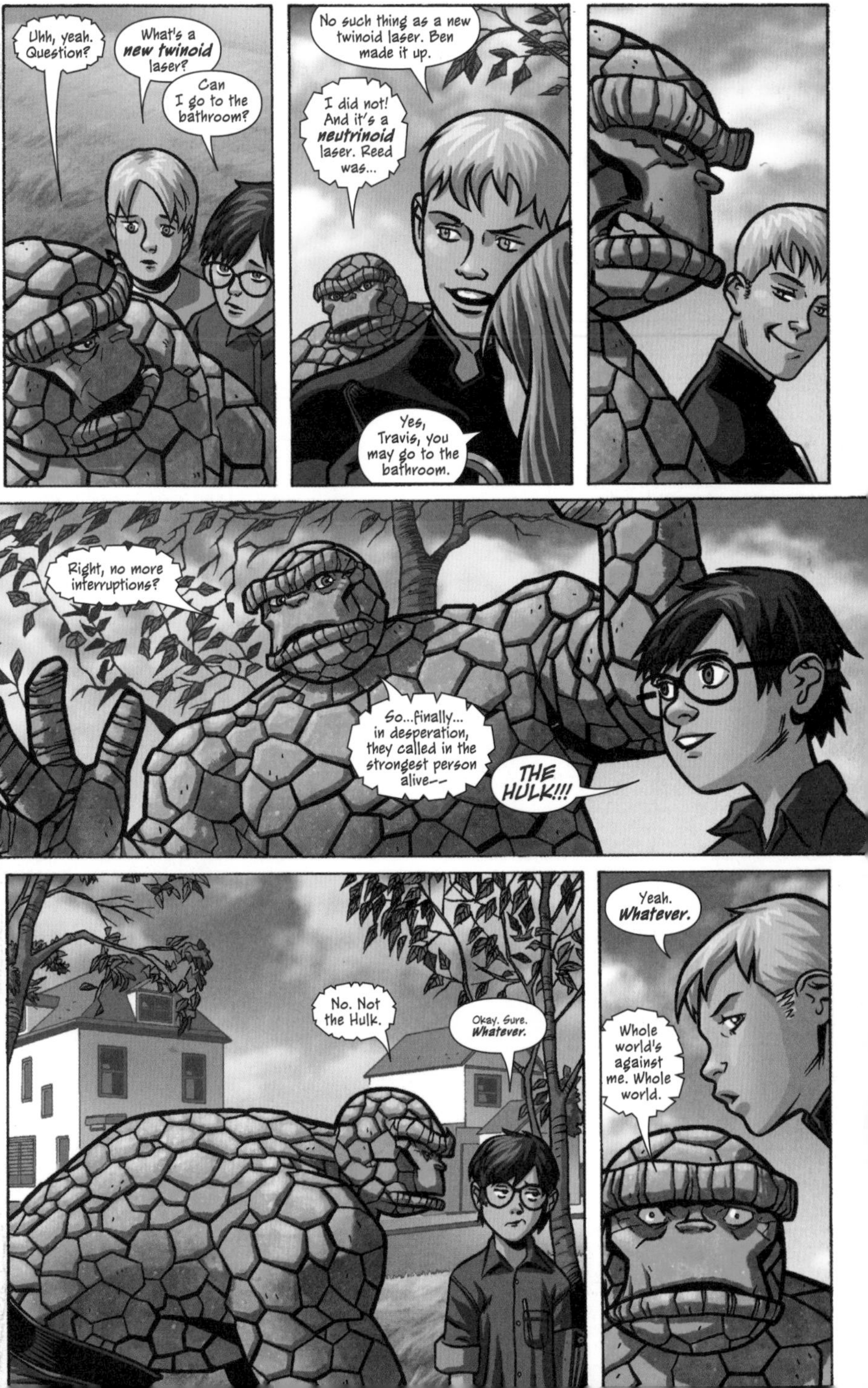

Uhh, yeah. Question?
What's a **new twinoid** laser?
Can I go to the bathroom?
No such thing as a new twinoid laser. Ben made it up.
I did not! And it's a **neutrinoid** laser. Reed was...
Yes, Travis, you may go to the bathroom.
Right, no more interruptions?
So...finally... in desperation, they called in the strongest person alive--
THE HULK!!!
No. Not the Hulk.
Okay. Sure. **Whatever.**
Yeah. **Whatever.**
Whole world's against me. Whole world.

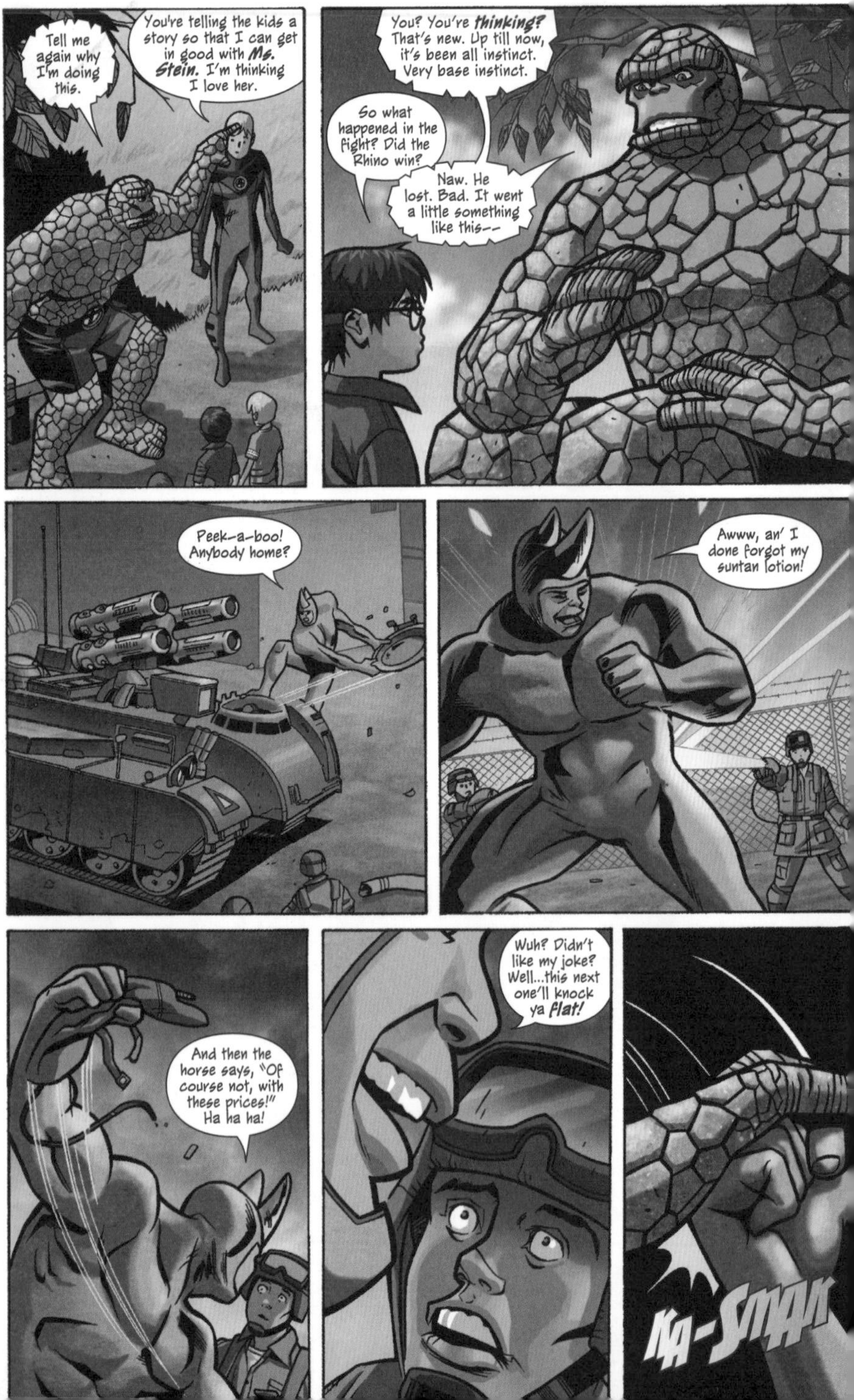
Tell me again why I'm doing this.
You're telling the kids a story so that I can get in good with *Ms. Stein.* I'm thinking I love her.
You? You're *thinking?* That's new. Up till now, it's been all instinct. Very base instinct.
So what happened in the fight? Did the Rhino win?
Naw. He lost. Bad. It went a little something like this--
Peek-a-boo! Anybody home?
Awww, an' I done forgot my suntan lotion!
And then the horse says, "Of course not, with these prices!" Ha ha ha!
Wuh? Didn't like my joke? Well...this next one'll knock ya *flat!*
KA-SMAK

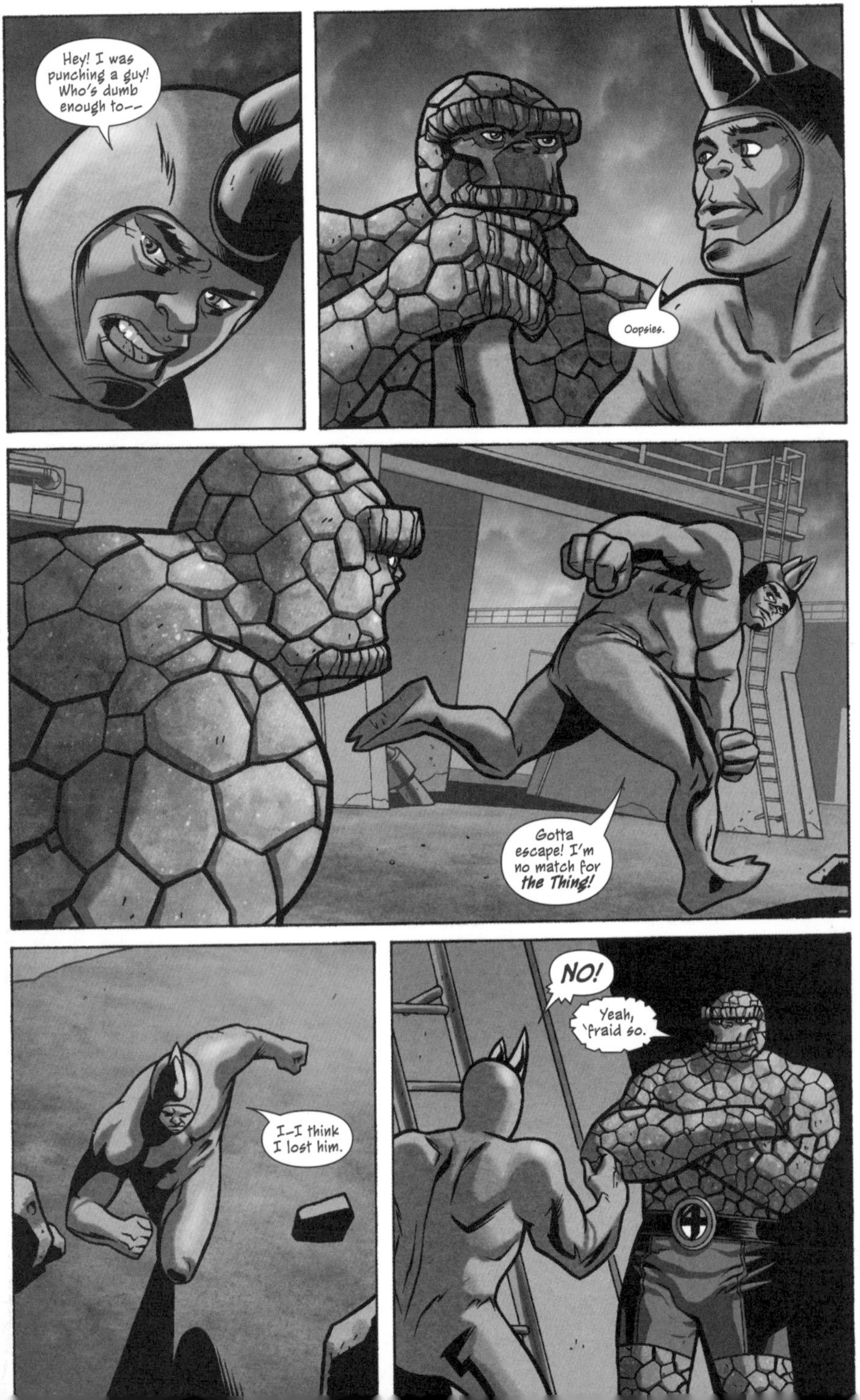
Hey! I was punching a guy! Who's dumb enough to--
Oopsies.
Gotta escape! I'm no match for *the Thing!*
I-I think I lost him.
NO!
Yeah, 'fraid so.

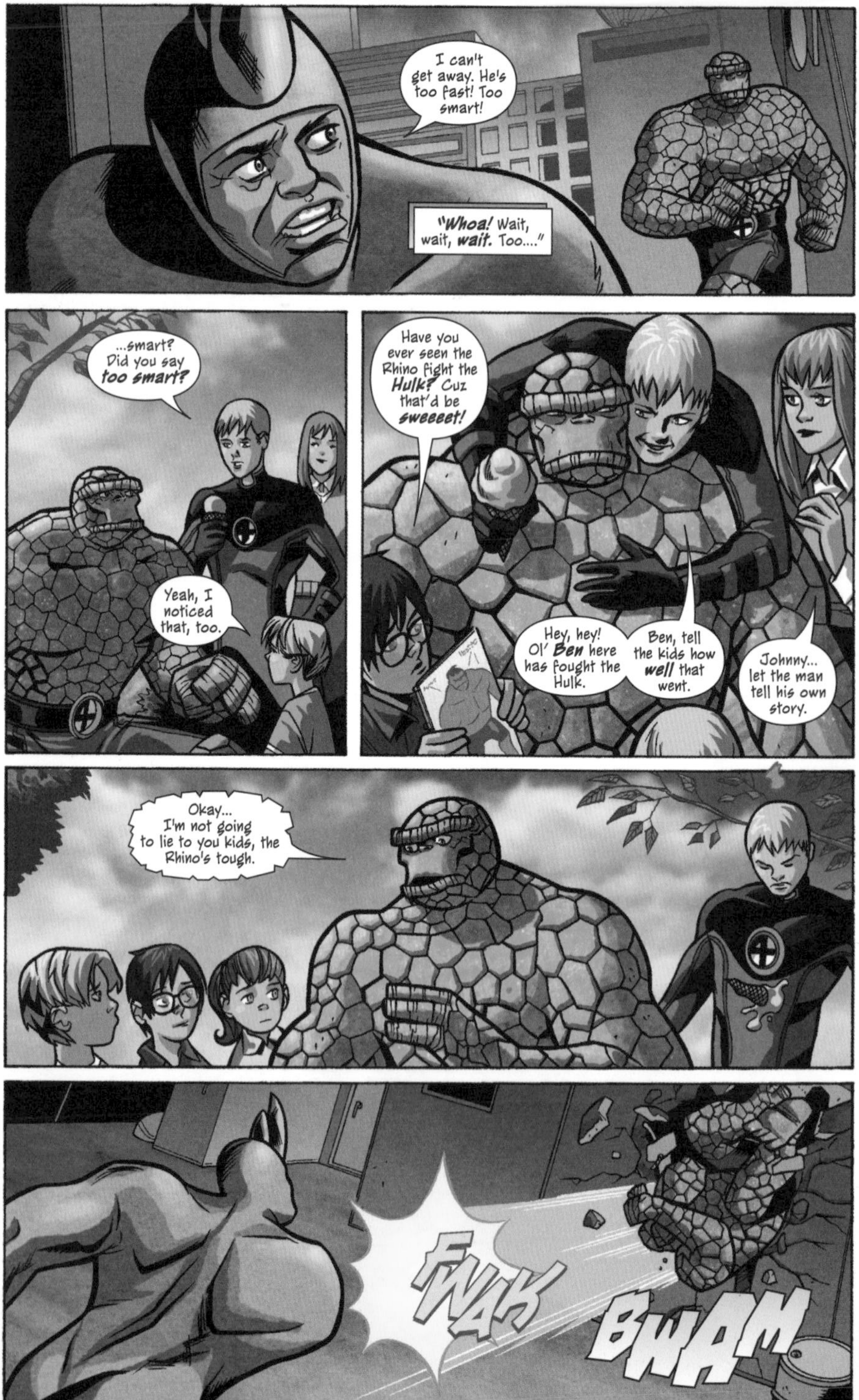

I can't get away. He's too fast! Too smart!
"Whoa! Wait, wait, wait. Too...."
...smart? Did you say too smart?
Yeah, I noticed that, too.
Have you ever seen the Rhino fight the Hulk? Cuz that'd be sweeeet!
Hey, hey! Ol' Ben here has fought the Hulk.
Ben, tell the kids how well that went.
Johnny... let the man tell his own story.
Okay... I'm not going to lie to you kids, the Rhino's tough.
FWAK
BWAM

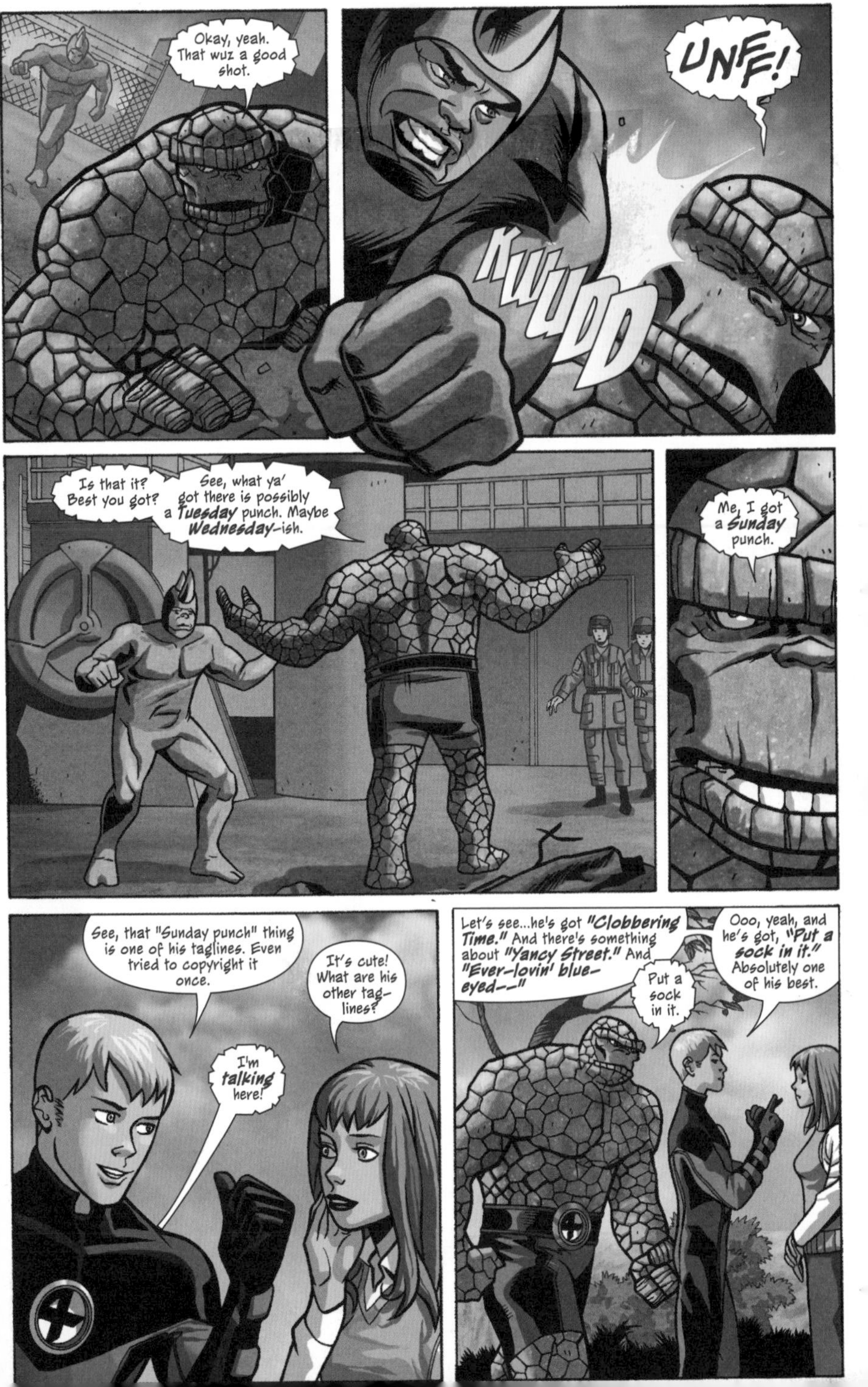

Okay, yeah. That wuz a good shot.
UNFF!
KWUDD
Is that it? Best you got?
See, what ya' got there is possibly a *Tuesday* punch. Maybe *Wednesday*-ish.
Me, I got a *Sunday* punch.
See, that "Sunday punch" thing is one of his taglines. Even tried to copyright it once.
It's cute! What are his other taglines?
I'm *talking* here!
Let's see...he's got *"Clobbering Time."* And there's something about *"Yancy Street."* And *"Ever-lovin' blue-eyed--"*
Put a sock in it.
Ooo, yeah, and he's got, *"Put a sock in it."* Absolutely one of his best.

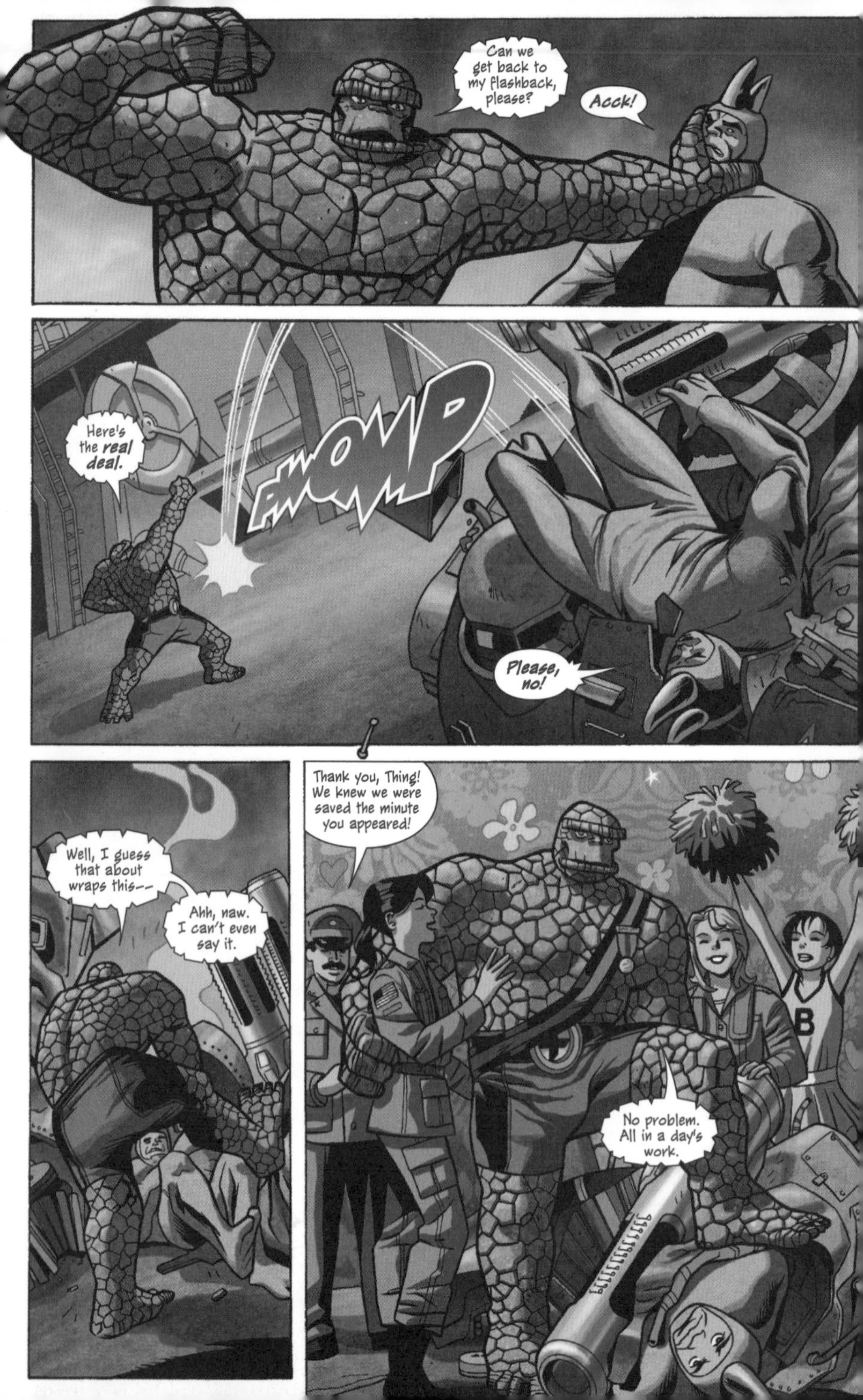
Can we get back to my flashback, please?
Acck!
Here's the real deal.
PWOMP
Please, no!
Well, I guess that about wraps this--
Ahh, naw. I can't even say it.
Thank you, Thing! We knew we were saved the minute you appeared!
No problem. All in a day's work.

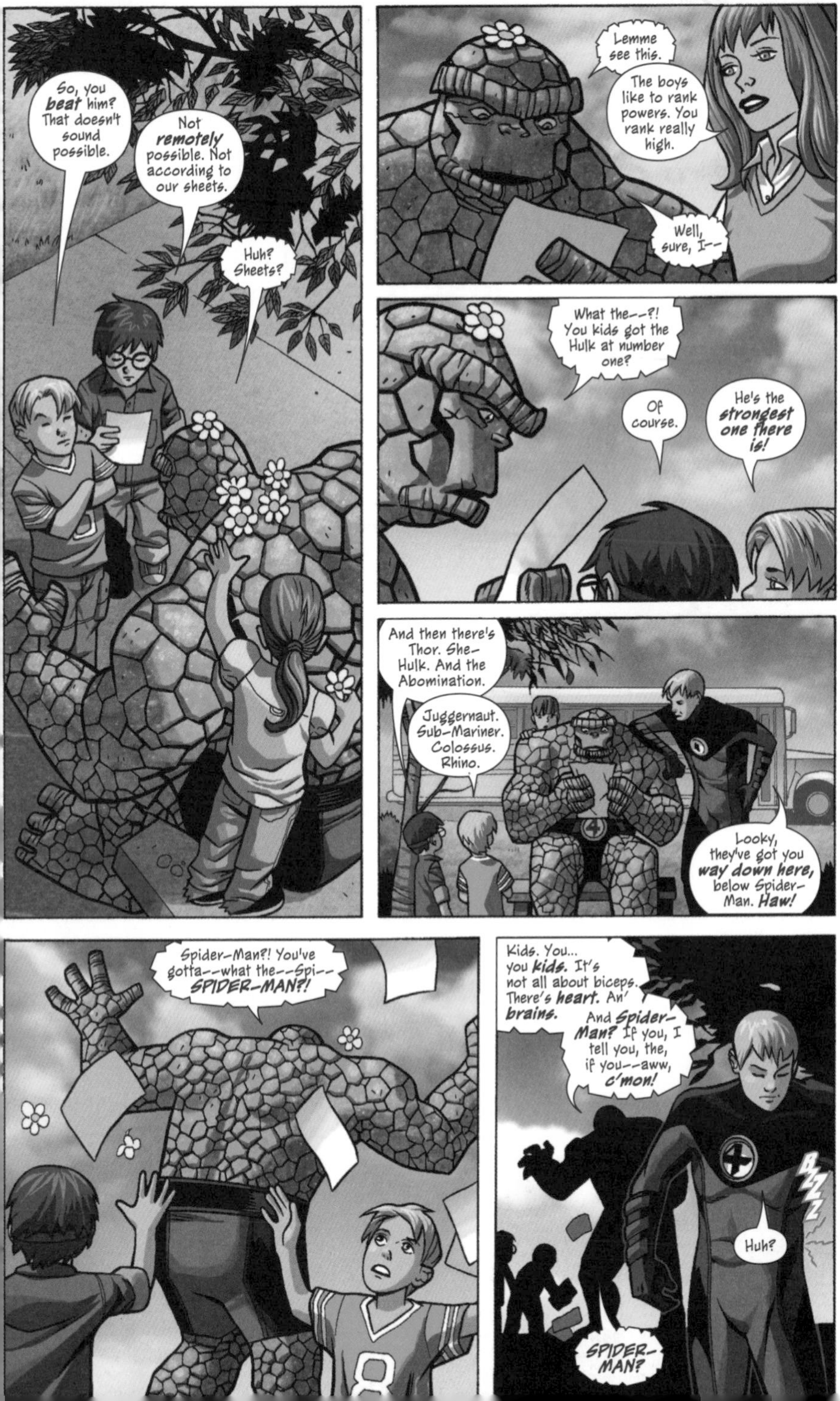
So, you beat him? That doesn't sound possible.
Not remotely possible. Not according to our sheets.
Huh? Sheets?
Lemme see this.
The boys like to rank powers. You rank really high.
Well, sure, I--
What the--?! You kids got the Hulk at number one?
Of course.
He's the strongest one there is!
And then there's Thor. She-Hulk. And the Abomination.
Juggernaut. Sub-Mariner. Colossus. Rhino.
Looky, they've got you way down here, below Spider-Man. Haw!
Spider-Man?! You've gotta--what the--Spi--SPIDER-MAN?!
Kids. You... you kids. It's not all about biceps. There's heart. An' brains.
And Spider-Man? If you, I tell you, the, if you--aww, c'mon!
BZZZ
Huh?
SPIDER-MAN?

Ben, hush.

Spidey ain't gone toe-to-toe with the Hulk, I'll tell ya' that!

He simply ain't.

Ben, shut up.

An' the Sub-Mariner outta water is a *pushover*. Colossus *looks* snazzy, but I breeze past him in pure power. And Spidey? My Aunt Petunia could--

Ben! *Shut it!*

What?

The Abomination. Downtown.

He's fighting Firestar.

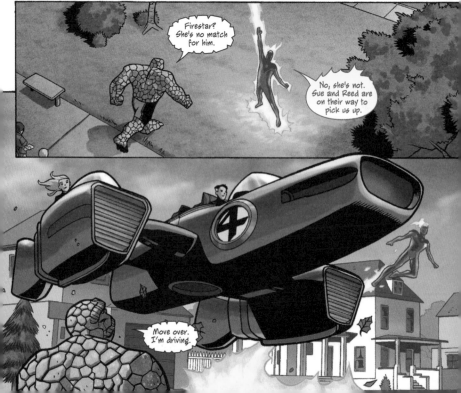

Firestar? She's no match for him.

No, she's not. Sue and Reed are on their way to pick us up.

Move over. I'm driving.

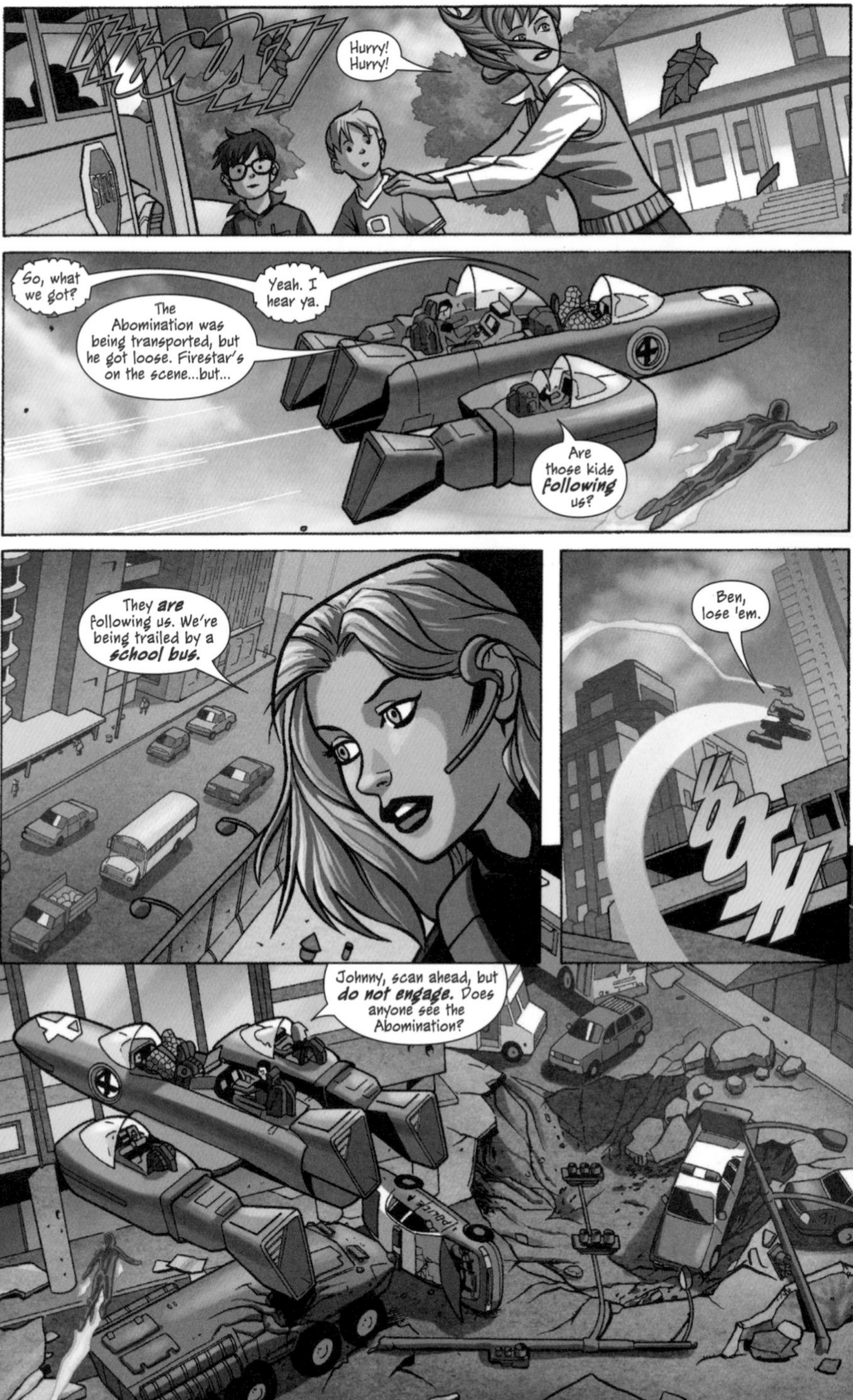
Hurry!
Hurry!
So, what we got?
Yeah. I hear ya.
The Abomination was being transported, but he got loose. Firestar's on the scene...but...
Are those kids *following* us?
They *are* following us. We're being trailed by a *school bus.*
Ben, lose 'em.
Johnny, scan ahead, but *do not engage.* Does anyone see the Abomination?

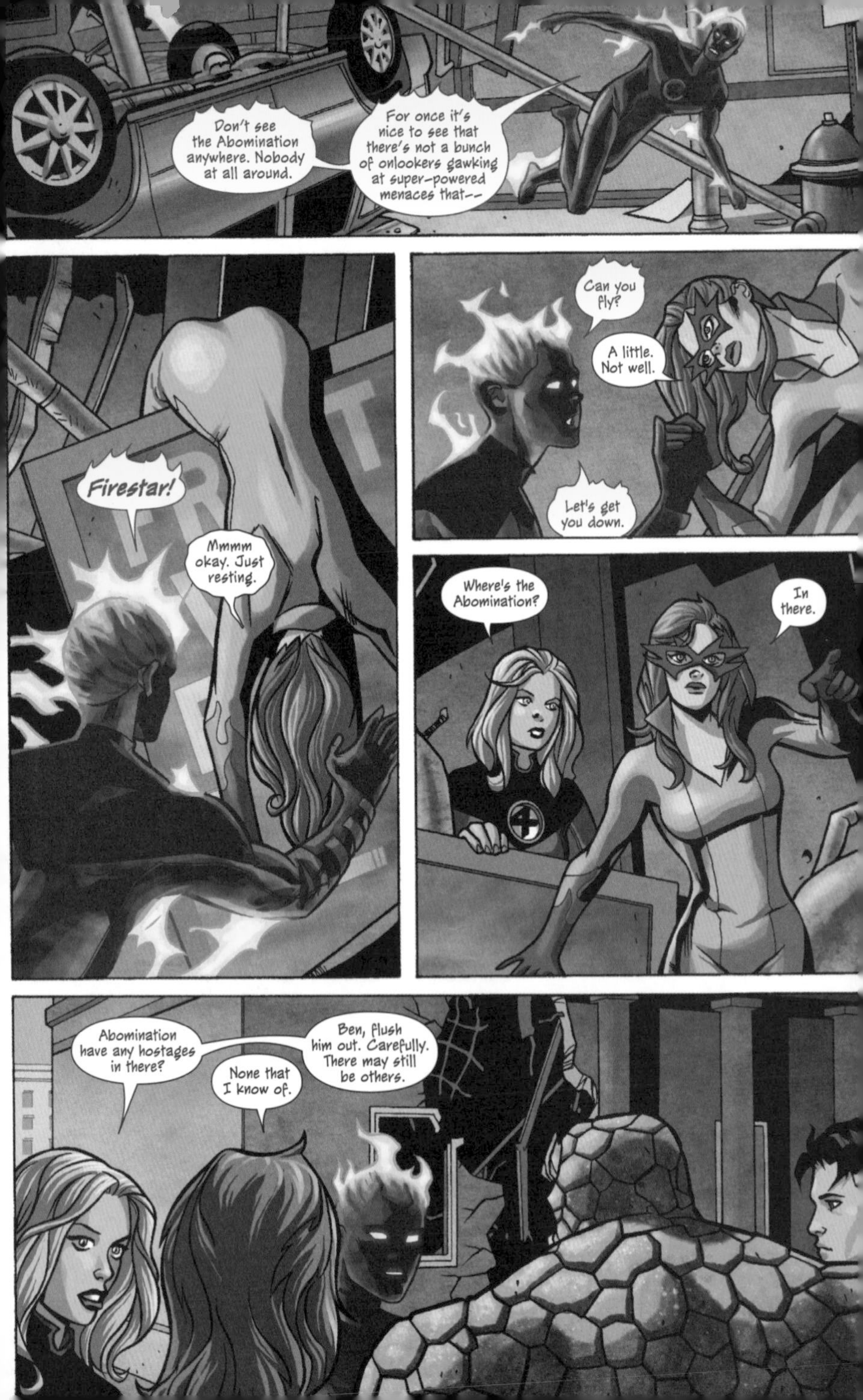

Don't see the Abomination anywhere. Nobody at all around.
For once it's nice to see that there's not a bunch of onlookers gawking at super-powered menaces that--
Firestar!
Mmmm okay. Just resting.
Can you fly?
A little. Not well.
Let's get you down.
Where's the Abomination?
In there.
Abomination have any hostages in there?
None that I know of.
Ben, flush him out. Carefully. There may still be others.

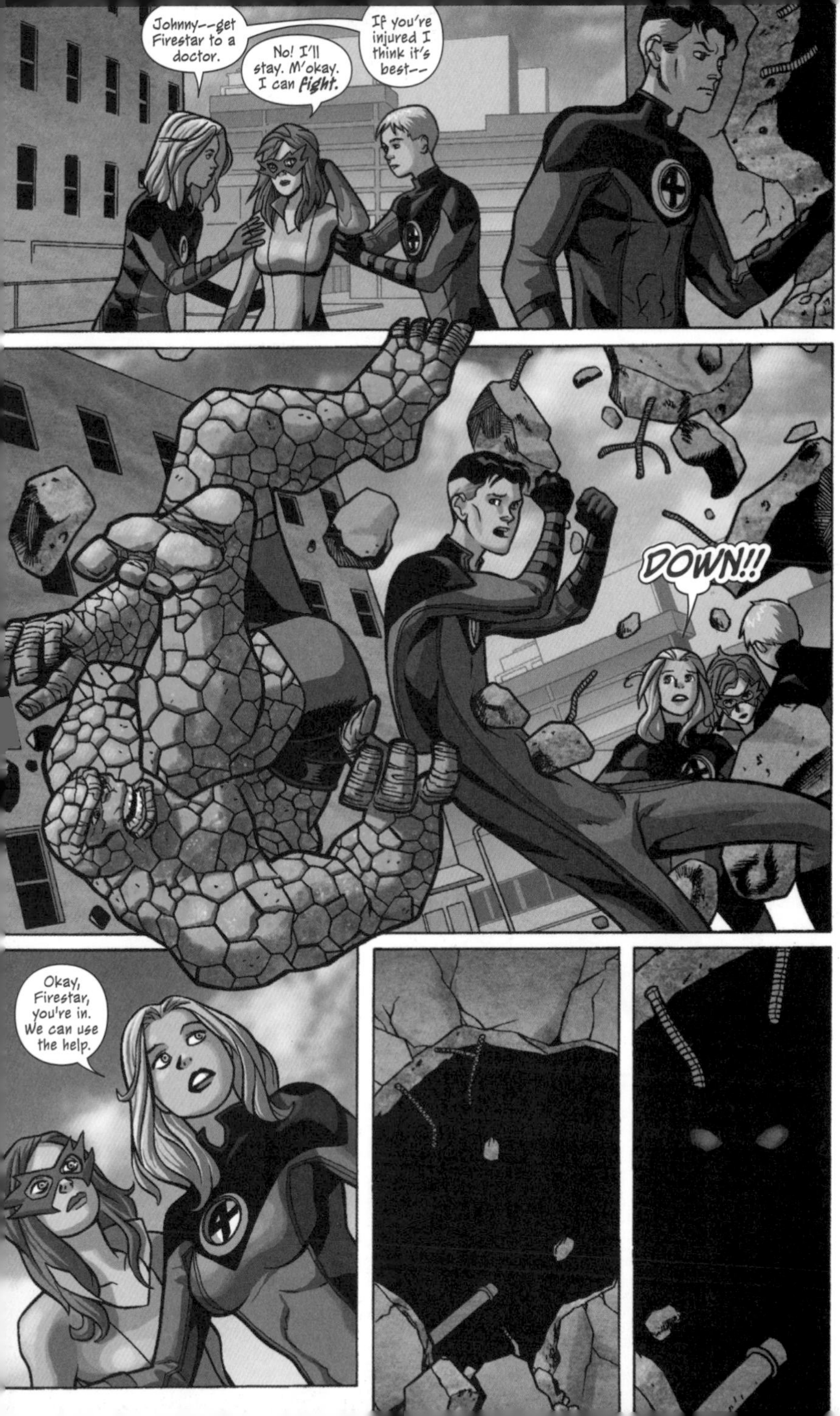

Johnny--get Firestar to a doctor.
No! I'll stay. M'okay. I can fight.
If you're injured I think it's best--
DOWN!!
Okay, Firestar, you're in. We can use the help.

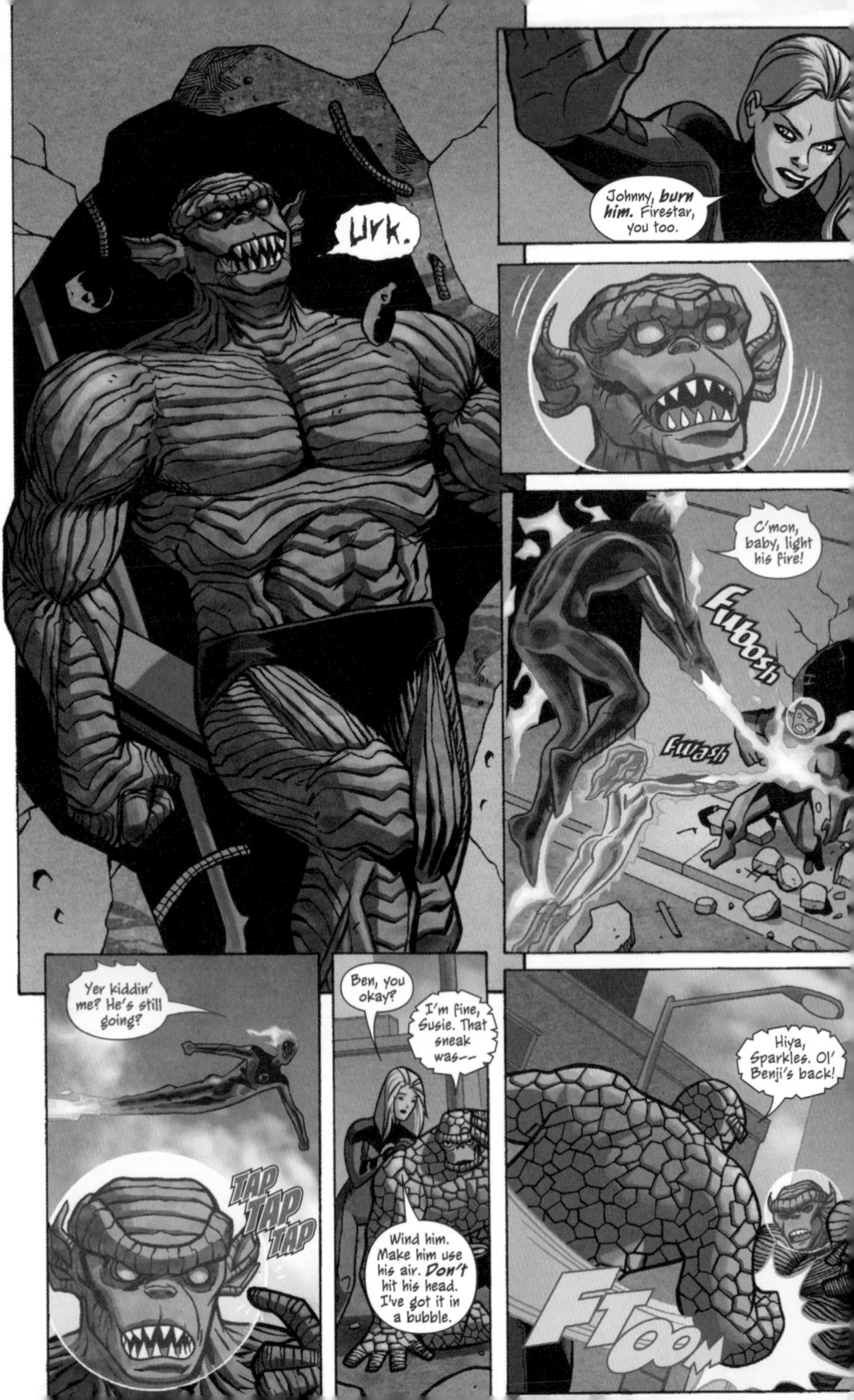
Urk.
Johnny, burn him. Firestar, you too.
C'mon, baby, light his fire!
Fuboosh
Fwash
Yer kiddin' me? He's still going?
TAP TAP TAP
Ben, you okay?
I'm fine, Susie. That sneak was--
Wind him. Make him use his air. Don't hit his head. I've got it in a bubble.
Hiya, Sparkles. Ol' Benji's back!
FTOOM

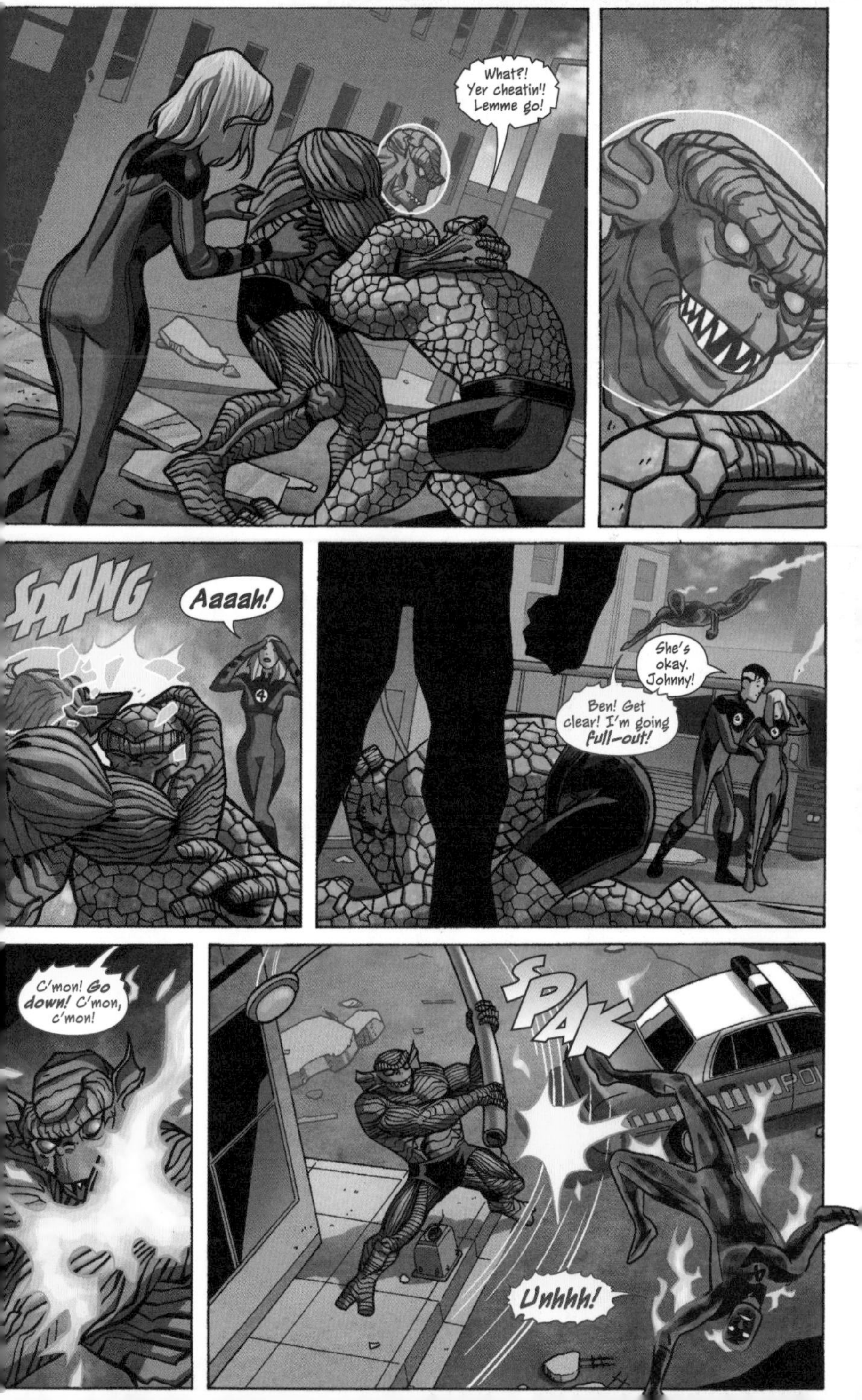

What?! Yer cheatin'! Lemme go!
SPANG
Aaaah!
She's okay. Johnny!
Ben! Get clear! I'm going full-out!
C'mon! Go down! C'mon, c'mon!
SPAK
Unhhh!

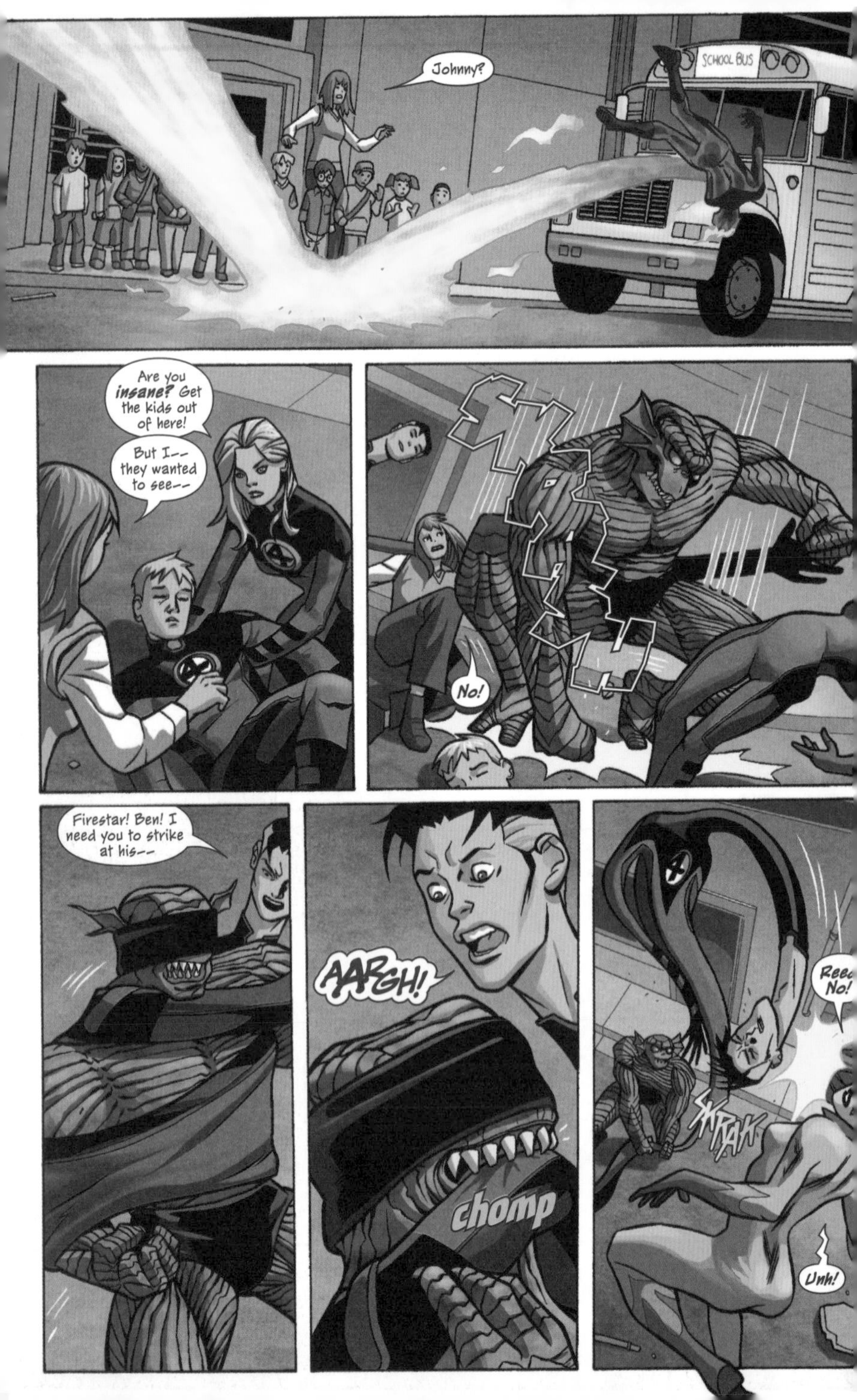
Johnny?
SCHOOL BUS
Are you insane? Get the kids out of here!
But I-- they wanted to see--
No!
Firestar! Ben! I need you to strike at his--
AARGH!
chomp
SKRAK
Unh!

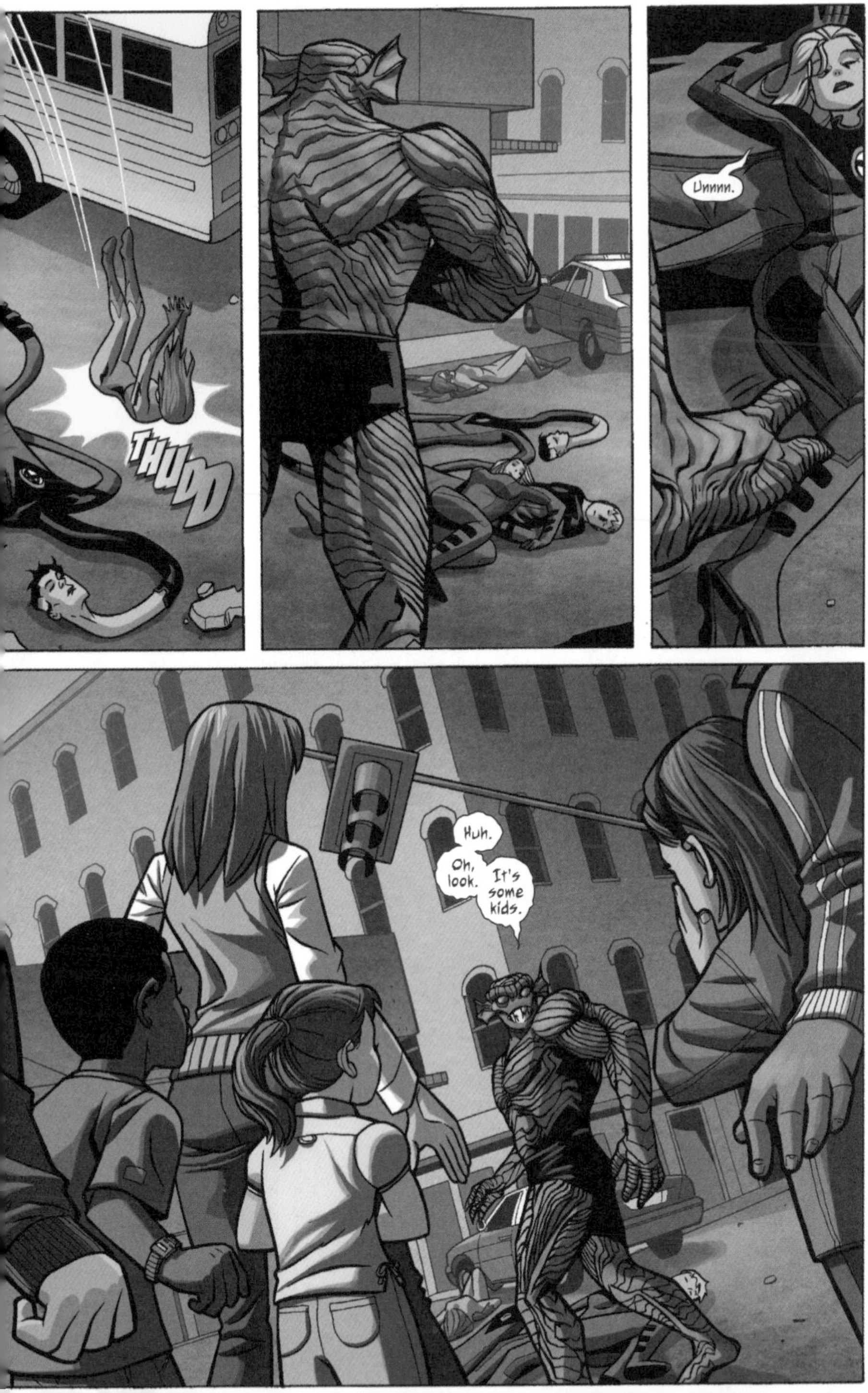
THUDD
Unnnn.
Huh.
Oh, look.
It's some kids.

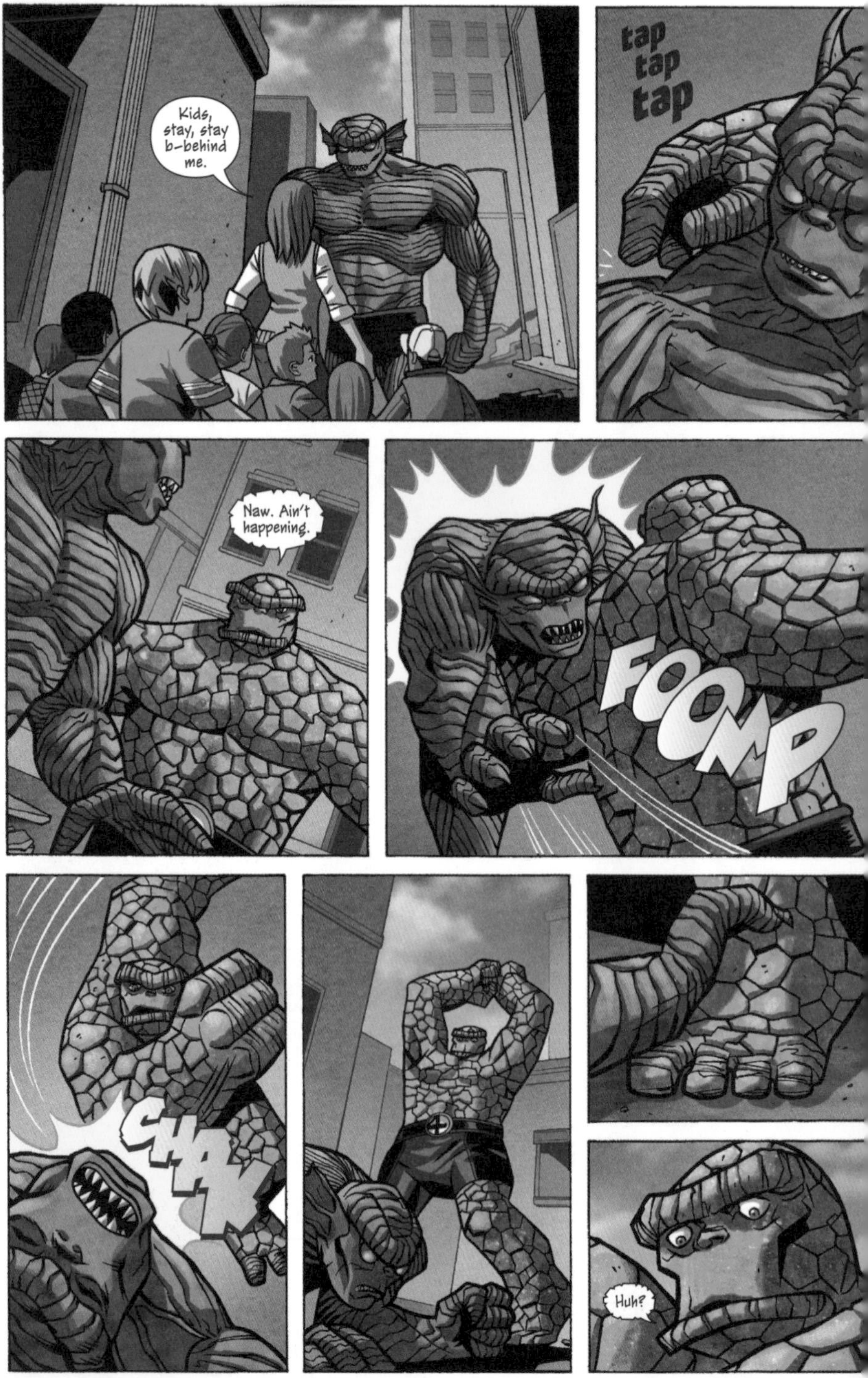
Kids, stay, stay b-behind me.
tap tap tap
Naw. Ain't happening.
FOOMP
CHAK
Huh?

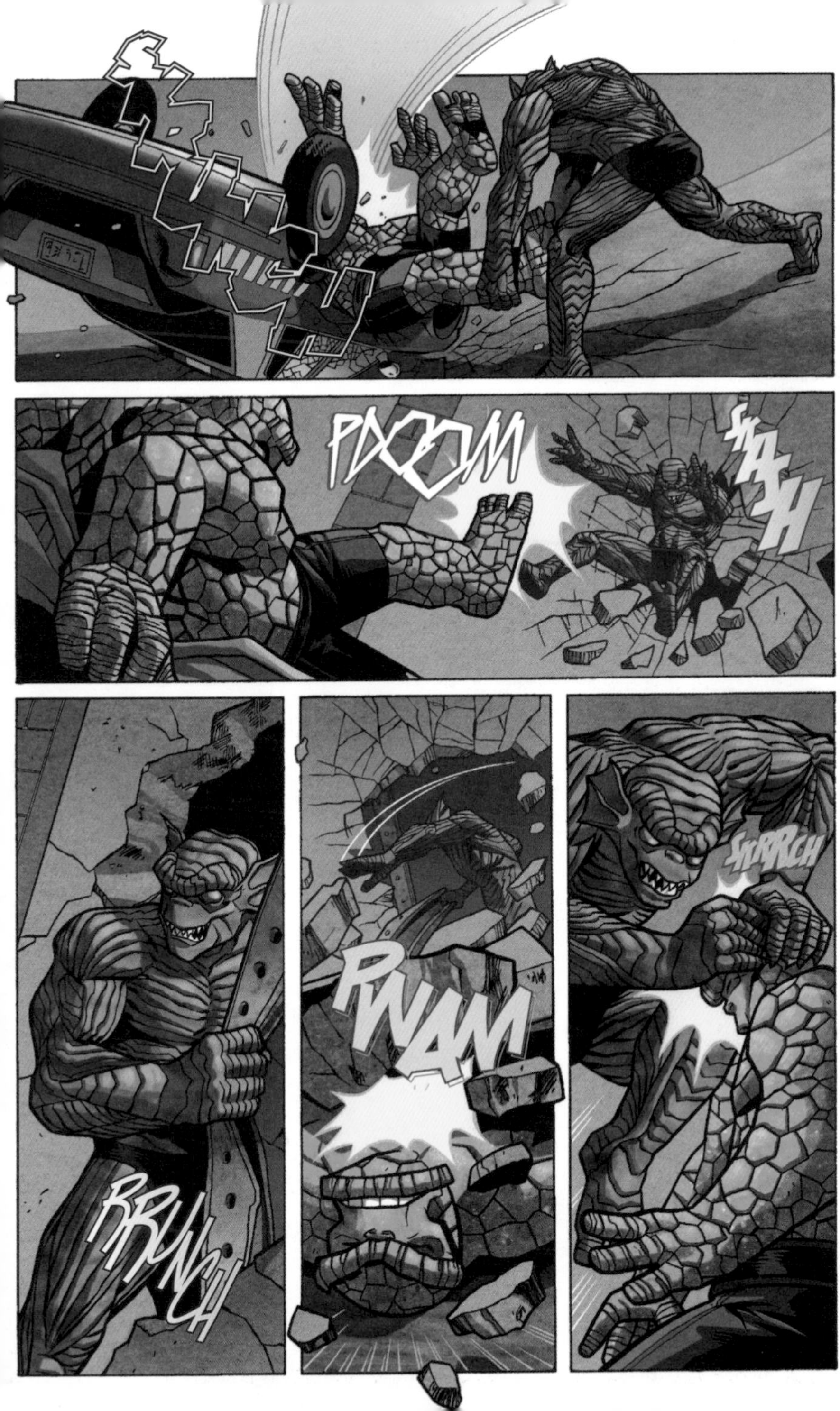
PDOOM
RRUNCH
PWAM

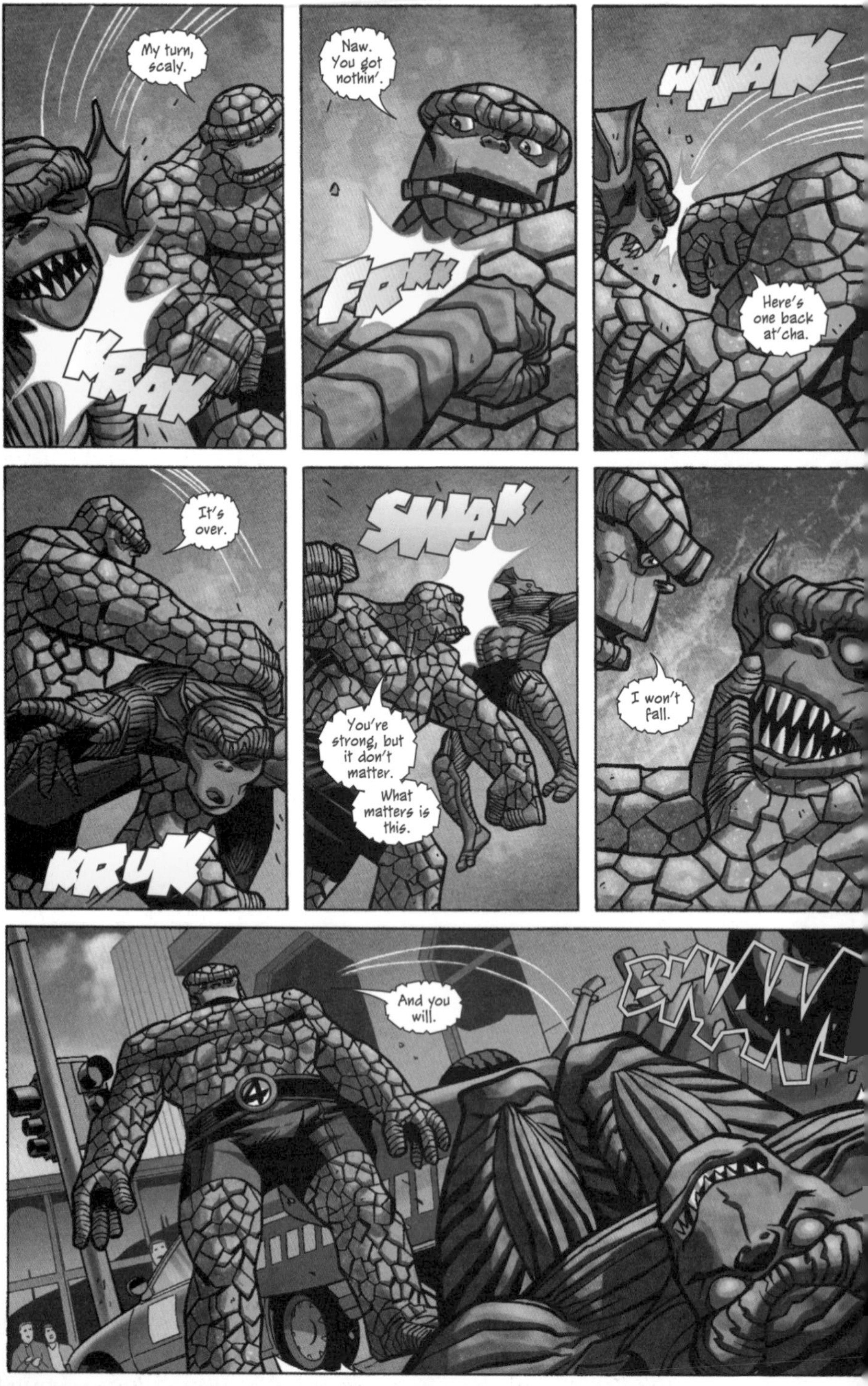
My turn, scaly.
KRAK
Naw. You got nothin'.
FRKK
WHAK
Here's one back at'cha.
It's over.
KRUK
SWAK
You're strong, but it don't matter.
What matters is this.
I won't fall.
And you will.
BWAM

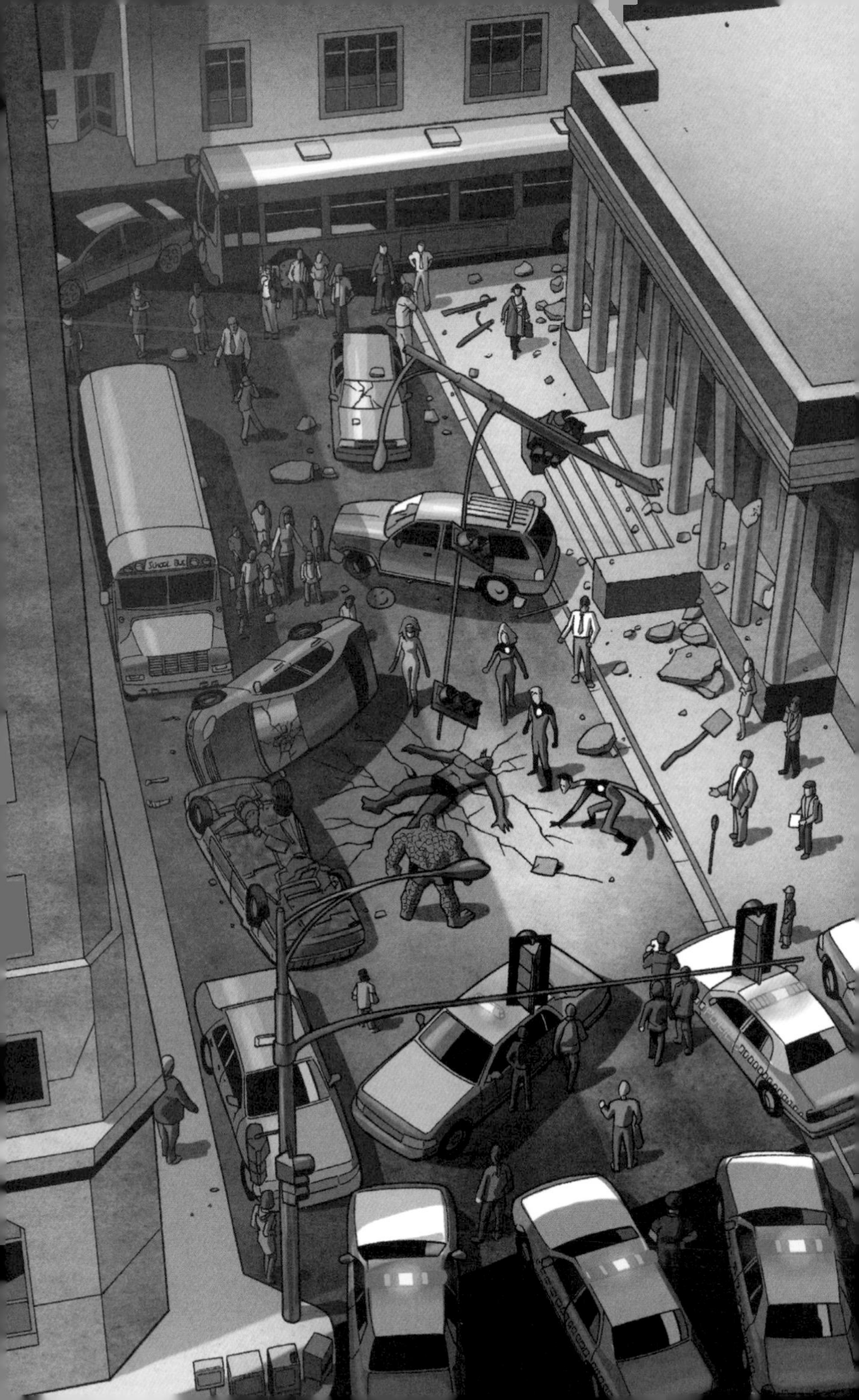
SCHOOL BUS

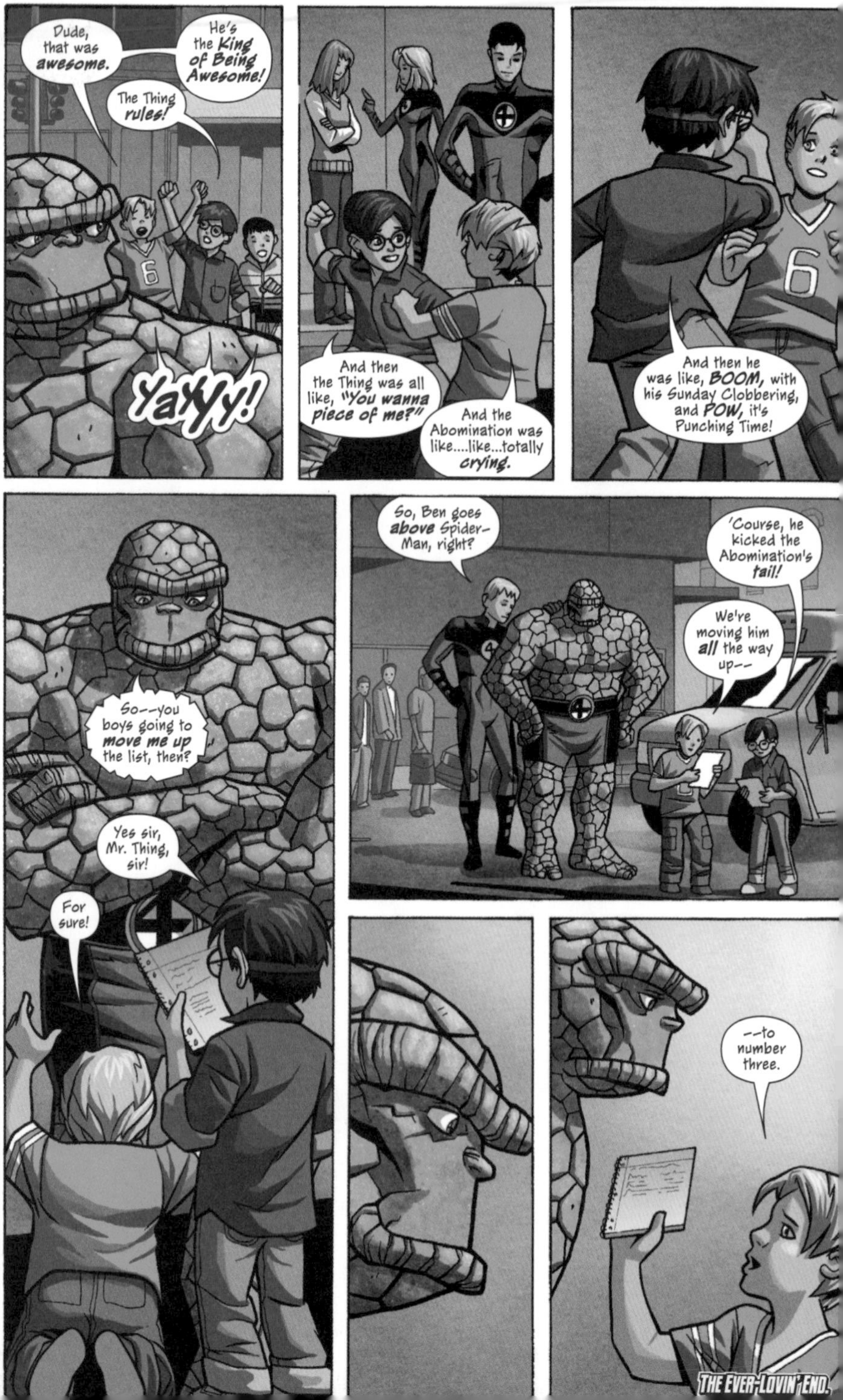

Dude, that was awesome.
He's the King of Being Awesome!
The Thing rules!
Yayyy!
And then the Thing was all like, "You wanna piece of me?"
And the Abomination was like....like...totally crying.
And then he was like, BOOM, with his Sunday Clobbering, and POW, it's Punching Time!
So--you boys going to move me up the list, then?
Yes sir, Mr. Thing, sir!
For sure!
So, Ben goes above Spider-Man, right?
'Course, he kicked the Abomination's tail!
We're moving him all the way up--
--to number three.
THE EVER-LOVIN' END.

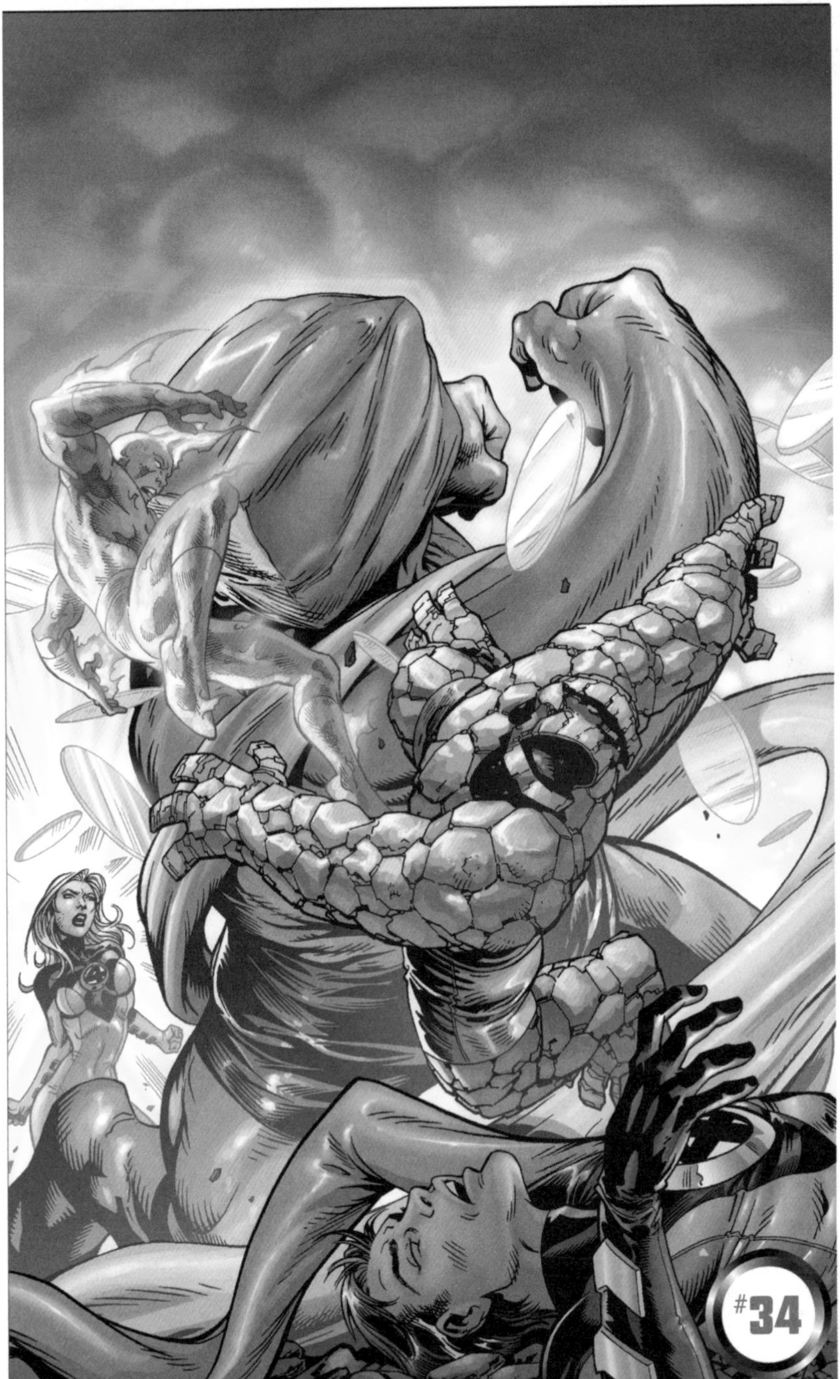
#34

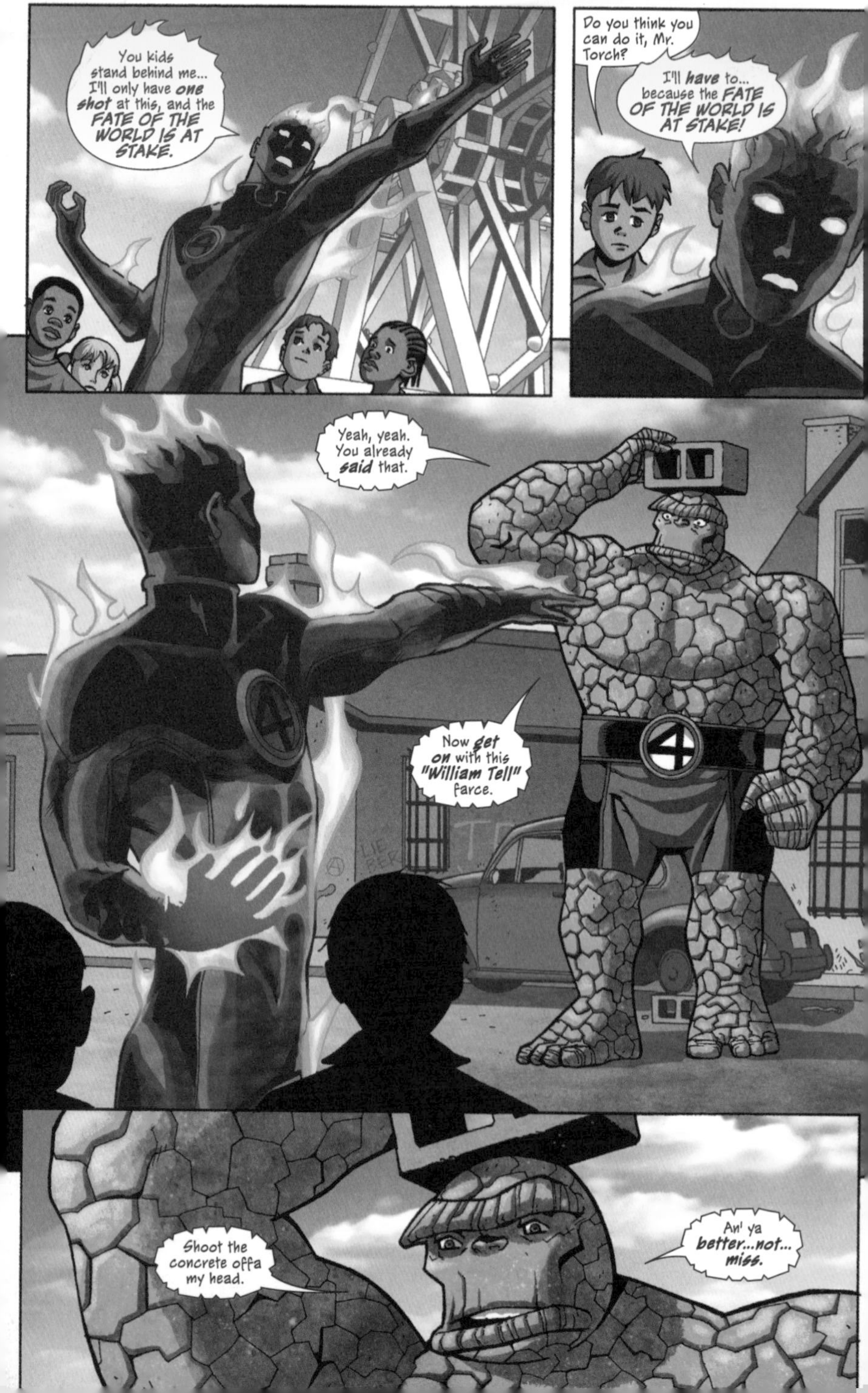
You kids stand behind me... I'll only have one shot at this, and the FATE OF THE WORLD IS AT STAKE.
Do you think you can do it, Mr. Torch?
I'll have to... because the FATE OF THE WORLD IS AT STAKE!
Yeah, yeah. You already said that.
Now get on with this "William Tell" farce.
Shoot the concrete offa my head.
An' ya better...not... miss.

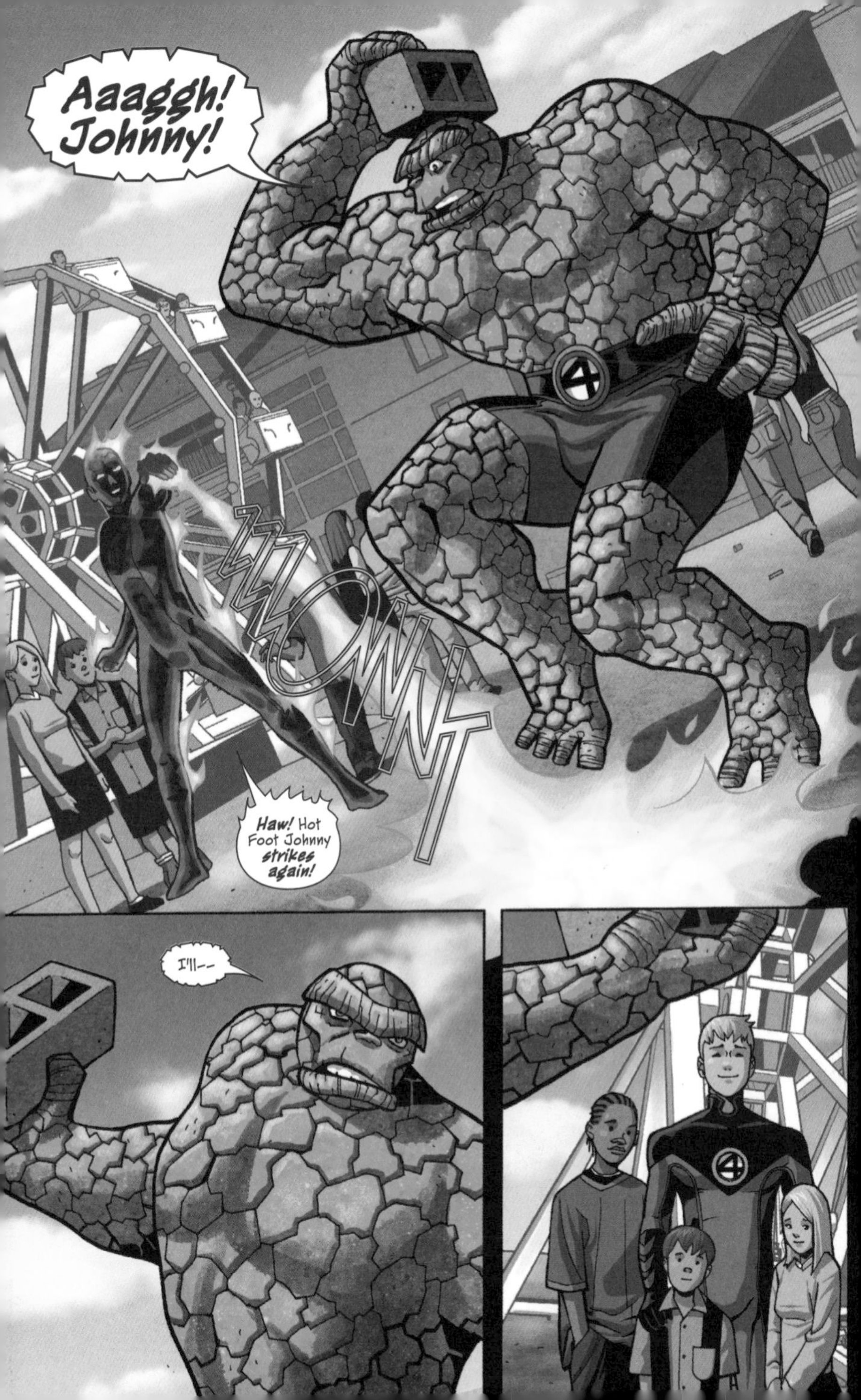
Aaaggh! Johnny!
WOOMP!
Haw! Hot Foot Johnny strikes again!
I'll--

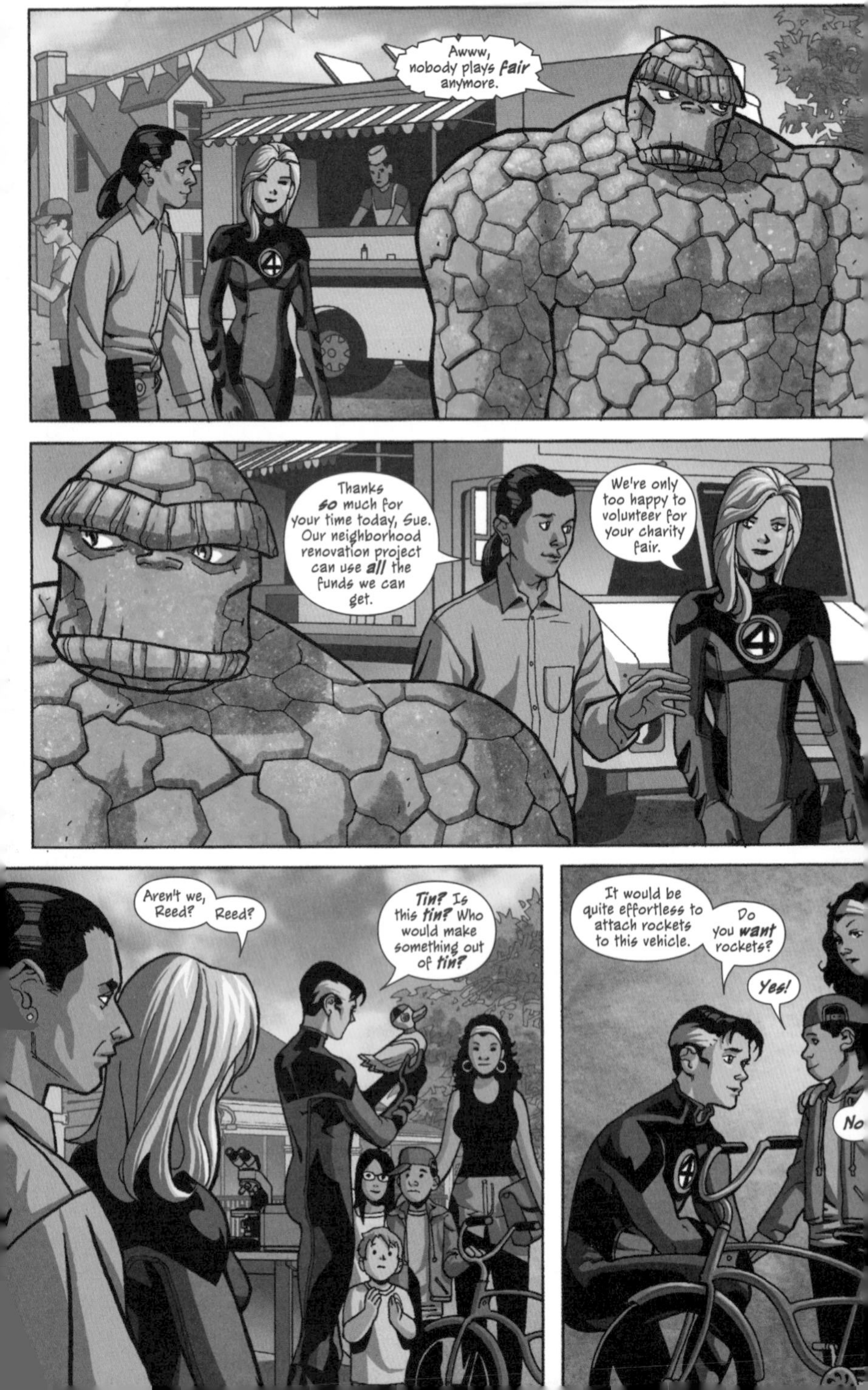

Awww, nobody plays fair anymore.
Thanks so much for your time today, Sue. Our neighborhood renovation project can use all the funds we can get.
We're only too happy to volunteer for your charity fair.
Aren't we, Reed?
Reed?
Tin? Is this tin? Who would make something out of tin?
It would be quite effortless to attach rockets to this vehicle.
Do you want rockets?
Yes!
No

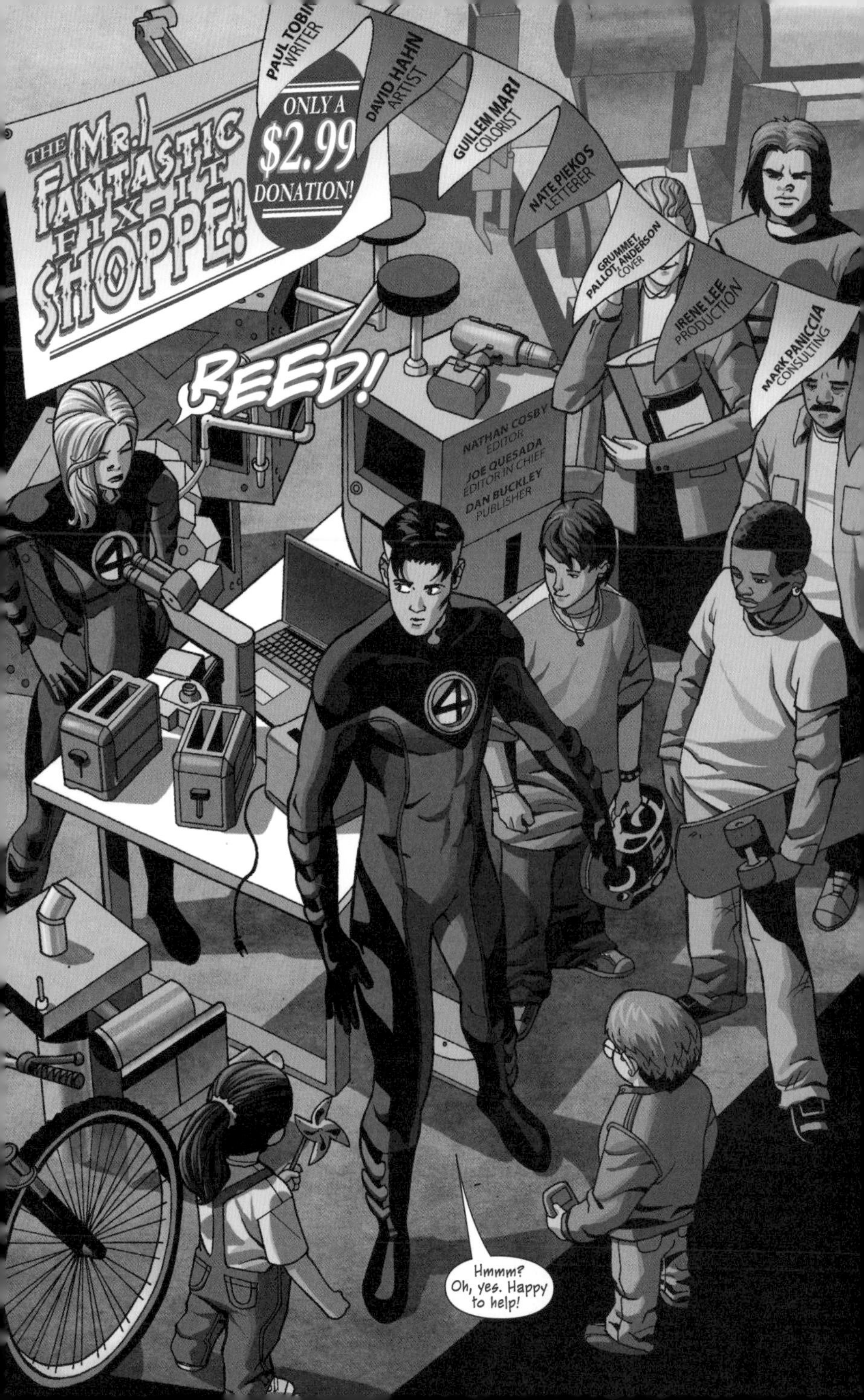

THE (Mr.) FANTASTIC FIX-IT SHOPPE!
ONLY A $2.99 DONATION!
PAUL TOBIN WRITER
DAVID HAHN ARTIST
GUILLEM MARI COLORIST
NATE PIEKOS LETTERER
GRUMMETT, PALLOT, ANDERSON COVER
IRENE LEE PRODUCTION
MARK PANICCIA CONSULTING
NATHAN COSBY EDITOR
JOE QUESADA EDITOR IN CHIEF
DAN BUCKLEY PUBLISHER
REED!
Hmmm? Oh, yes. Happy to help!

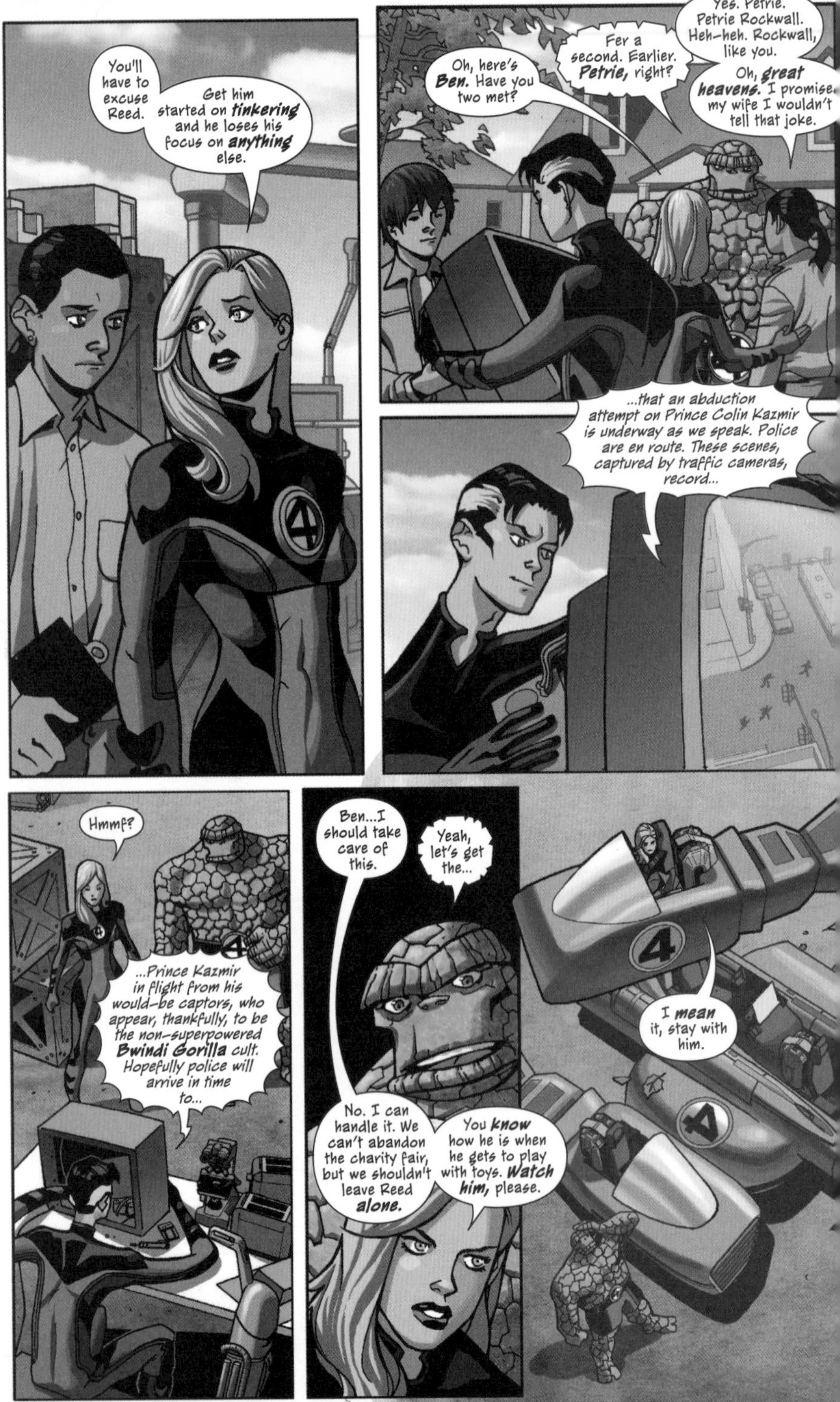

You'll have to excuse Reed.
Get him started on tinkering and he loses his focus on anything else.
Oh, here's Ben. Have you two met?
Fer a second. Earlier. Petrie, right?
Yes. Petrie. Petrie Rockwall. Heh-heh. Rockwall, like you.
Oh, great heavens. I promised my wife I wouldn't tell that joke.
...that an abduction attempt on Prince Colin Kazmir is underway as we speak. Police are en route. These scenes, captured by traffic cameras, record...
Hmmf?
...Prince Kazmir in flight from his would-be captors, who appear, thankfully, to be the non-superpowered Bwindi Gorilla cult. Hopefully police will arrive in time to...
Ben...I should take care of this.
Yeah, let's get the...
No. I can handle it. We can't abandon the charity fair, but we shouldn't leave Reed alone.
You know how he is when he gets to play with toys. Watch him, please.
I mean it, stay with him.

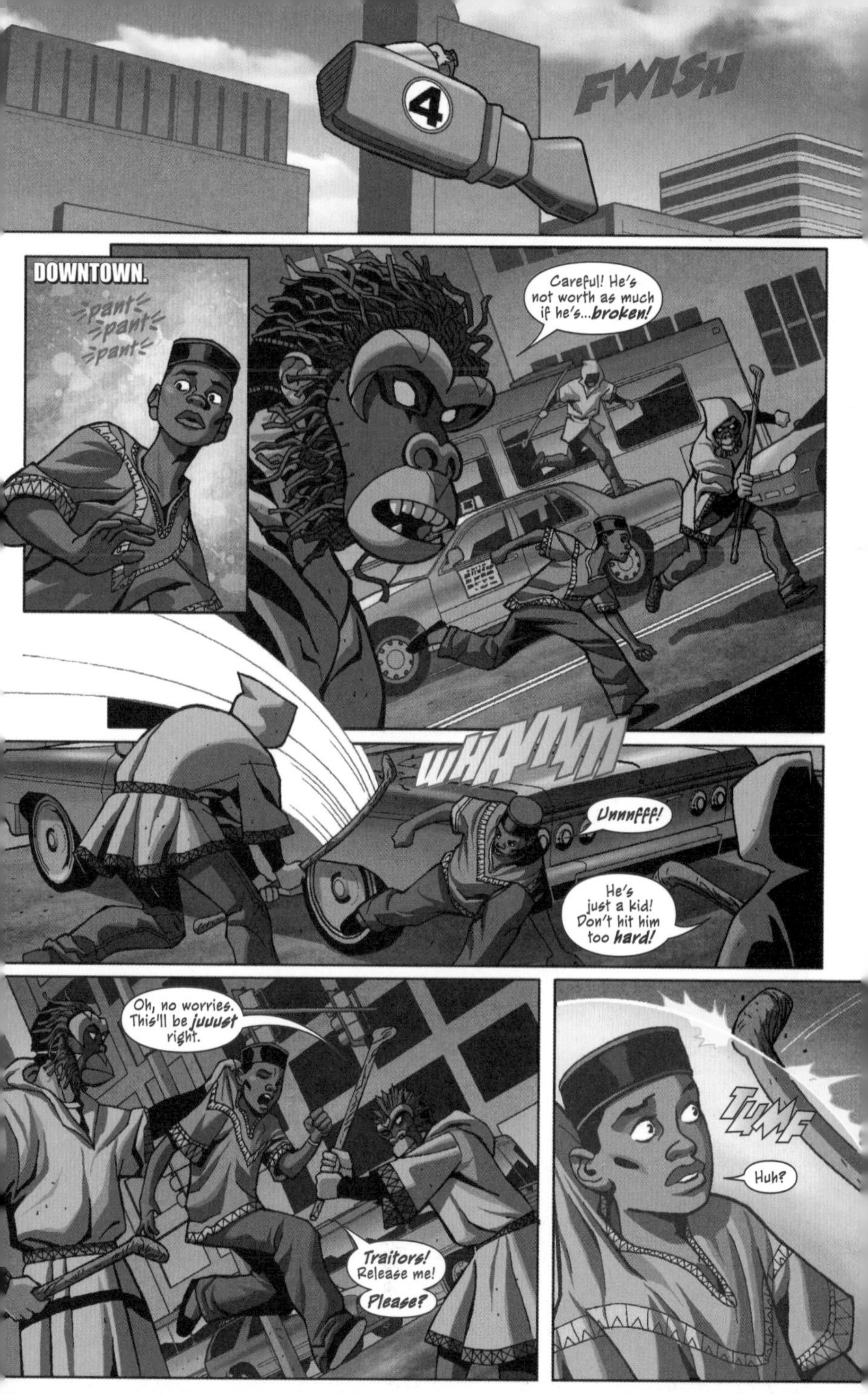
FWISH
DOWNTOWN.
pant pant pant
Careful! He's not worth as much if he's...broken!
WHAMM
Unnnfff!
He's just a kid! Don't hit him too hard!
Oh, no worries. This'll be juuust right.
Traitors! Release me!
Please?
THWMF
Huh?

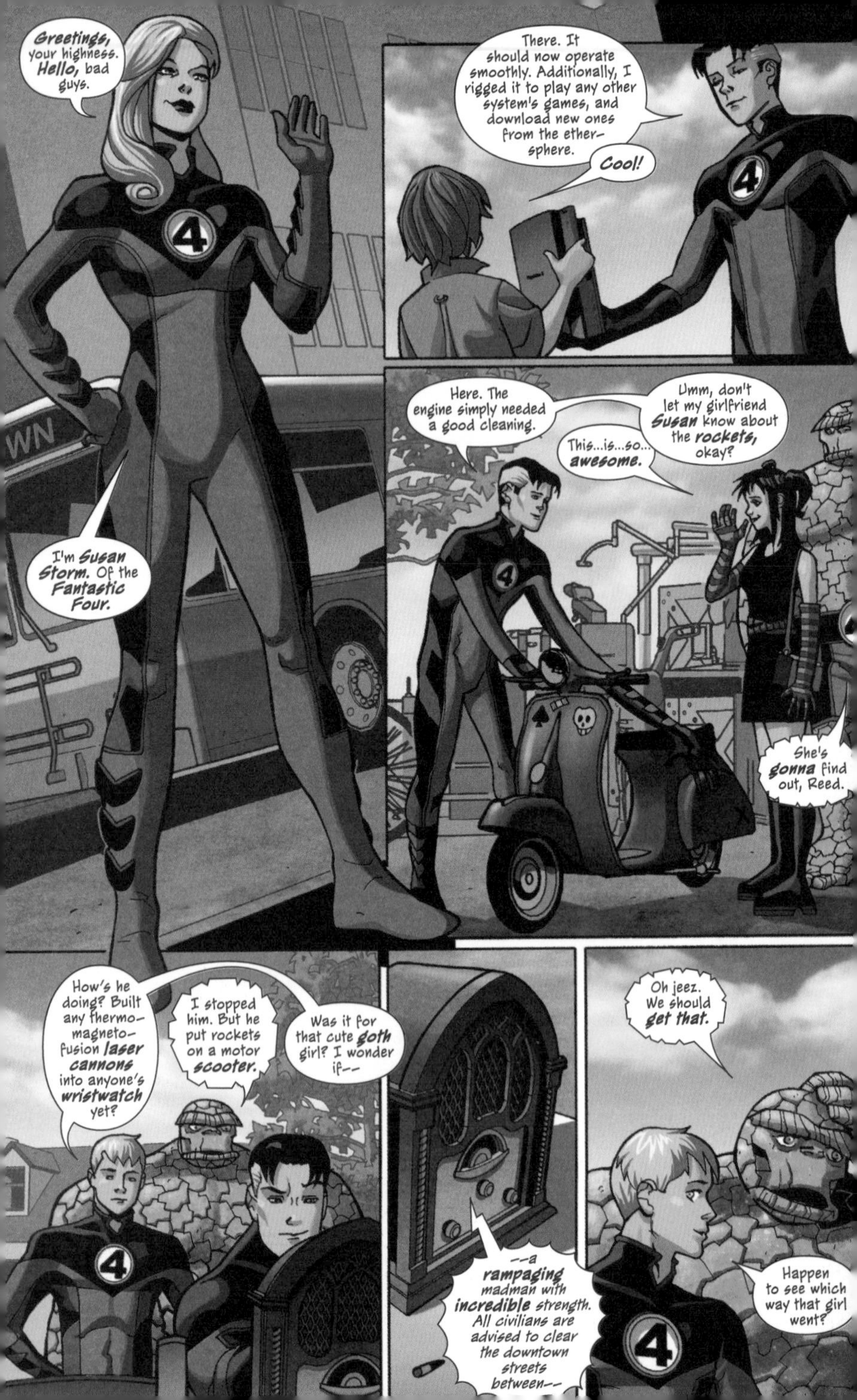
Greetings, your highness. Hello, bad guys.
I'm Susan Storm. Of the Fantastic Four.
There. It should now operate smoothly. Additionally, I rigged it to play any other system's games, and download new ones from the ether-sphere.
Cool!
Here. The engine simply needed a good cleaning.
Umm, don't let my girlfriend Susan know about the rockets, okay?
This...is...so... awesome.
She's gonna find out, Reed.
How's he doing? Built any thermo-magneto-fusion laser cannons into anyone's wristwatch yet?
I stopped him. But he put rockets on a motor scooter.
Was it for that cute goth girl? I wonder if--
--a rampaging madman with incredible strength. All civilians are advised to clear the downtown streets between--
Oh jeez. We should get that.
Happen to see which way that girl went?

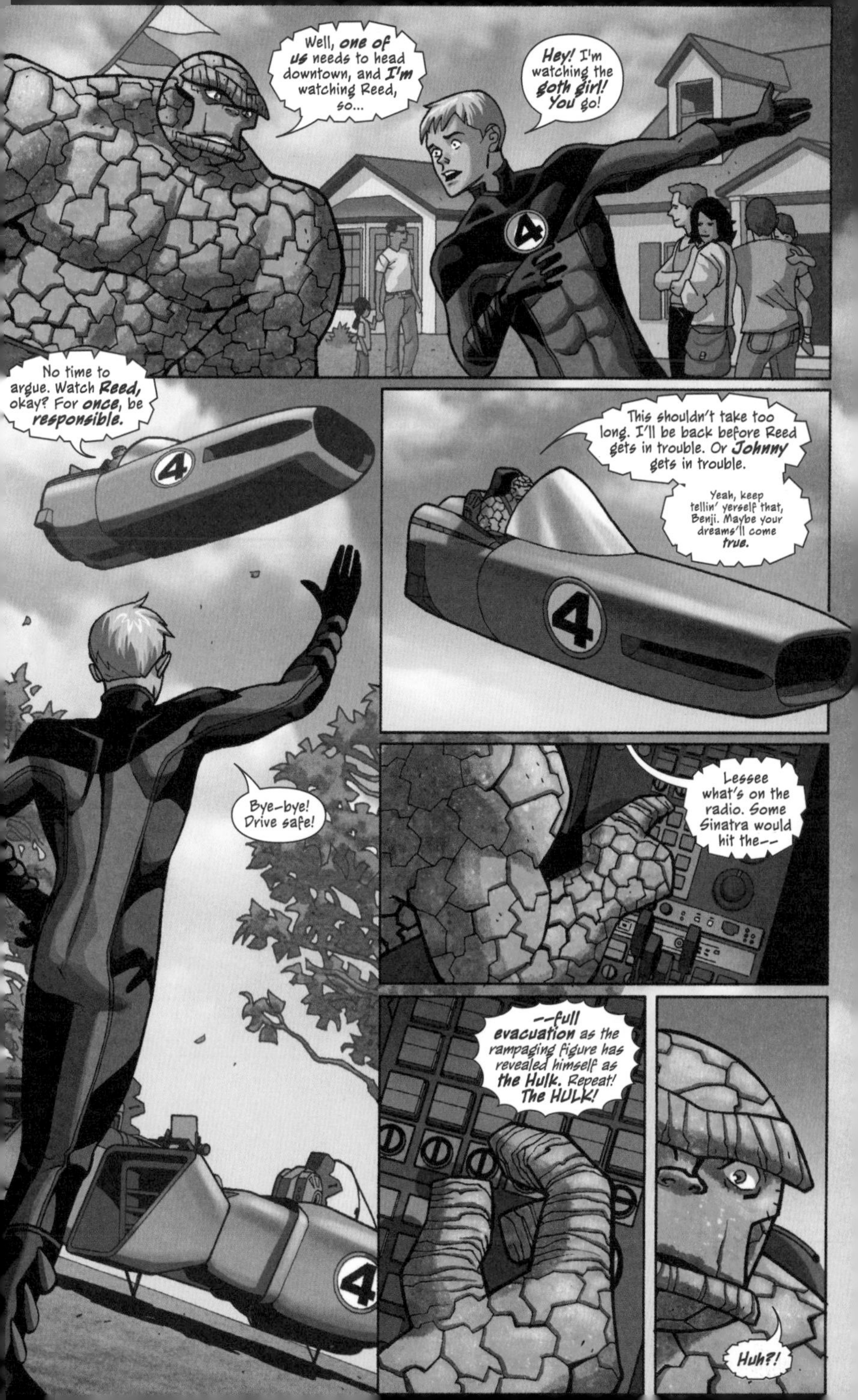
Well, one of us needs to head downtown, and I'm watching Reed, so...
Hey! I'm watching the goth girl! You go!
No time to argue. Watch Reed, okay? For once, be responsible.
This shouldn't take too long. I'll be back before Reed gets in trouble. Or Johnny gets in trouble.
Yeah, keep tellin' yerself that, Benji. Maybe your dreams'll come true.
Bye-bye! Drive safe!
Lessee what's on the radio. Some Sinatra would hit the--
--full evacuation as the rampaging figure has revealed himself as the Hulk. Repeat! The HULK!
Huh?!

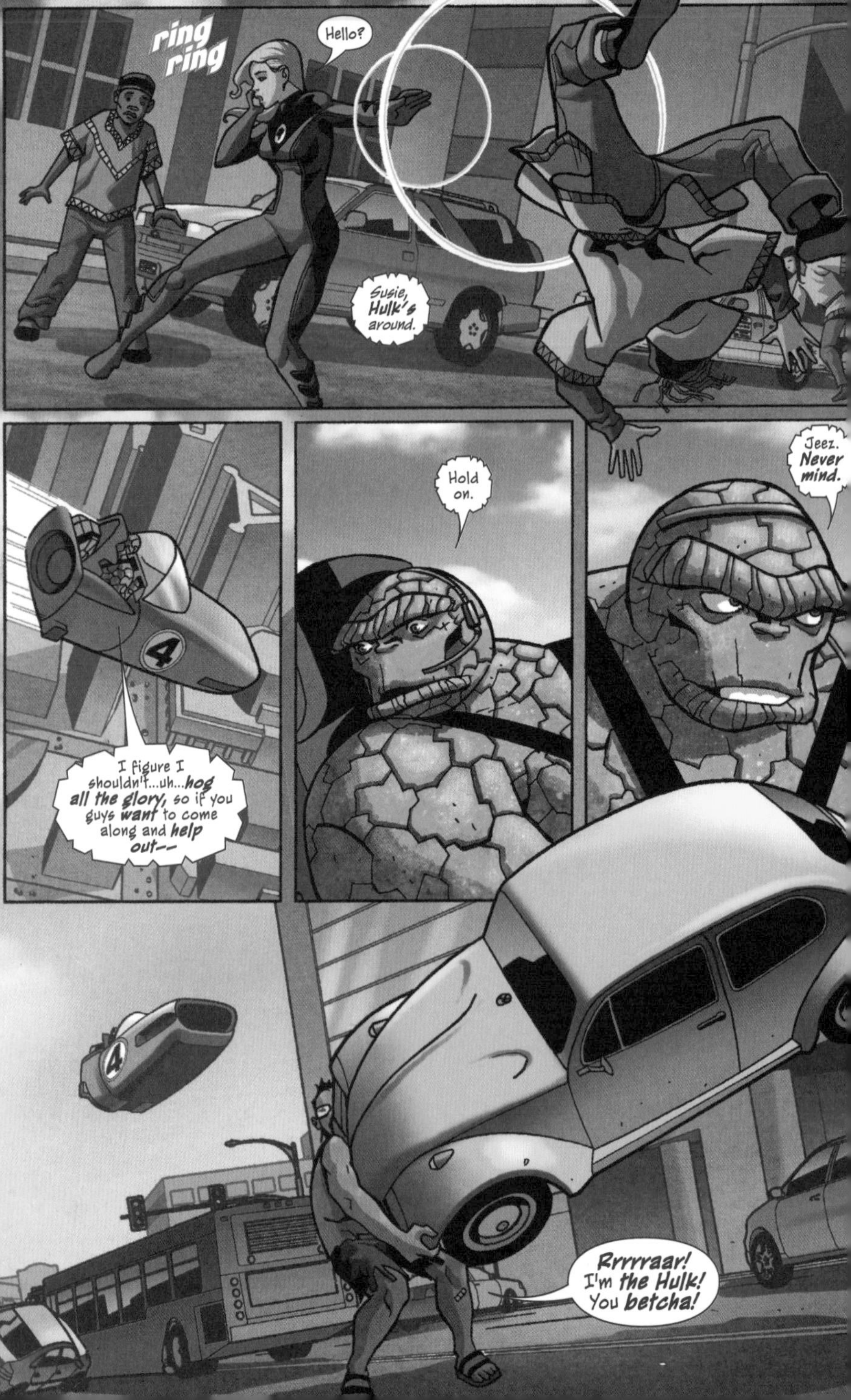
ring ring
Hello?
Susie, Hulk's around.
I figure I shouldn't...uh...hog all the glory, so if you guys want to come along and help out--
Hold on.
Jeez. Never mind.
Rrrrraar! I'm the Hulk! You betcha!

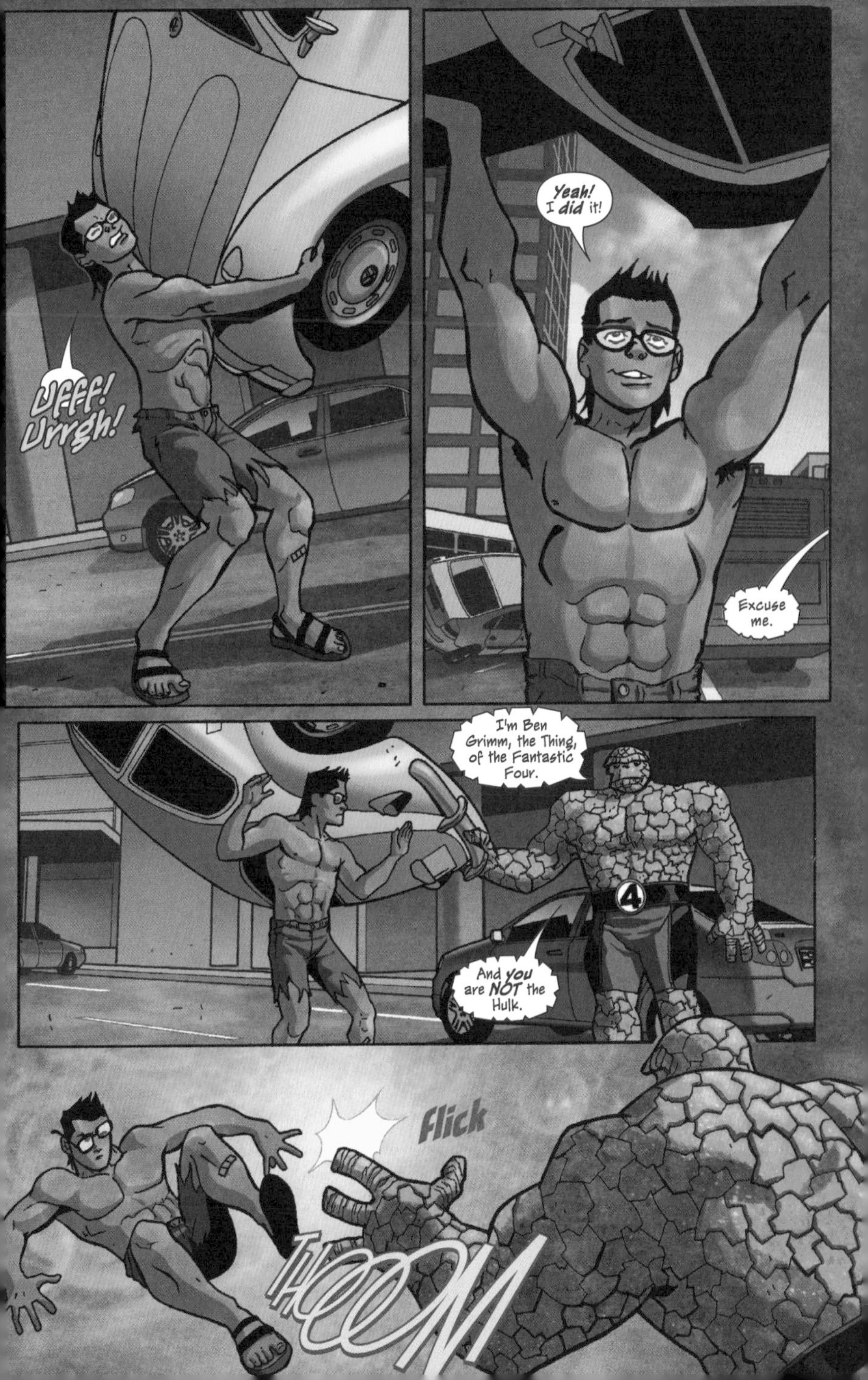
Ufff! Urrgh!
Yeah! I did it!
Excuse me.
I'm Ben Grimm, the Thing, of the Fantastic Four.
And you are NOT the Hulk.
Flick
THOOOM

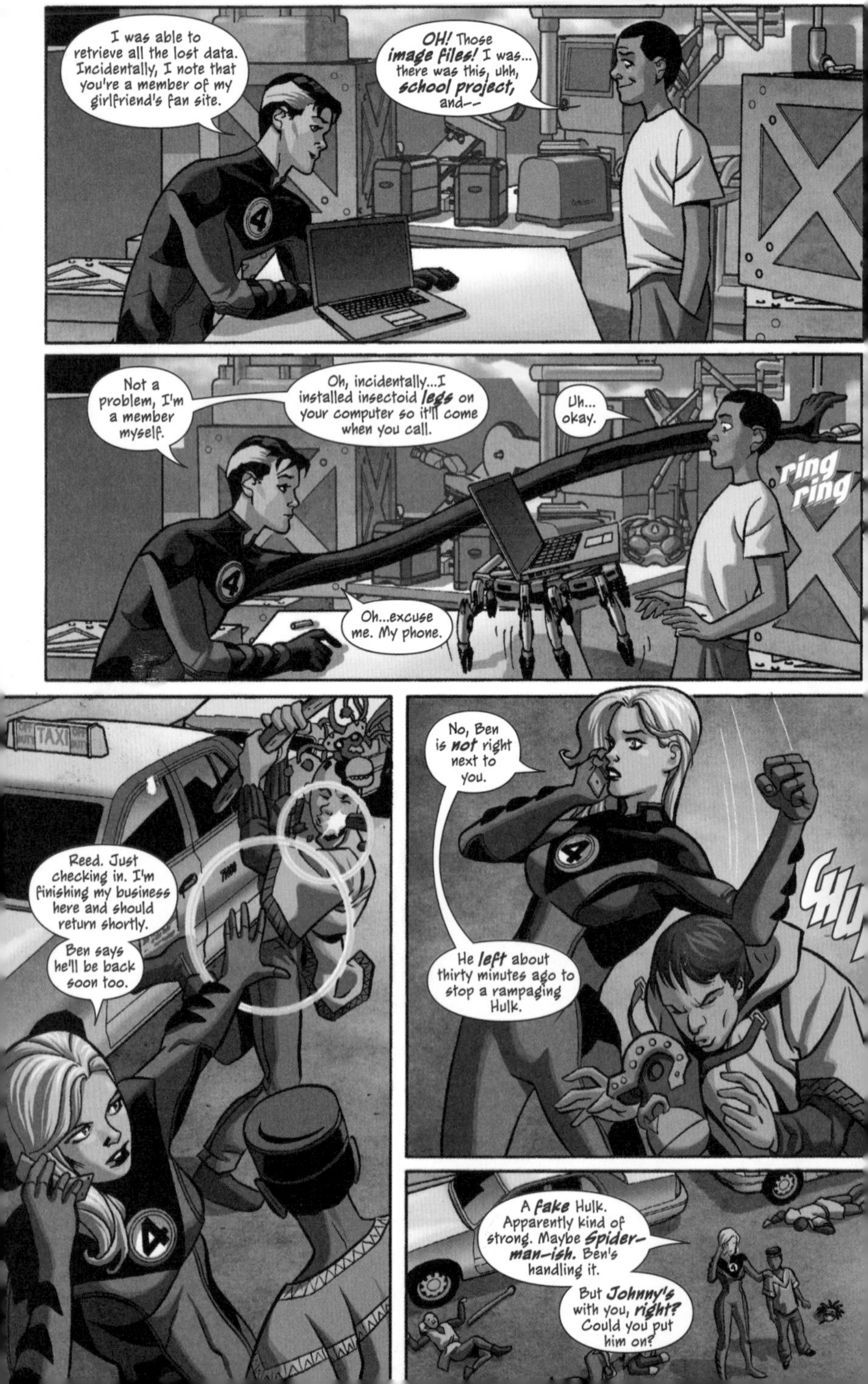
I was able to retrieve all the lost data. Incidentally, I note that you're a member of my girlfriend's fan site.
OH! Those image files! I was... there was this, uhh, school project, and--
Not a problem, I'm a member myself.
Oh, incidentally...I installed insectoid legs on your computer so it'll come when you call.
Uh... okay.
ring ring
Oh...excuse me. My phone.
TAXI
Reed. Just checking in. I'm finishing my business here and should return shortly.
Ben says he'll be back soon too.
No, Ben is not right next to you.
He left about thirty minutes ago to stop a rampaging Hulk.
A fake Hulk. Apparently kind of strong. Maybe Spider-man-ish. Ben's handling it.
But Johnny's with you, right? Could you put him on?

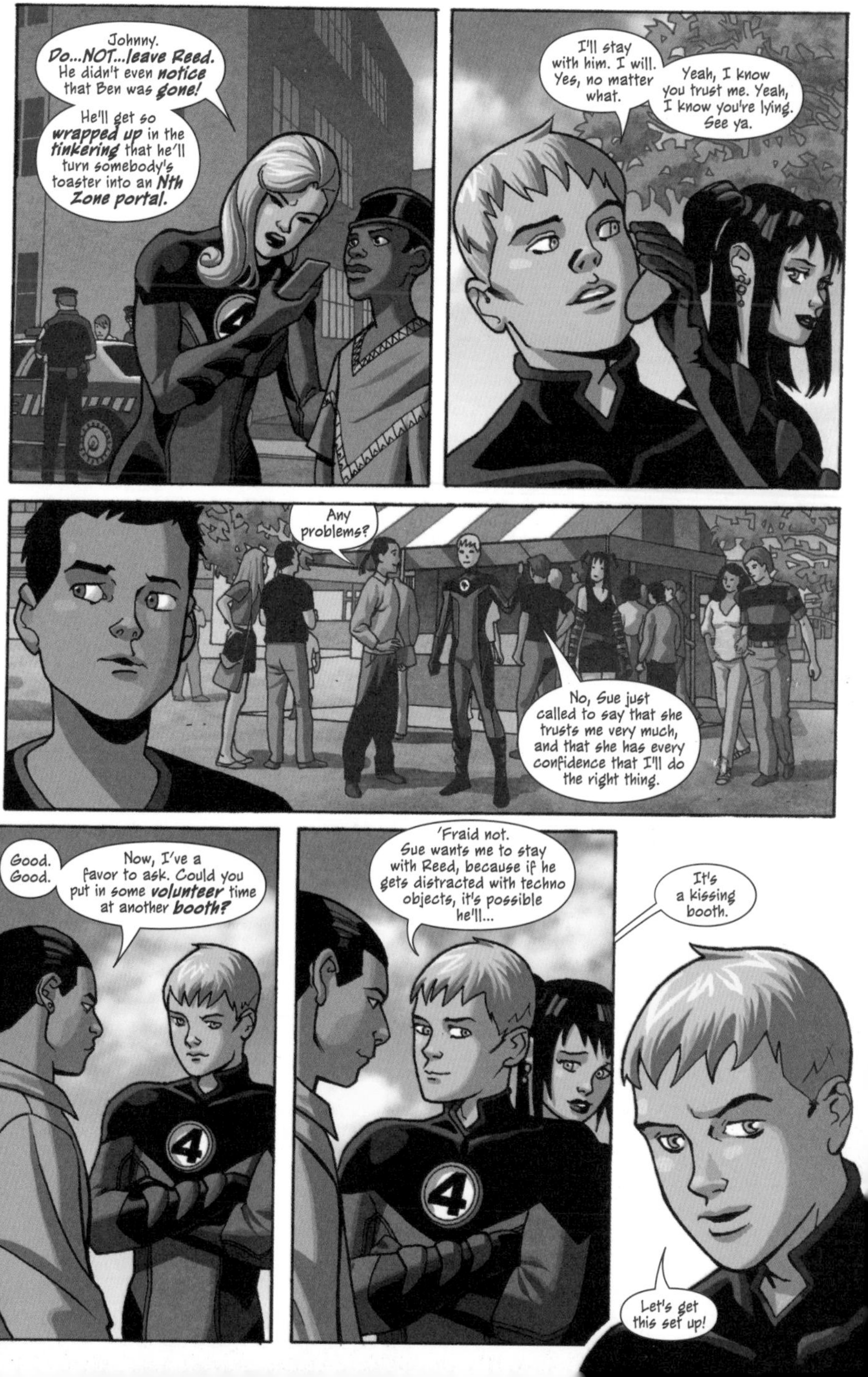
Johnny.
Do...NOT...leave Reed. He didn't even notice that Ben was gone!
He'll get so wrapped up in the tinkering that he'll turn somebody's toaster into an Nth Zone portal.
I'll stay with him. I will. Yes, no matter what.
Yeah, I know you trust me. Yeah, I know you're lying. See ya.
Any problems?
No, Sue just called to say that she trusts me very much, and that she has every confidence that I'll do the right thing.
Good. Good.
Now, I've a favor to ask. Could you put in some volunteer time at another booth?
'Fraid not. Sue wants me to stay with Reed, because if he gets distracted with techno objects, it's possible he'll...
It's a kissing booth.
Let's get this set up!

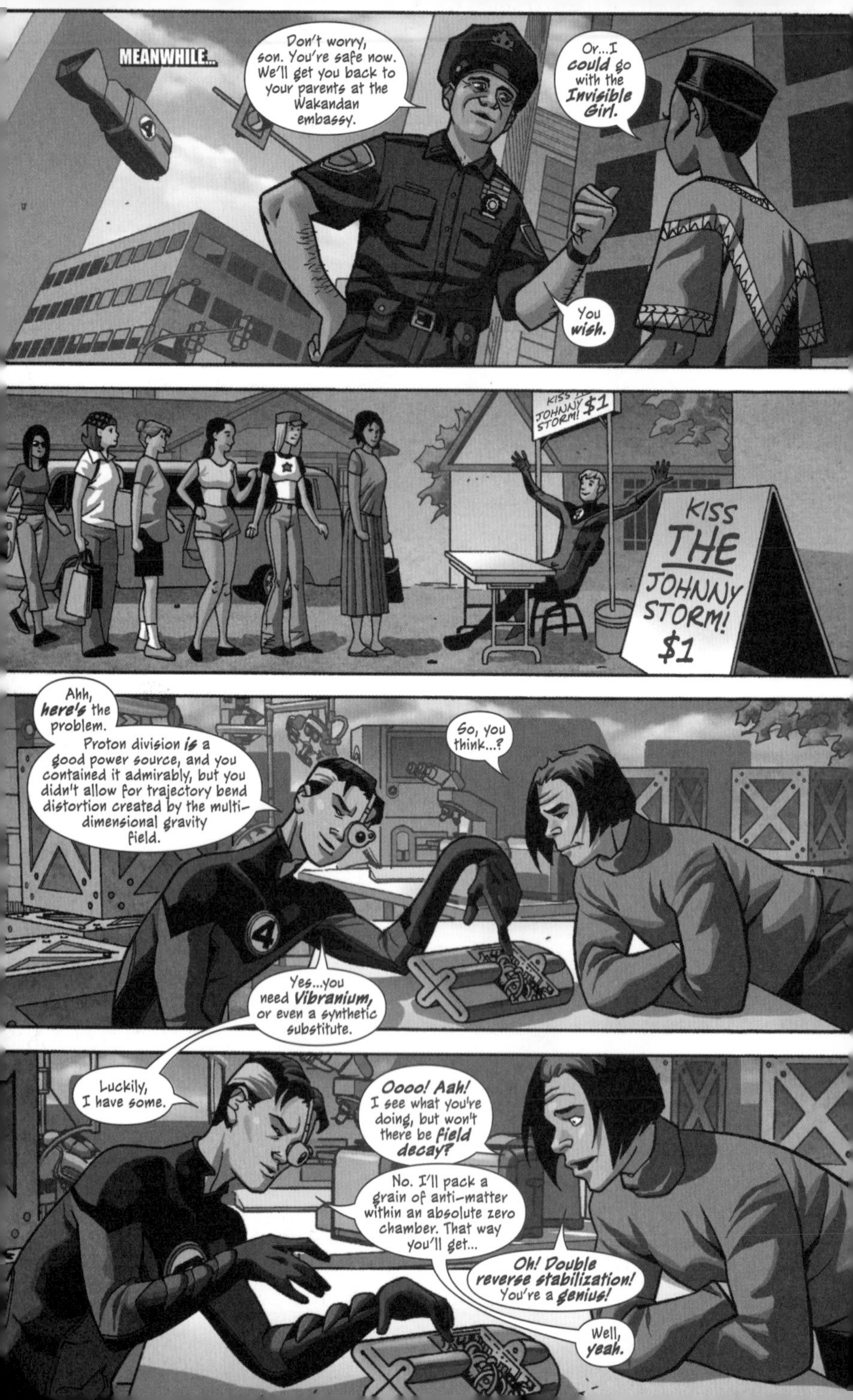
MEANWHILE...
Don't worry, son. You're safe now. We'll get you back to your parents at the Wakandan embassy.
Or...I could go with the Invisible Girl.
You wish.
KISS JOHNNY STORM! $1
KISS THE JOHNNY STORM! $1
Ahh, here's the problem.
Proton division is a good power source, and you contained it admirably, but you didn't allow for trajectory bend distortion created by the multi-dimensional gravity field.
So, you think...?
Yes...you need Vibranium, or even a synthetic substitute.
Luckily, I have some.
Oooo! Aah! I see what you're doing, but won't there be field decay?
No. I'll pack a grain of anti-matter within an absolute zero chamber. That way you'll get...
Oh! Double reverse stabilization! You're a genius!
Well, yeah.

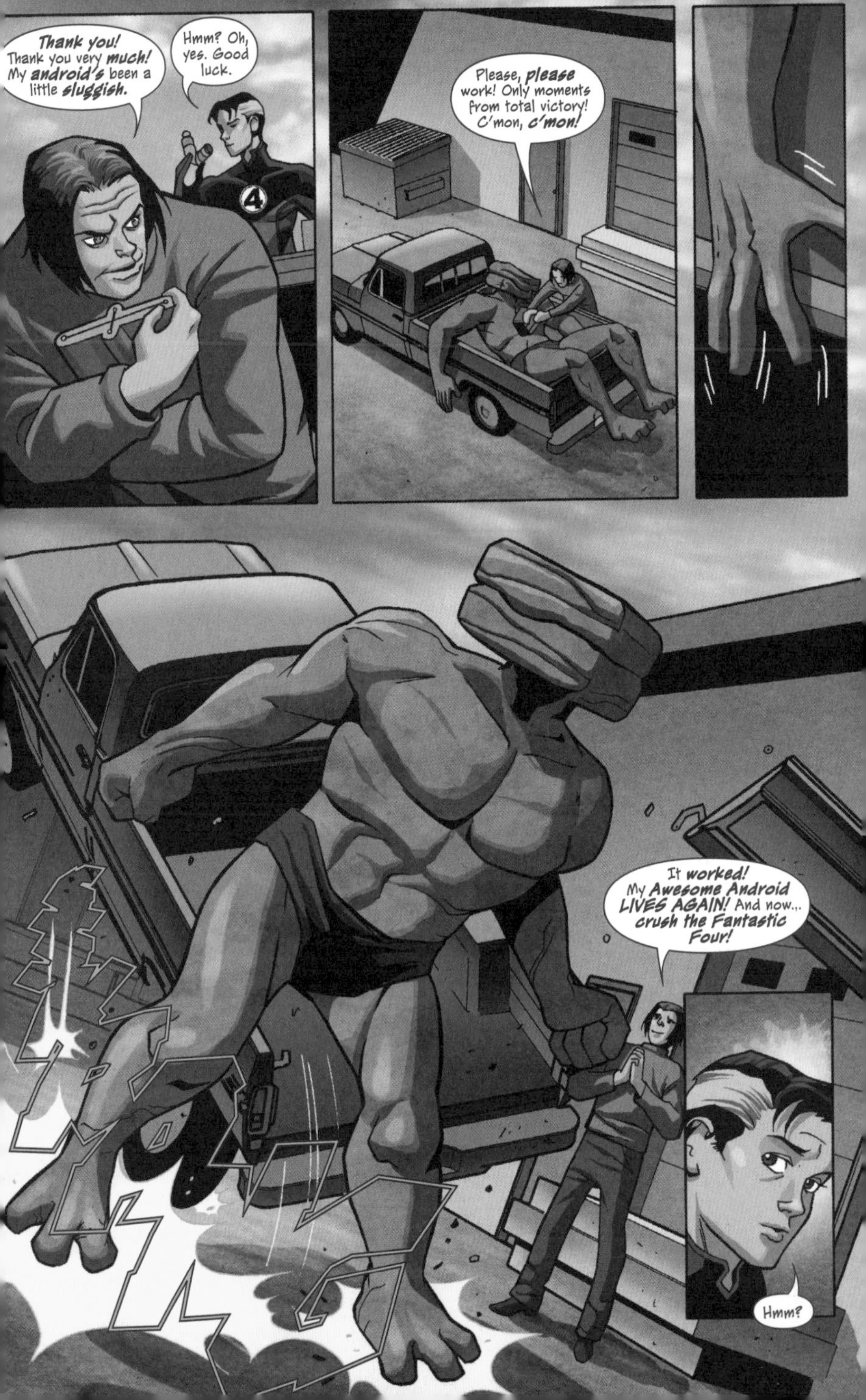
Thank you! Thank you very much! My android's been a little sluggish.
Hmm? Oh, yes. Good luck.
Please, please work! Only moments from total victory! C'mon, c'mon!
It worked! My Awesome Android LIVES AGAIN! And now... crush the Fantastic Four!
Hmm?

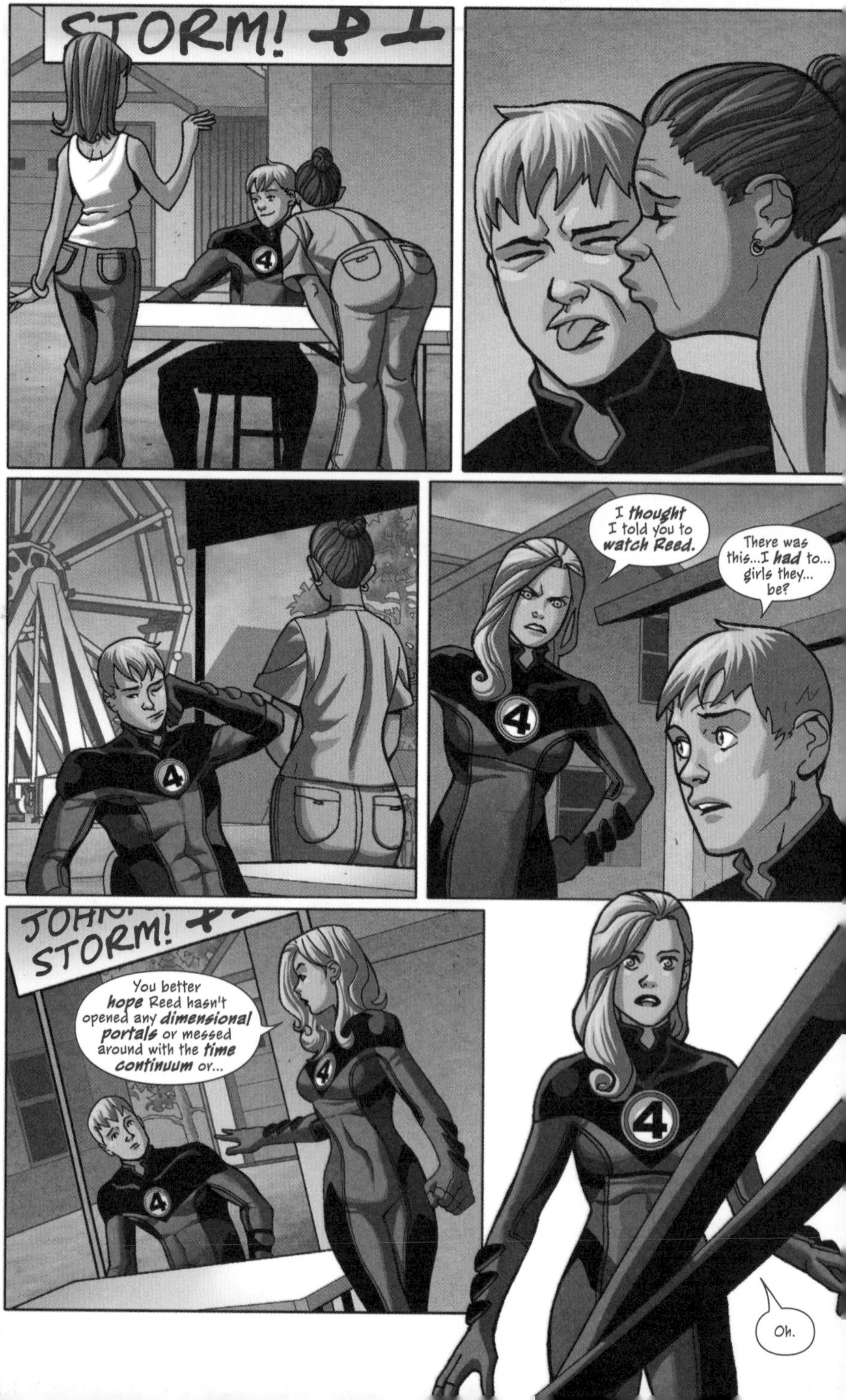
STORM!
I thought I told you to watch Reed.
There was this...I had to... girls they... be?
STORM!
You better hope Reed hasn't opened any dimensional portals or messed around with the time continuum or...
Oh.

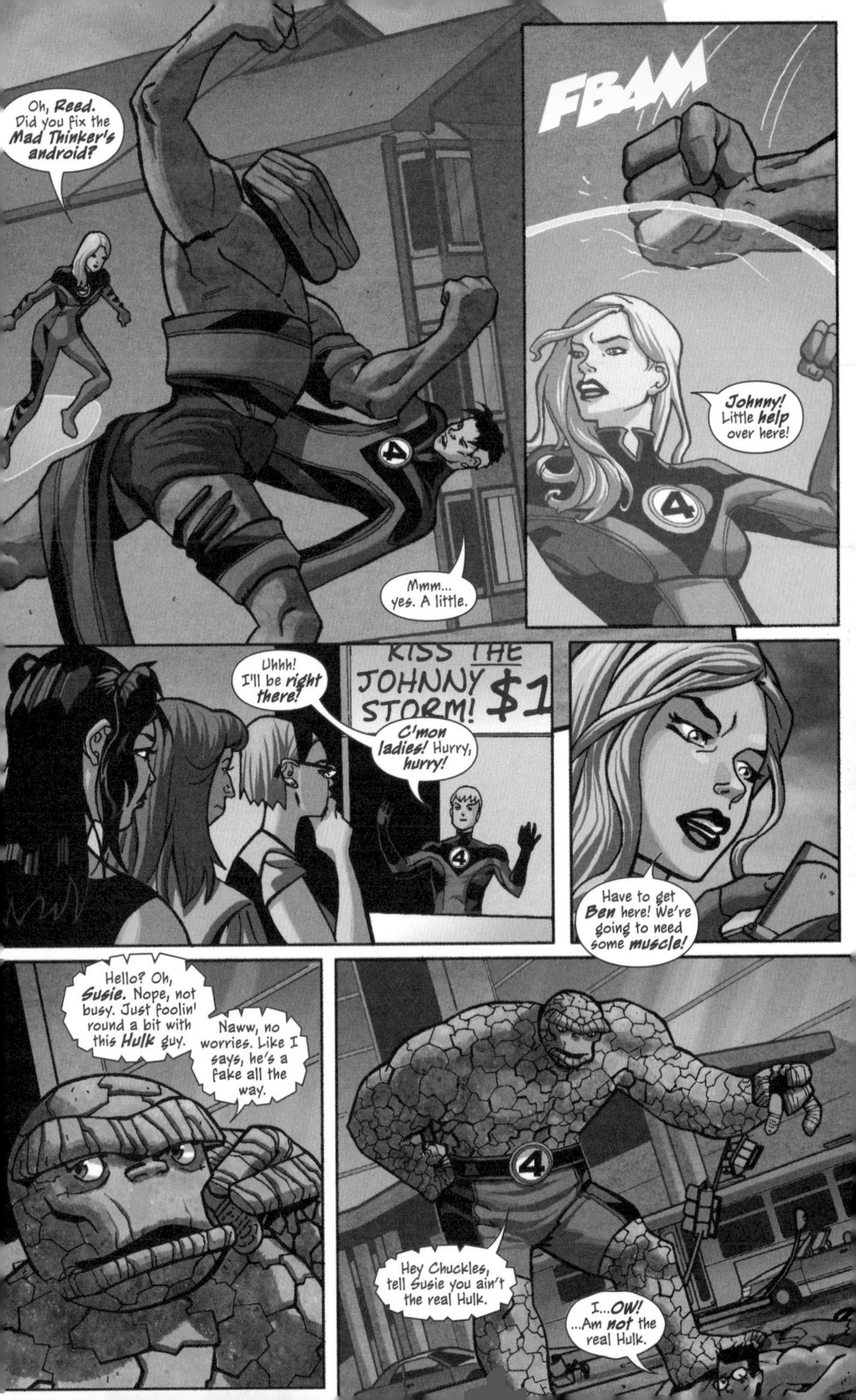

Oh, Reed. Did you fix the Mad Thinker's android?
Mmm... yes. A little.
FBAM
Johnny! Little help over here!
KISS THE JOHNNY STORM! $1
Uhhh! I'll be right there!
C'mon ladies! Hurry, hurry!
Have to get Ben here! We're going to need some muscle!
Hello? Oh, Susie. Nope, not busy. Just foolin' round a bit with this Hulk guy.
Naww, no worries. Like I says, he's a fake all the way.
Hey Chuckles, tell Susie you ain't the real Hulk.
I...OW! ...Am not the real Hulk.

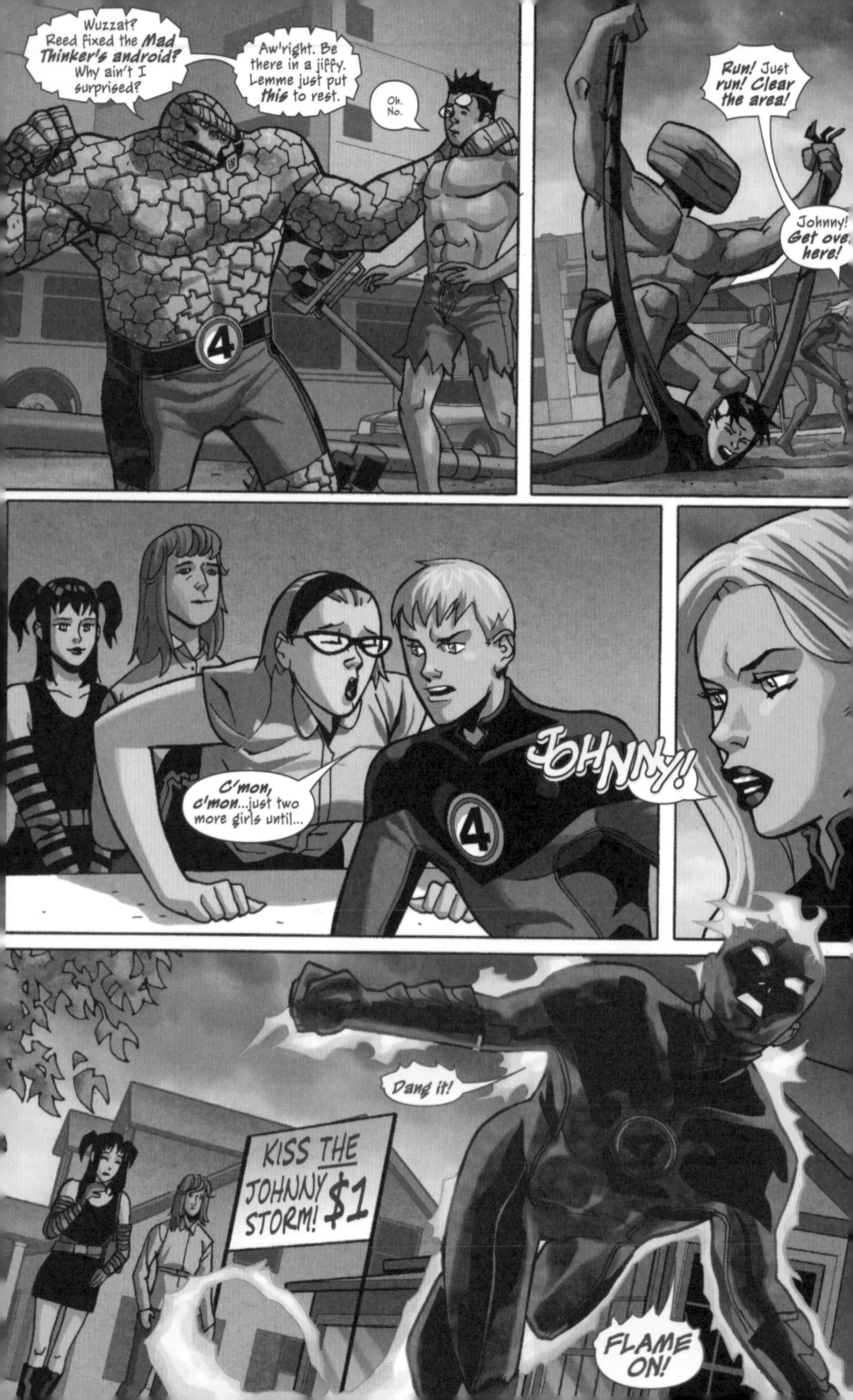
Wuzzat? Reed fixed the Mad Thinker's android? Why ain't I surprised?
Aw'right. Be there in a jiffy. Lemme just put this to rest.
Oh. No.
Run! Just run! Clear the area!
Johnny! Get ove here!
C'mon, c'mon...just two more girls until...
JOHNNY!
Dang it!
KISS THE JOHNNY STORM! $1
FLAME ON!

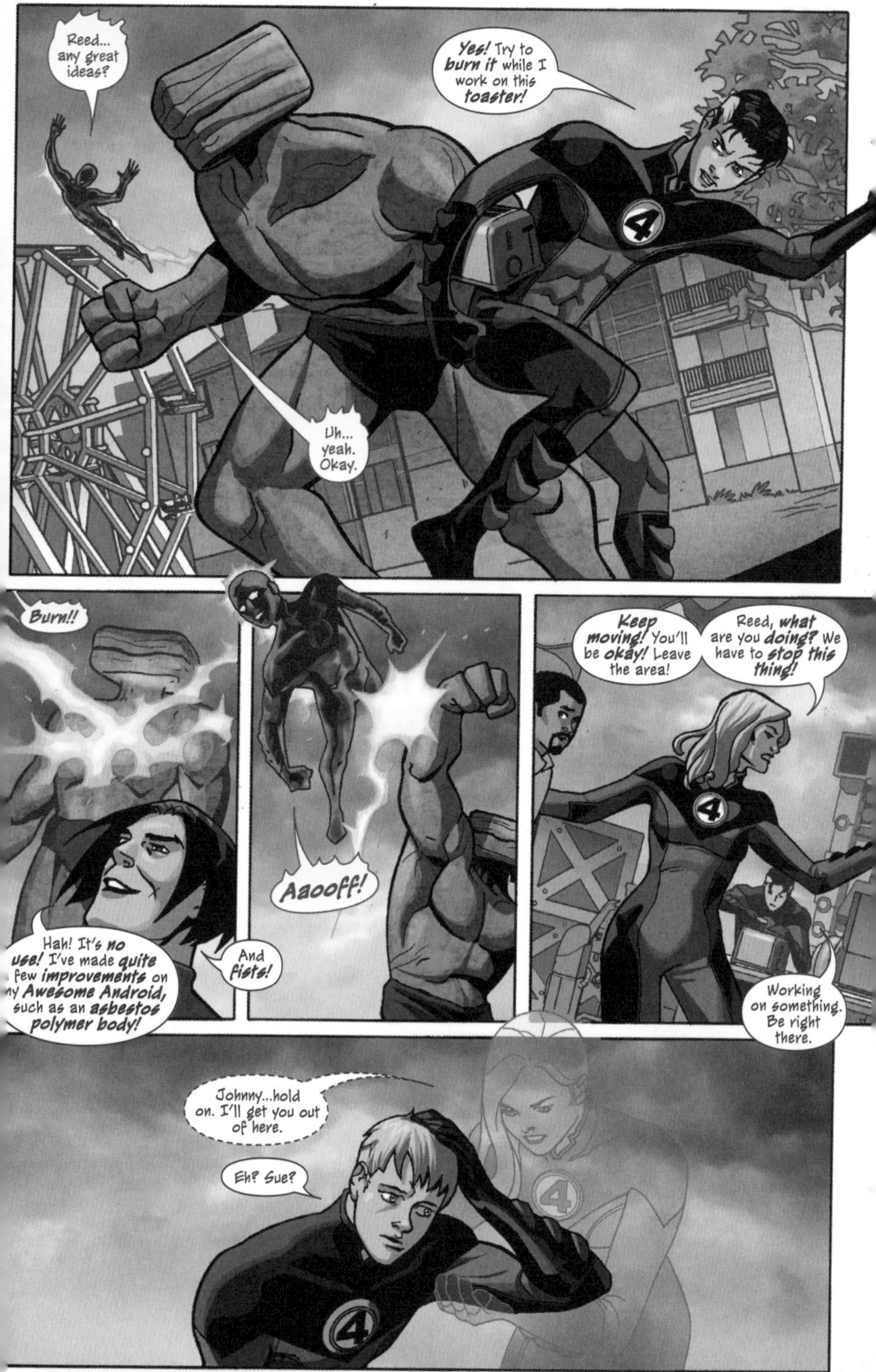
Reed... any great ideas?
Yes! Try to burn it while I work on this toaster!
Uh... yeah. Okay.
Burn!!
Hah! It's no use! I've made quite a few improvements on my Awesome Android, such as an asbestos polymer body!
And fists!
Aaooff!
Keep moving! You'll be okay! Leave the area!
Reed, what are you doing? We have to stop this thing!
Working on something. Be right there.
Johnny...hold on. I'll get you out of here.
Eh? Sue?

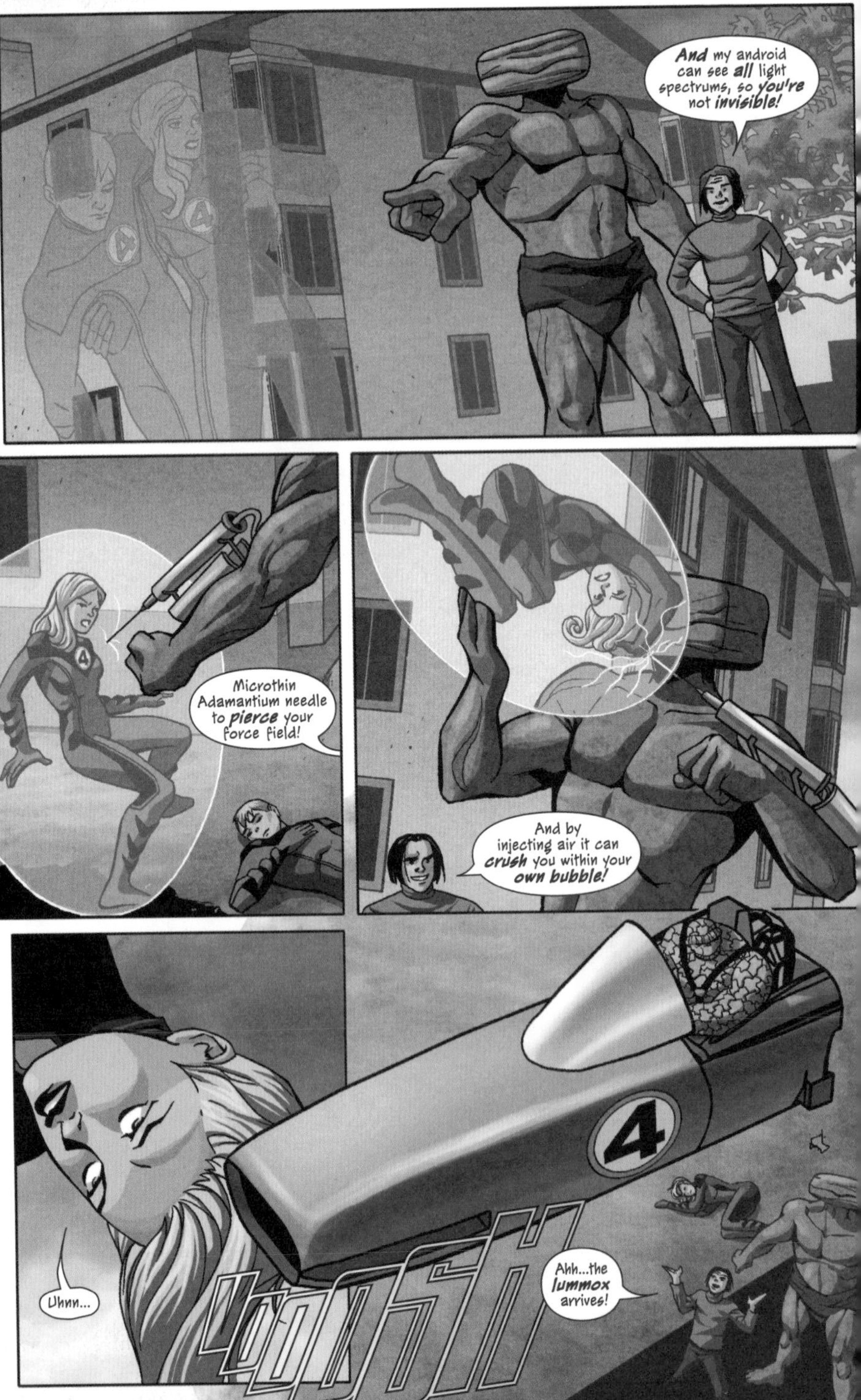
And my android can see all light spectrums, so you're not invisible!
Microthin Adamantium needle to pierce your force field!
And by injecting air it can crush you within your own bubble!
Uhnn...
Ahh...the lummox arrives!

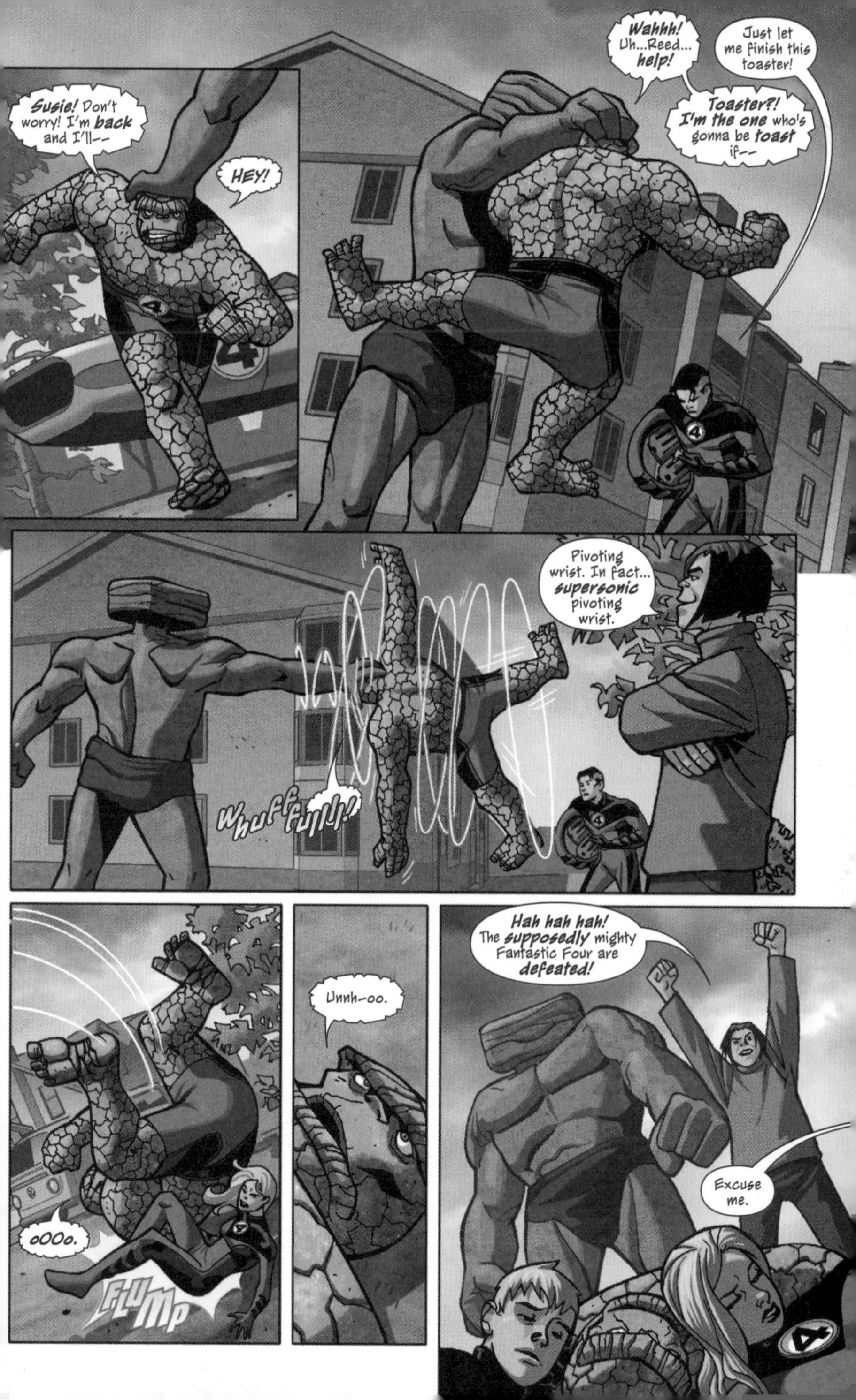

Susie! Don't worry! I'm back and I'll--
HEY!
Wahhh! Uh...Reed... help!
Just let me finish this toaster!
Toaster?! I'm the one who's gonna be toast if--
Pivoting wrist. In fact... supersonic pivoting wrist.
Whufffulllp!
oOOo.
FLUMP
Unnh-oo.
Hah hah hah! The supposedly mighty Fantastic Four are defeated!
Excuse me.

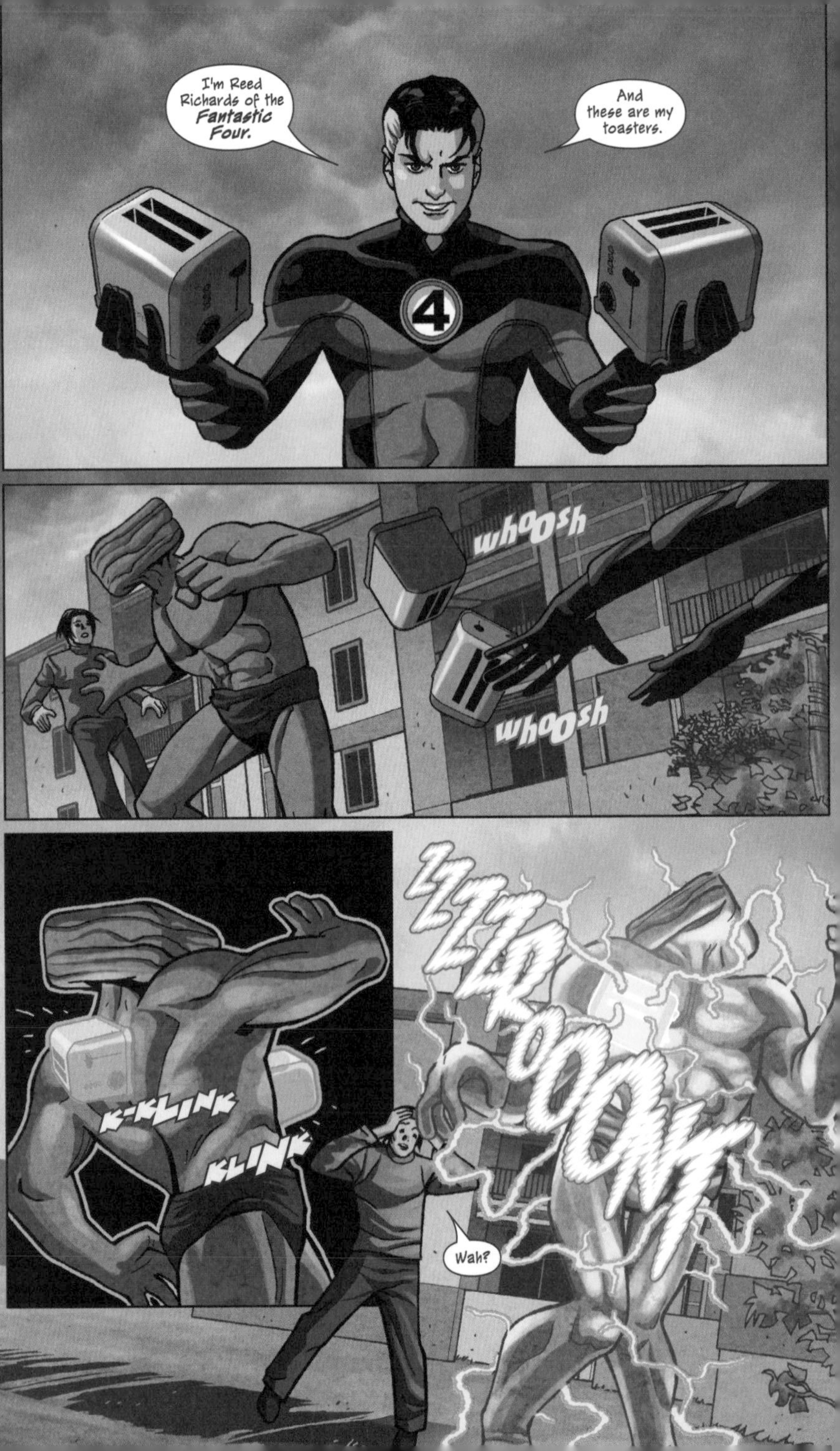
I'm Reed Richards of the *Fantastic Four.*
And these are my toasters.
whoosh
whoosh
K-KLINK
KLINK
ZZZZROOOOM
Wah?

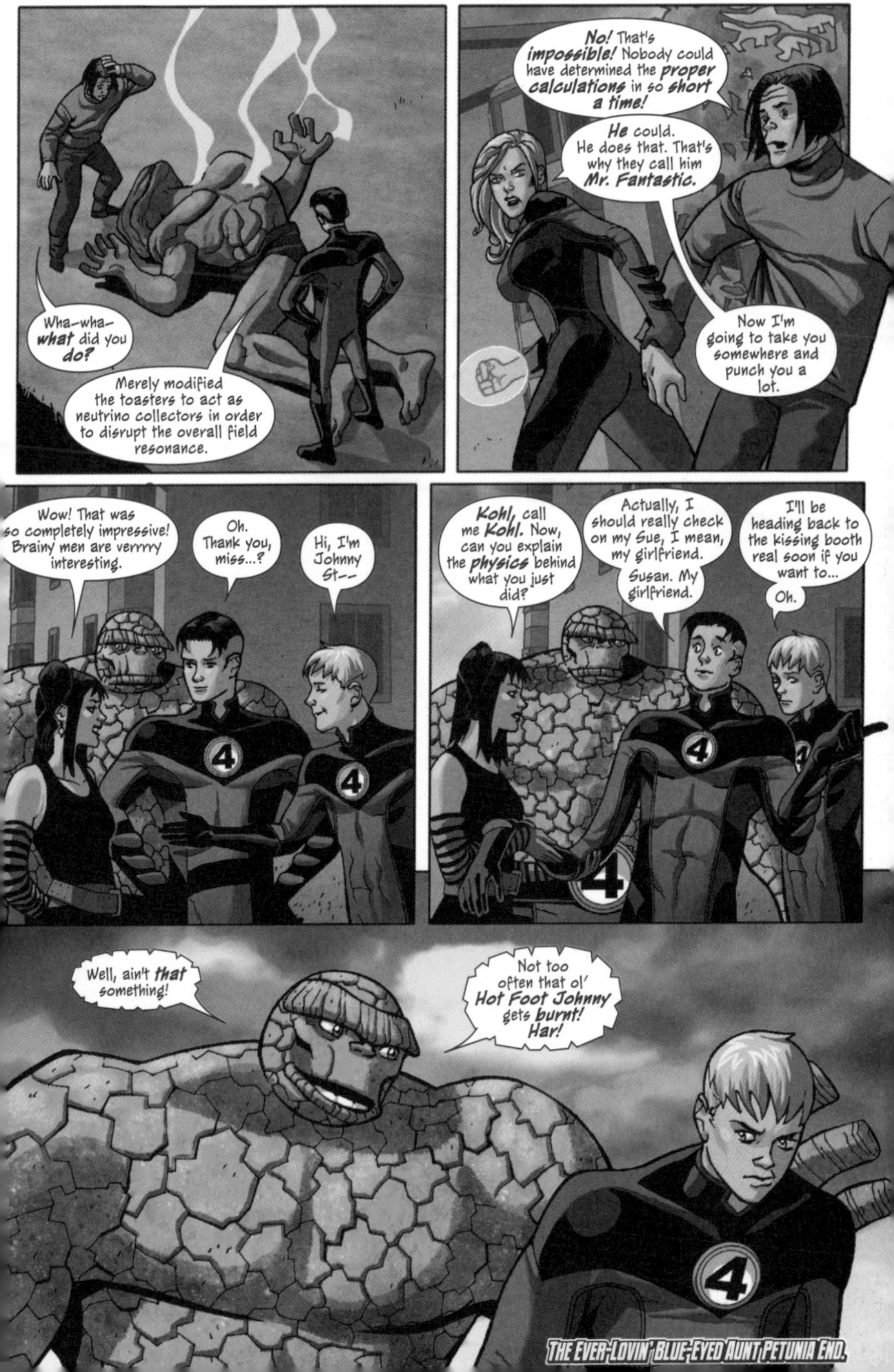

Wha-wha-what did you do?
Merely modified the toasters to act as neutrino collectors in order to disrupt the overall field resonance.
No! That's impossible! Nobody could have determined the proper calculations in so short a time!
He could. He does that. That's why they call him Mr. Fantastic.
Now I'm going to take you somewhere and punch you a lot.
Wow! That was so completely impressive! Brainy men are verrrry interesting.
Oh. Thank you, miss...?
Hi, I'm Johnny St--
Kohl, call me Kohl. Now, can you explain the physics behind what you just did?
Actually, I should really check on my Sue, I mean, my girlfriend.
Susan. My girlfriend.
I'll be heading back to the kissing booth real soon if you want to...
Oh.
Well, ain't that something!
Not too often that ol' Hot Foot Johnny gets burnt! Har!
THE EVER-LOVIN' BLUE-EYED AUNT PETUNIA END.

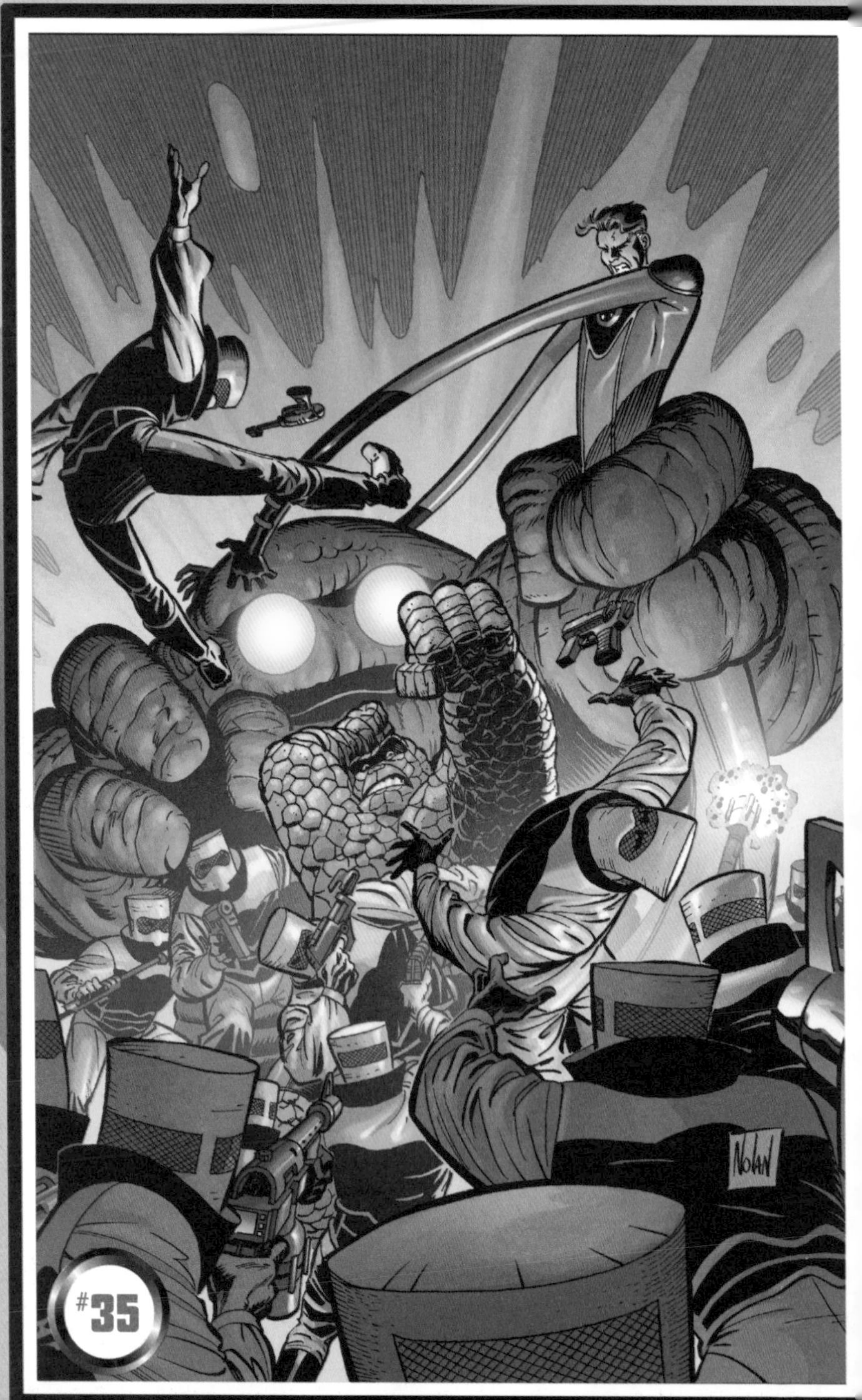
#35
NOLAN

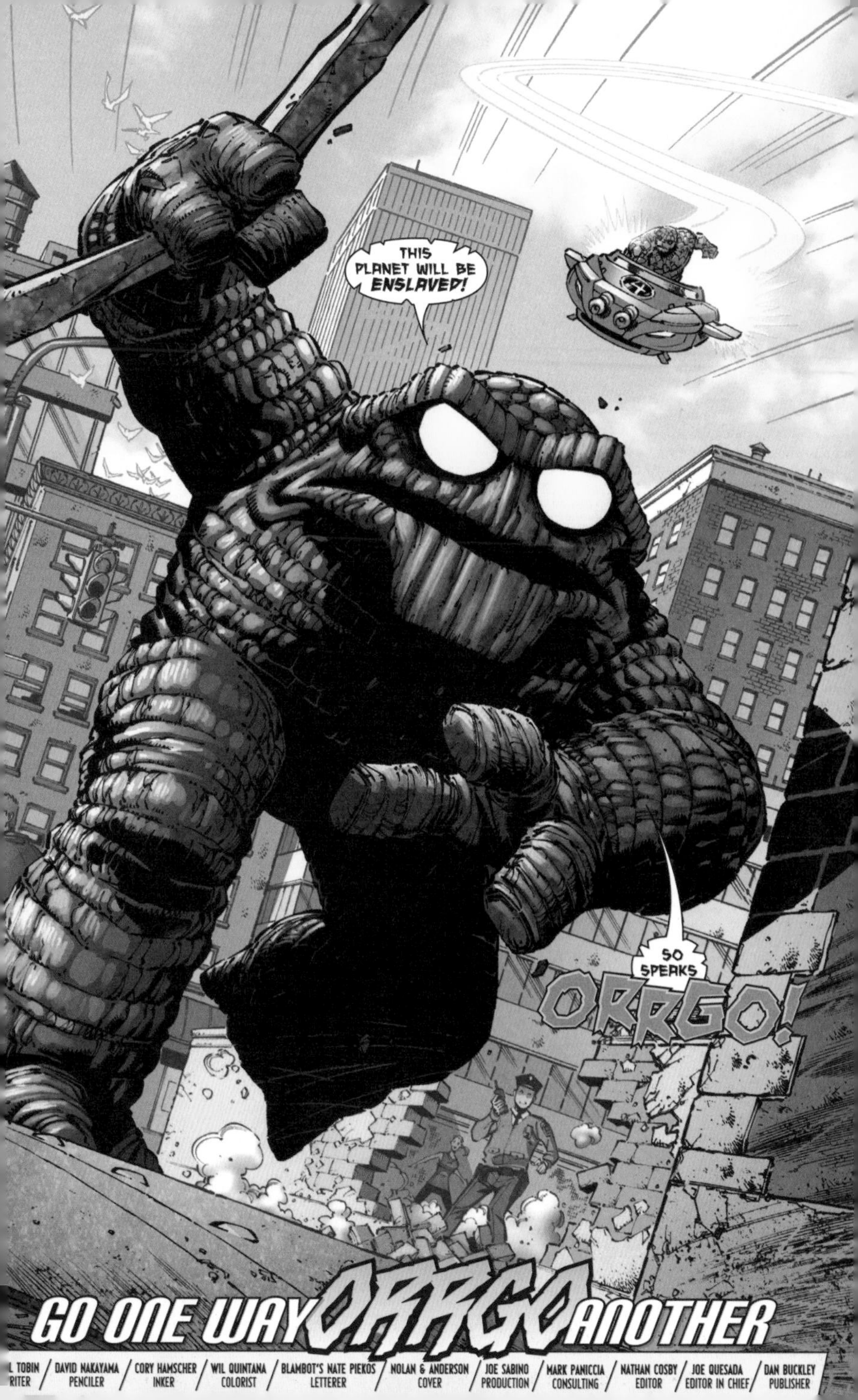
THIS PLANET WILL BE ENSLAVED!
SO SPEAKS
ORRGO!
GO ONE WAY ORRGO ANOTHER
L TOBIN / DAVID NAKAYAMA / CORY HAMSCHER / WIL QUINTANA / BLAMBOT'S NATE PIEKOS / NOLAN & ANDERSON / JOE SABINO / MARK PANICCIA / NATHAN COSBY / JOE QUESADA / DAN BUCKLEY
RITER / PENCILER / INKER / COLORIST / LETTERER / COVER / PRODUCTION / CONSULTING / EDITOR / EDITOR IN CHIEF / PUBLISHER

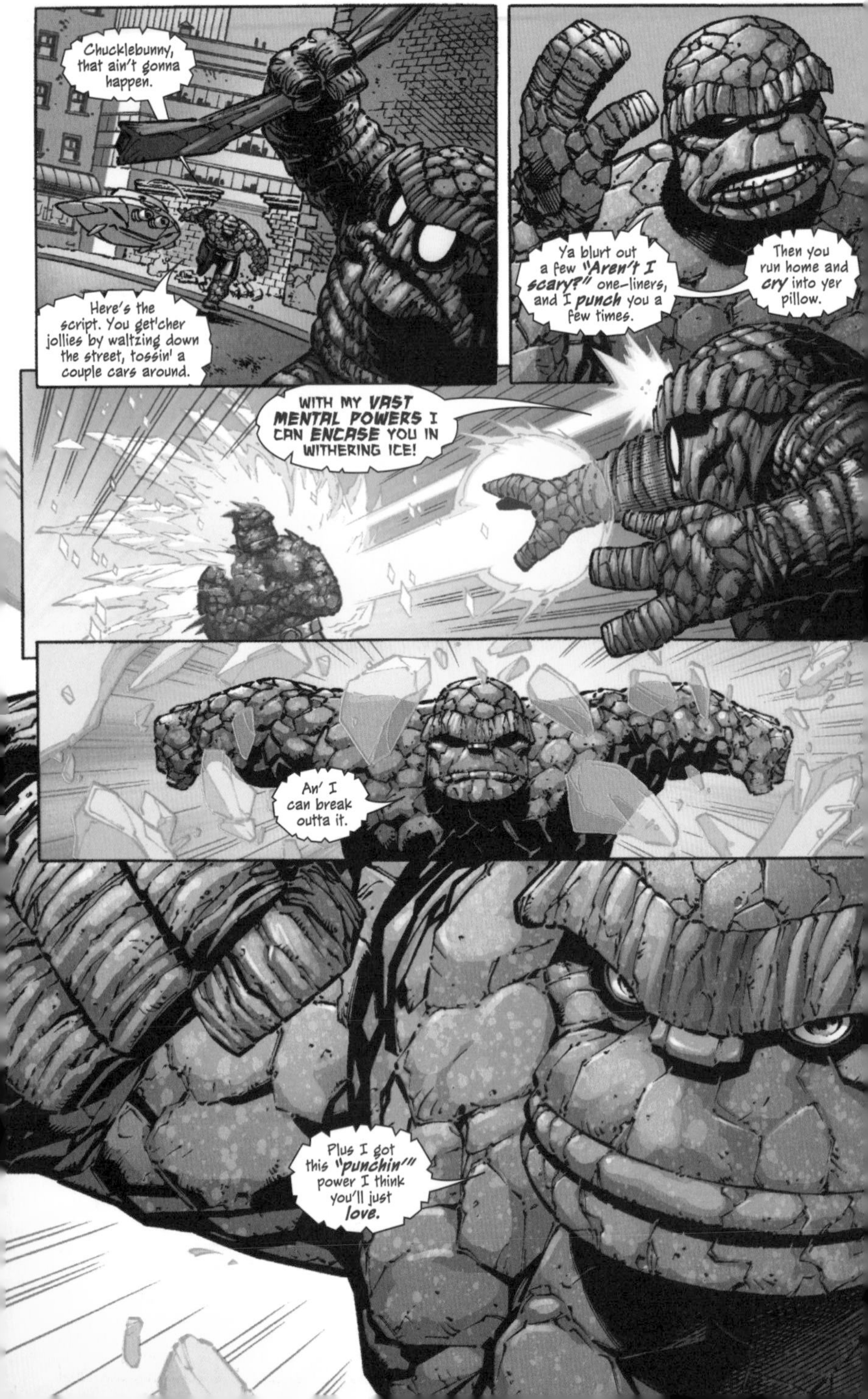
Chucklebunny, that ain't gonna happen.
Here's the script. You get'cher jollies by waltzing down the street, tossin' a couple cars around.
Ya blurt out a few "Aren't I scary?" one-liners, and I punch you a few times.
Then you run home and cry into yer pillow.
WITH MY VAST MENTAL POWERS I CAN ENCASE YOU IN WITHERING ICE!
An' I can break outta it.
Plus I got this "punchin'" power I think you'll just love.

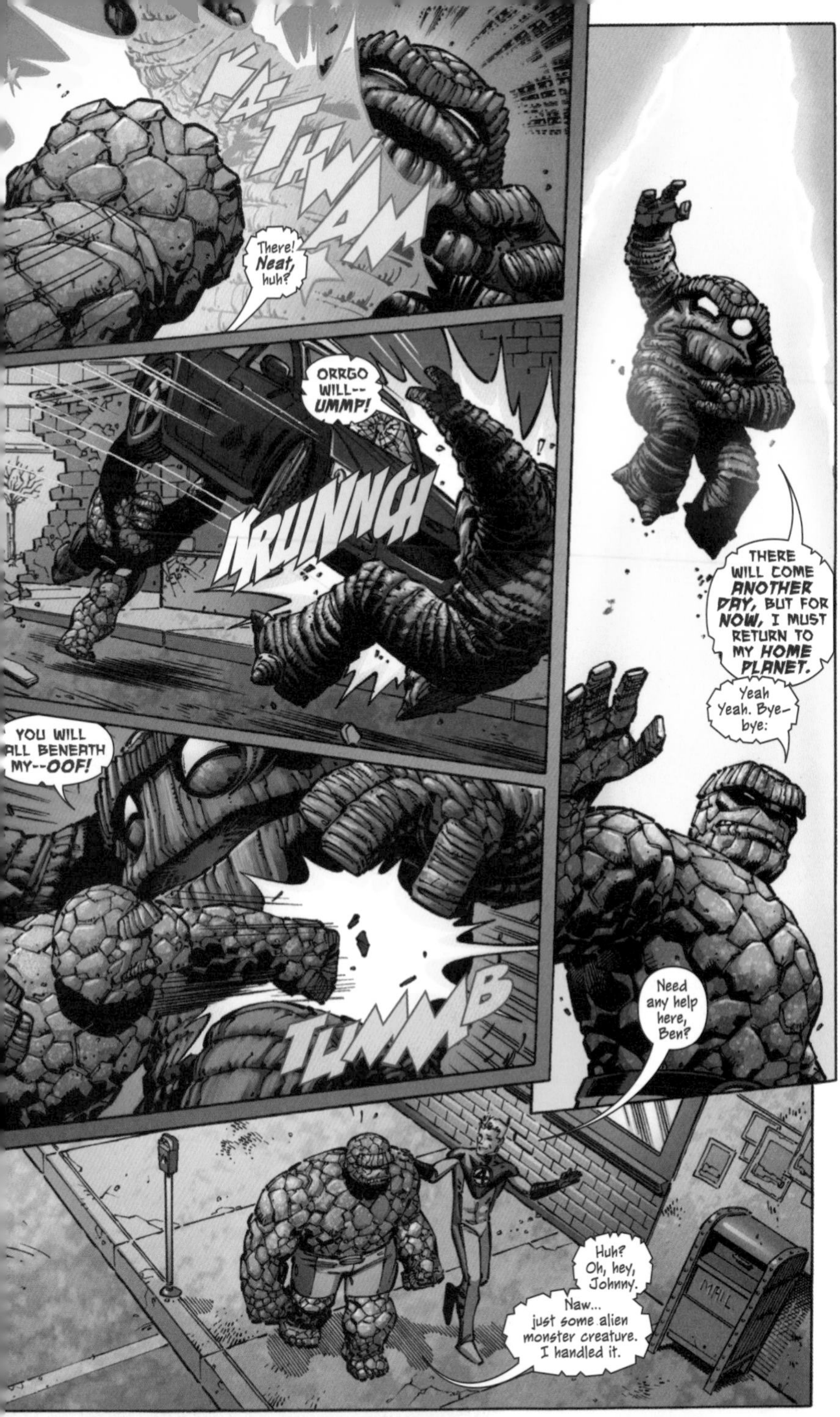
KA-THWAM
There! Neat, huh?
ORRGO WILL-- UMMP!
KRUNNCH
YOU WILL ALL BENEATH MY--OOF!
TUMMB
THERE WILL COME ANOTHER DAY, BUT FOR NOW, I MUST RETURN TO MY HOME PLANET.
Yeah Yeah. Bye-bye:
Need any help here, Ben?
Huh? Oh, hey, Johnny.
Naw... just some alien monster creature. I handled it.
MAIL

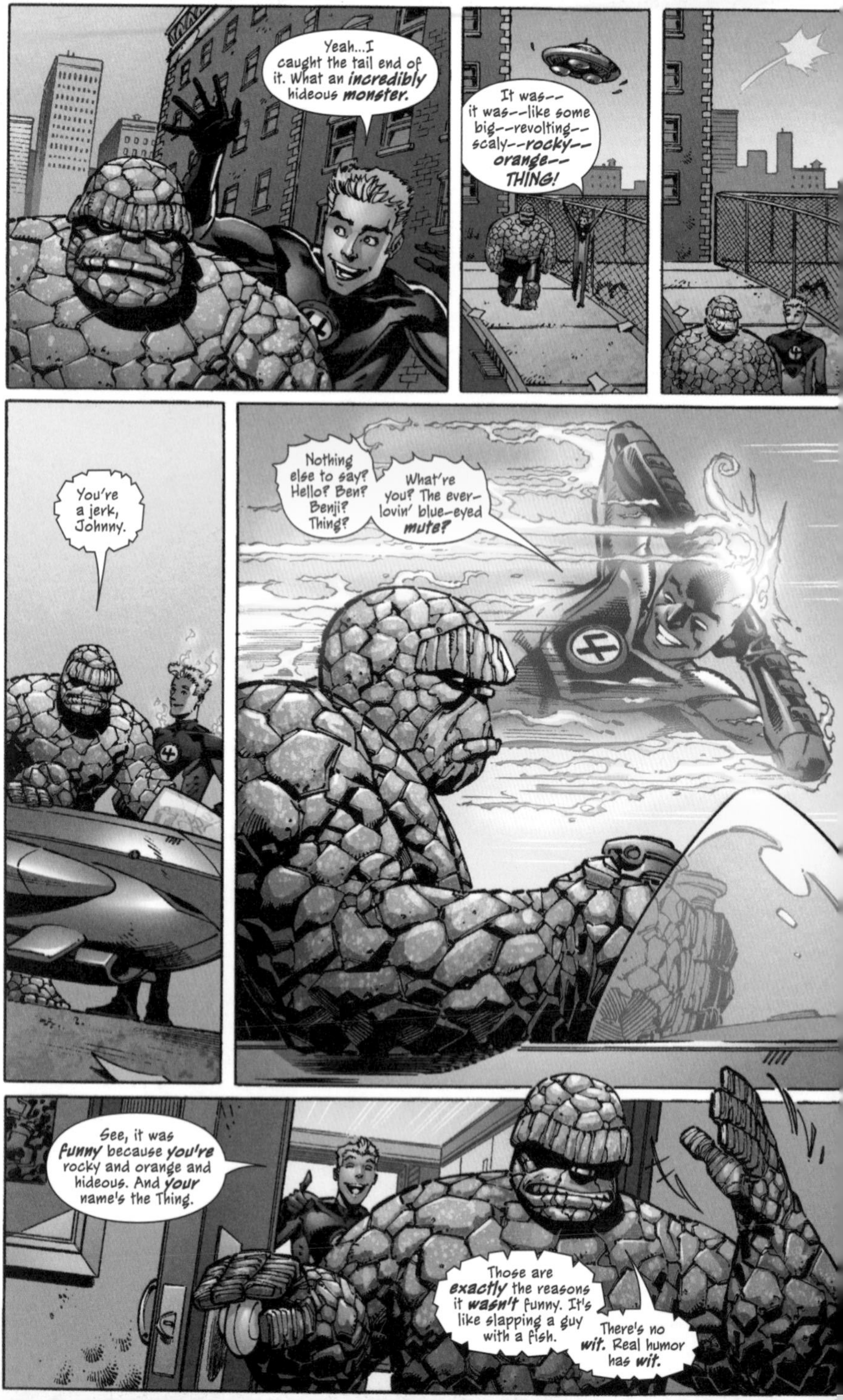
Yeah...I caught the tail end of it. What an incredibly hideous monster.
It was-- it was--like some big--revolting--scaly--rocky--orange--THING!
You're a jerk, Johnny.
Nothing else to say? Hello? Ben? Benji? Thing?
What're you? The ever-lovin' blue-eyed mute?
See, it was funny because you're rocky and orange and hideous. And your name's the Thing.
Those are exactly the reasons it wasn't funny. It's like slapping a guy with a fish.
There's no wit. Real humor has wit.

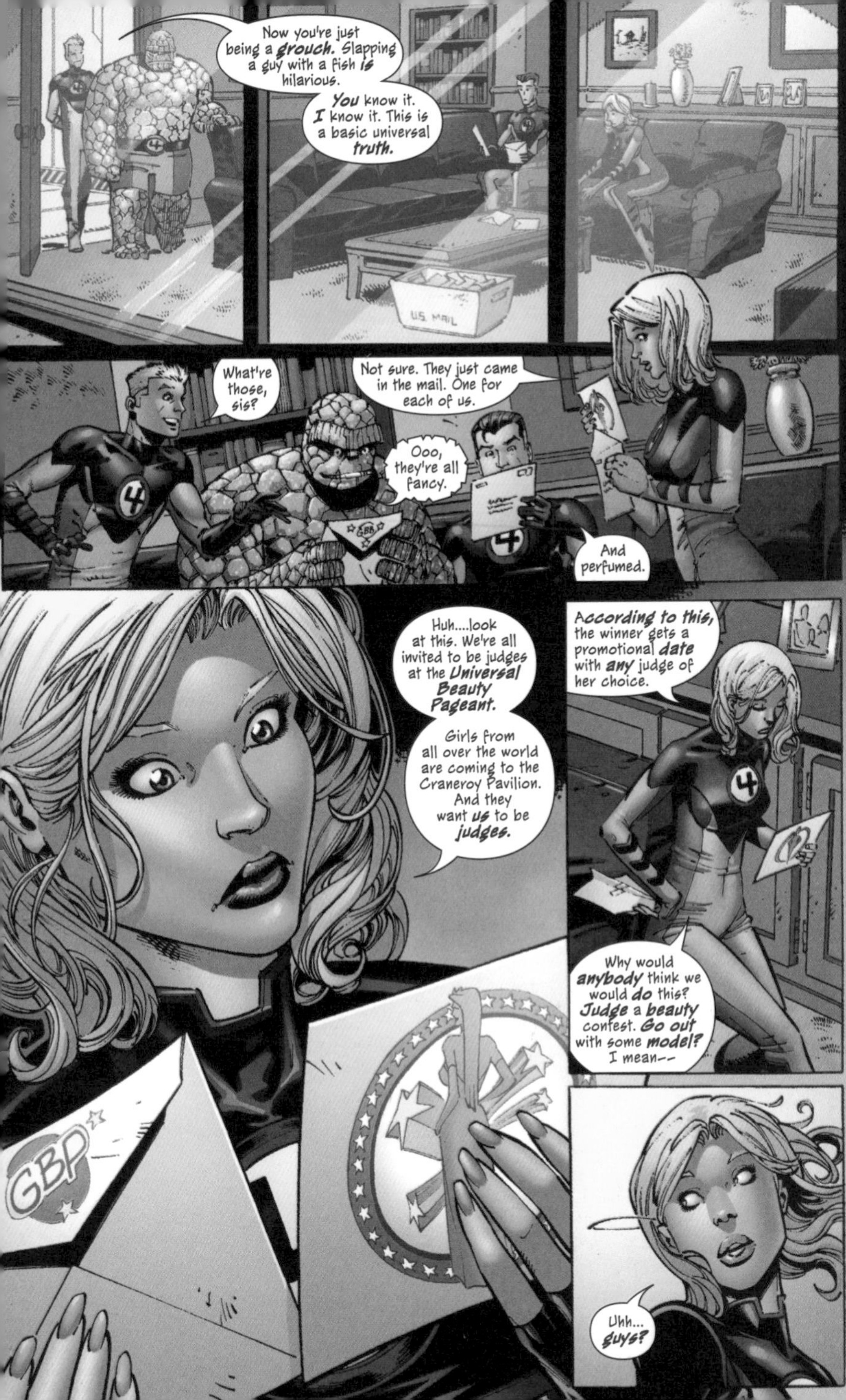
Now you're just being a grouch. Slapping a guy with a fish is hilarious.
You know it. I know it. This is a basic universal truth.
U.S. MAIL
What're those, sis?
Not sure. They just came in the mail. One for each of us.
Ooo, they're all fancy.
And perfumed.
Huh....look at this. We're all invited to be judges at the Universal Beauty Pageant.
Girls from all over the world are coming to the Craneroy Pavilion. And they want us to be judges.
According to this, the winner gets a promotional date with any judge of her choice.
Why would anybody think we would do this? Judge a beauty contest. Go out with some model? I mean--
GBP
Uhh... guys?

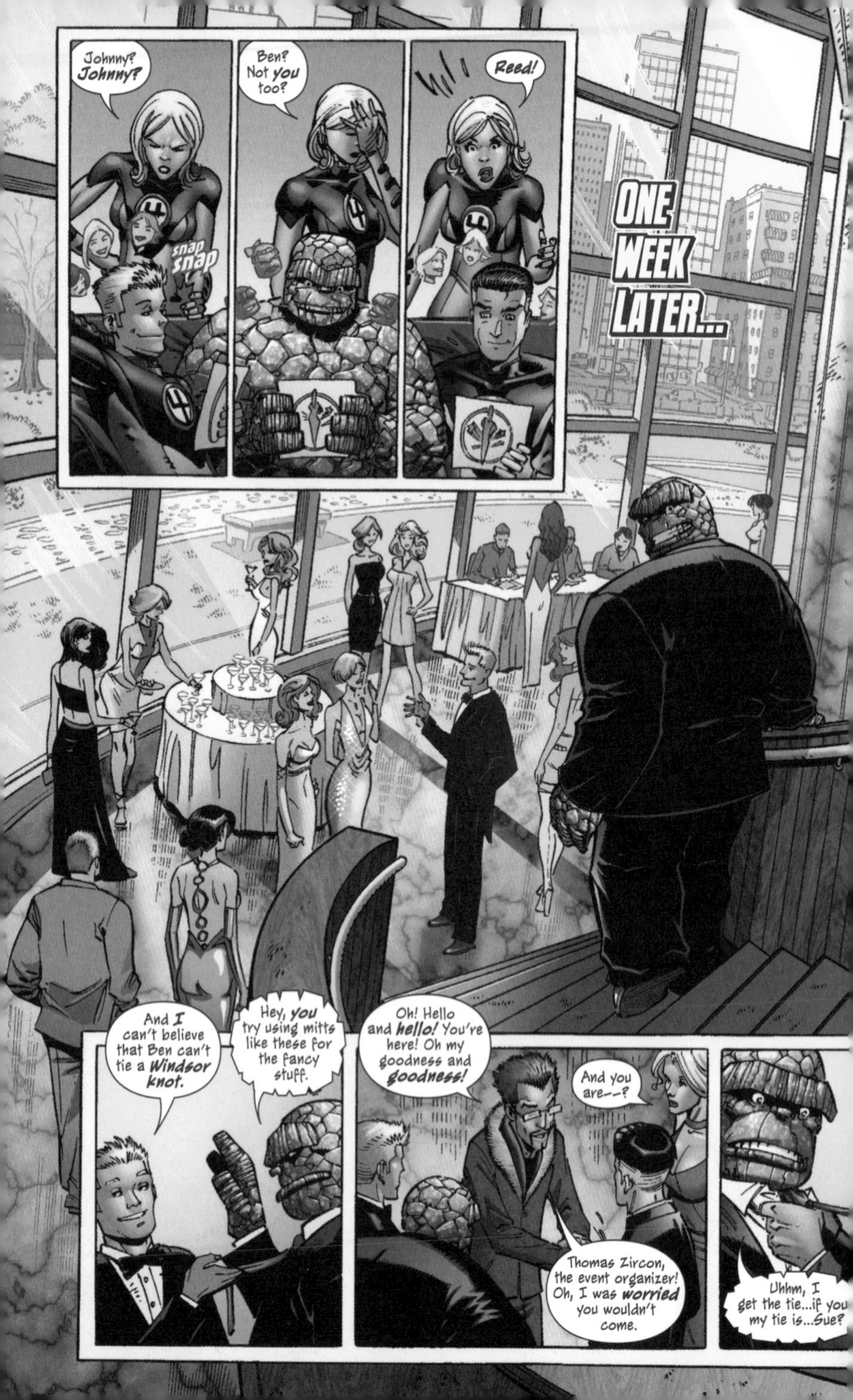
Johnny? Johnny?
snap snap
Ben? Not you too?
Reed!
ONE WEEK LATER...
And I can't believe that Ben can't tie a Windsor knot.
Hey, you try using mitts like these for the fancy stuff.
Oh! Hello and hello! You're here! Oh my goodness and goodness!
And you are--?
Thomas Zircon, the event organizer! Oh, I was worried you wouldn't come.
Uhhm, I get the tie...if you my tie is...Sue?

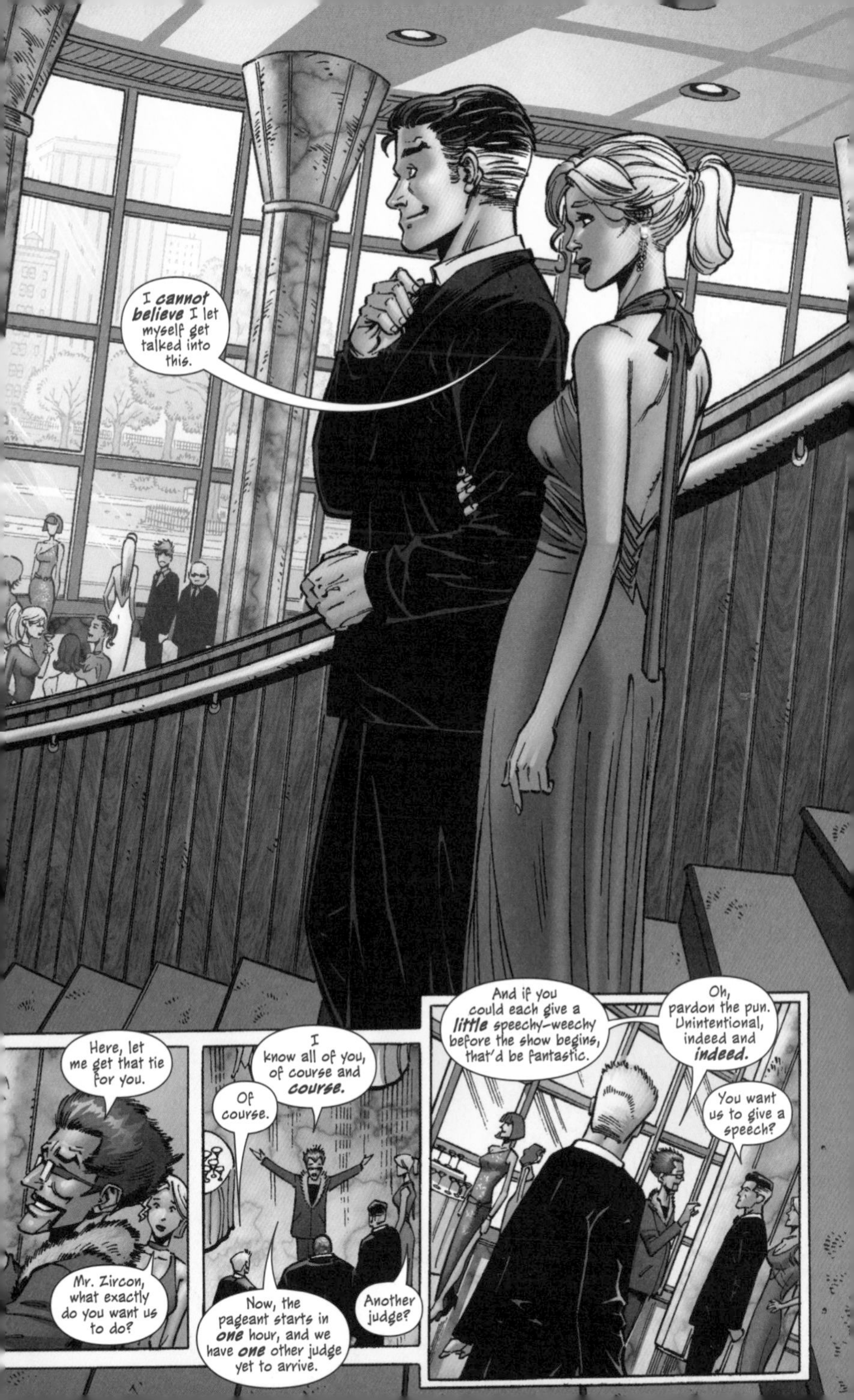

I cannot believe I let myself get talked into this.
Here, let me get that tie for you.
Mr. Zircon, what exactly do you want us to do?
I know all of you, of course and course.
Of course.
Now, the pageant starts in one hour, and we have one other judge yet to arrive.
Another judge?
And if you could each give a little speechy-weechy before the show begins, that'd be fantastic.
Oh, pardon the pun. Unintentional, indeed and indeed.
You want us to give a speech?

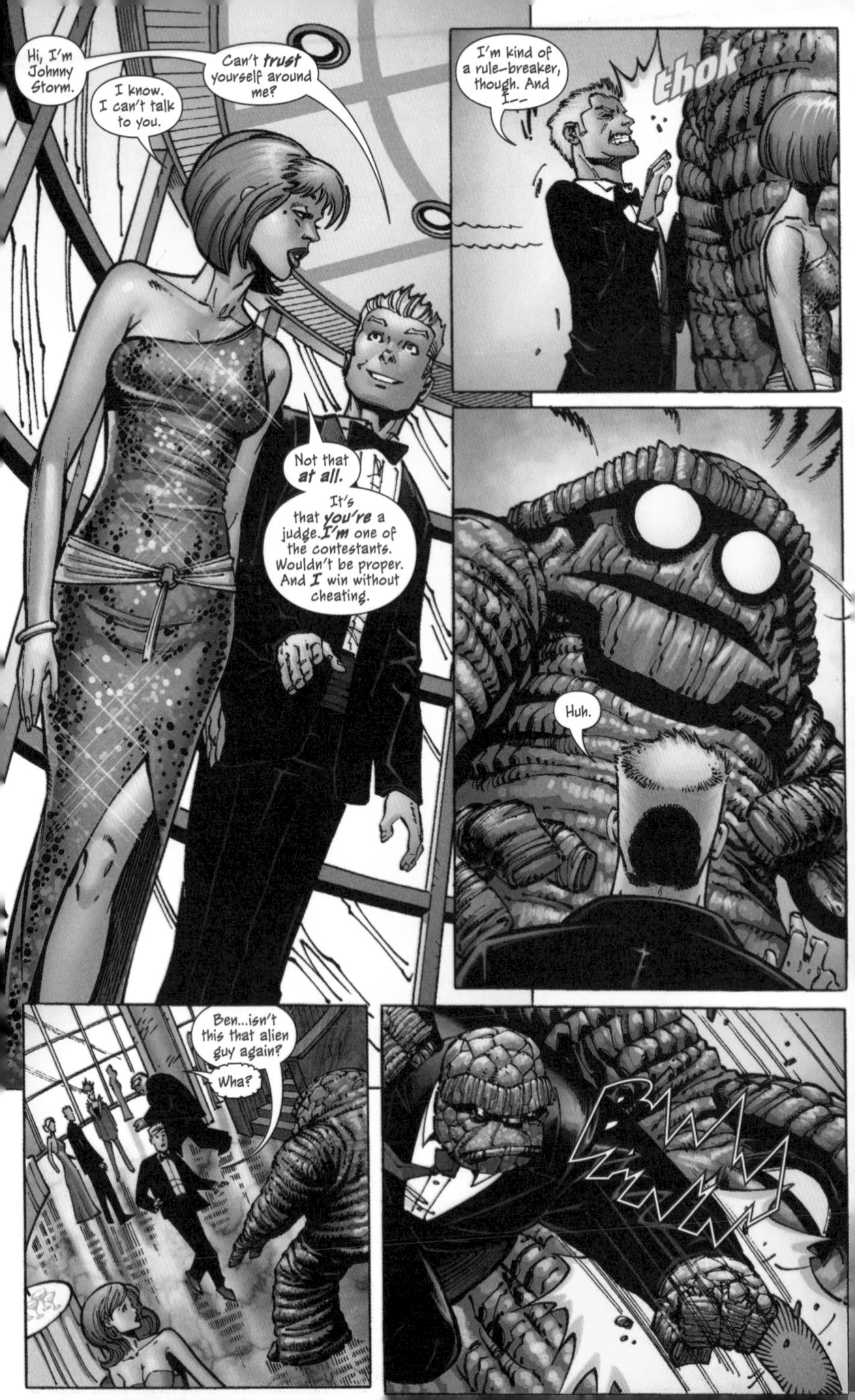
Hi, I'm Johnny Storm.
I know. I can't talk to you.
Can't trust yourself around me?
Not that at all.
It's that you're a judge. I'm one of the contestants. Wouldn't be proper. And I win without cheating.
I'm kind of a rule-breaker, though. And I--
thok
Huh.
Ben...isn't this that alien guy again?
Wha?

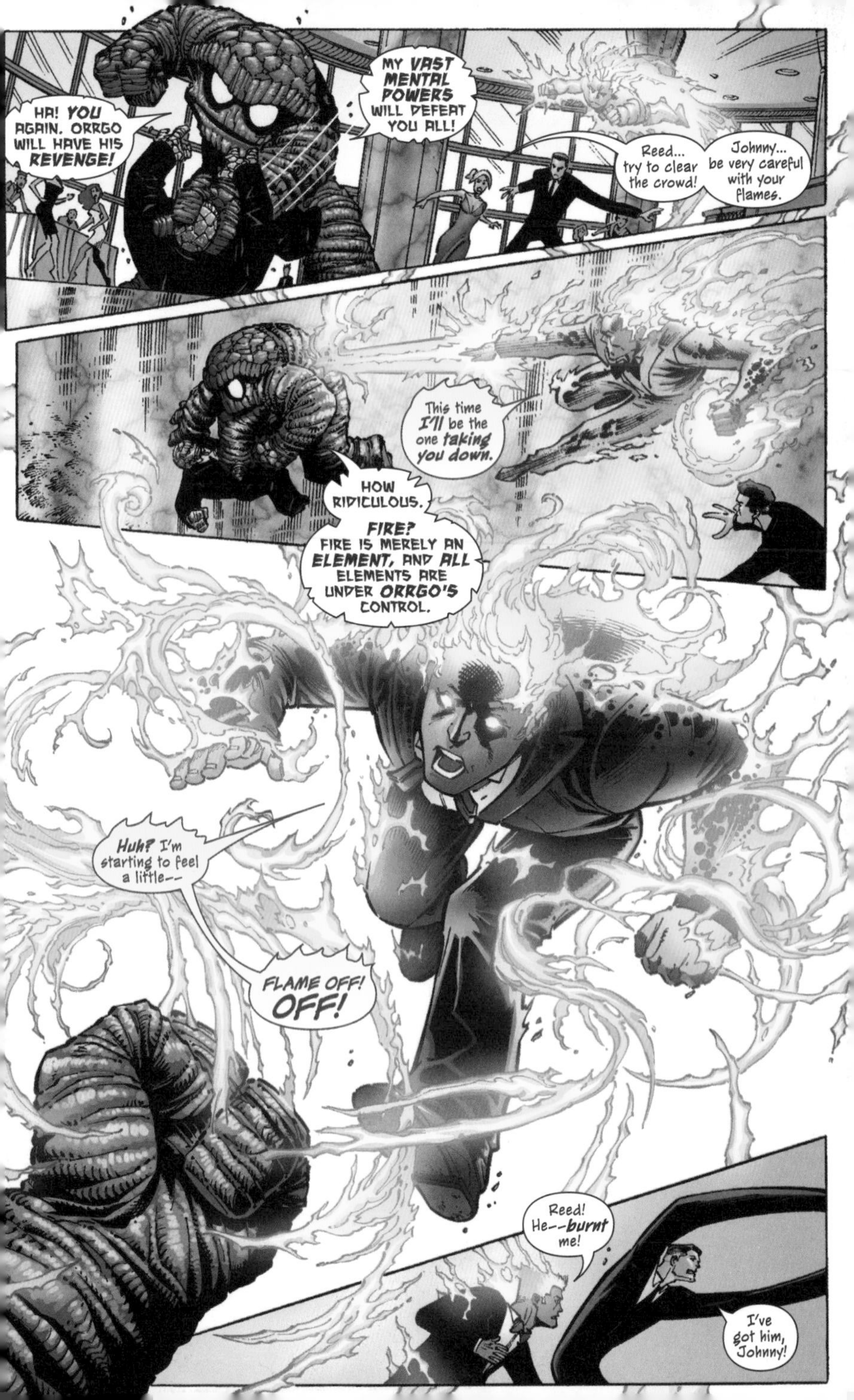
HA! YOU AGAIN. ORRGO WILL HAVE HIS REVENGE!
MY VAST MENTAL POWERS WILL DEFEAT YOU ALL!
Reed... try to clear the crowd!
Johnny... be very careful with your flames.
This time I'll be the one taking you down.
HOW RIDICULOUS.
FIRE? FIRE IS MERELY AN ELEMENT, AND ALL ELEMENTS ARE UNDER ORRGO'S CONTROL.
Huh? I'm starting to feel a little--
FLAME OFF! OFF!
Reed! He--burnt me!
I've got him, Johnny!

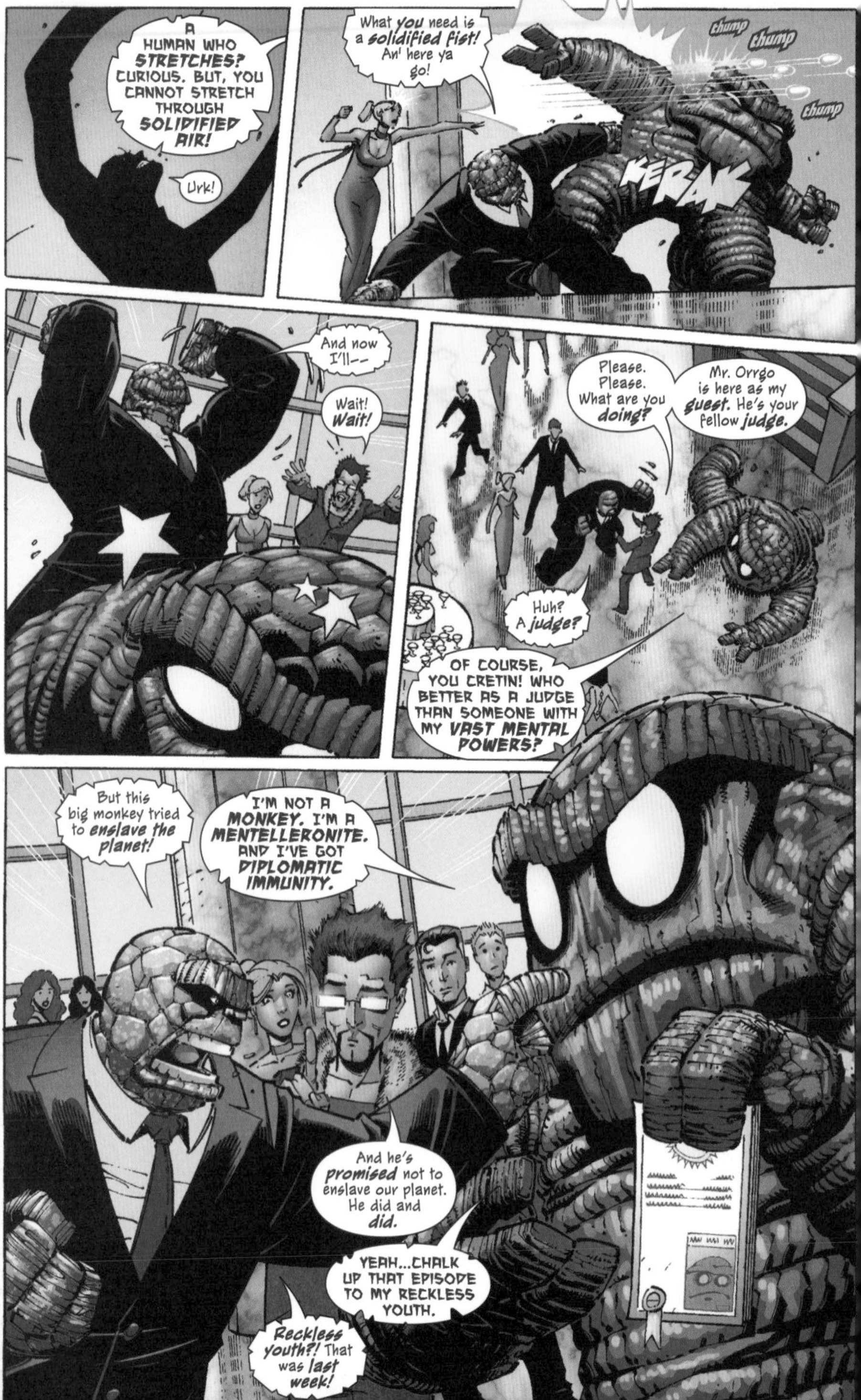

A HUMAN WHO STRETCHES? CURIOUS. BUT, YOU CANNOT STRETCH THROUGH SOLIDIFIED AIR!
Urk!
What you need is a solidified fist! An' here ya go!
thump
thump
thump
KERAK
And now I'll--
Wait! Wait!
Please. Please. What are you doing?
Mr. Orrgo is here as my guest. He's your fellow judge.
Huh? A judge?
OF COURSE, YOU CRETIN! WHO BETTER AS A JUDGE THAN SOMEONE WITH MY VAST MENTAL POWERS?
But this big monkey tried to enslave the planet!
I'M NOT A MONKEY. I'M A MENTELLERONITE. AND I'VE GOT DIPLOMATIC IMMUNITY.
And he's promised not to enslave our planet. He did and did.
YEAH...CHALK UP THAT EPISODE TO MY RECKLESS YOUTH.
Reckless youth?! That was last week!

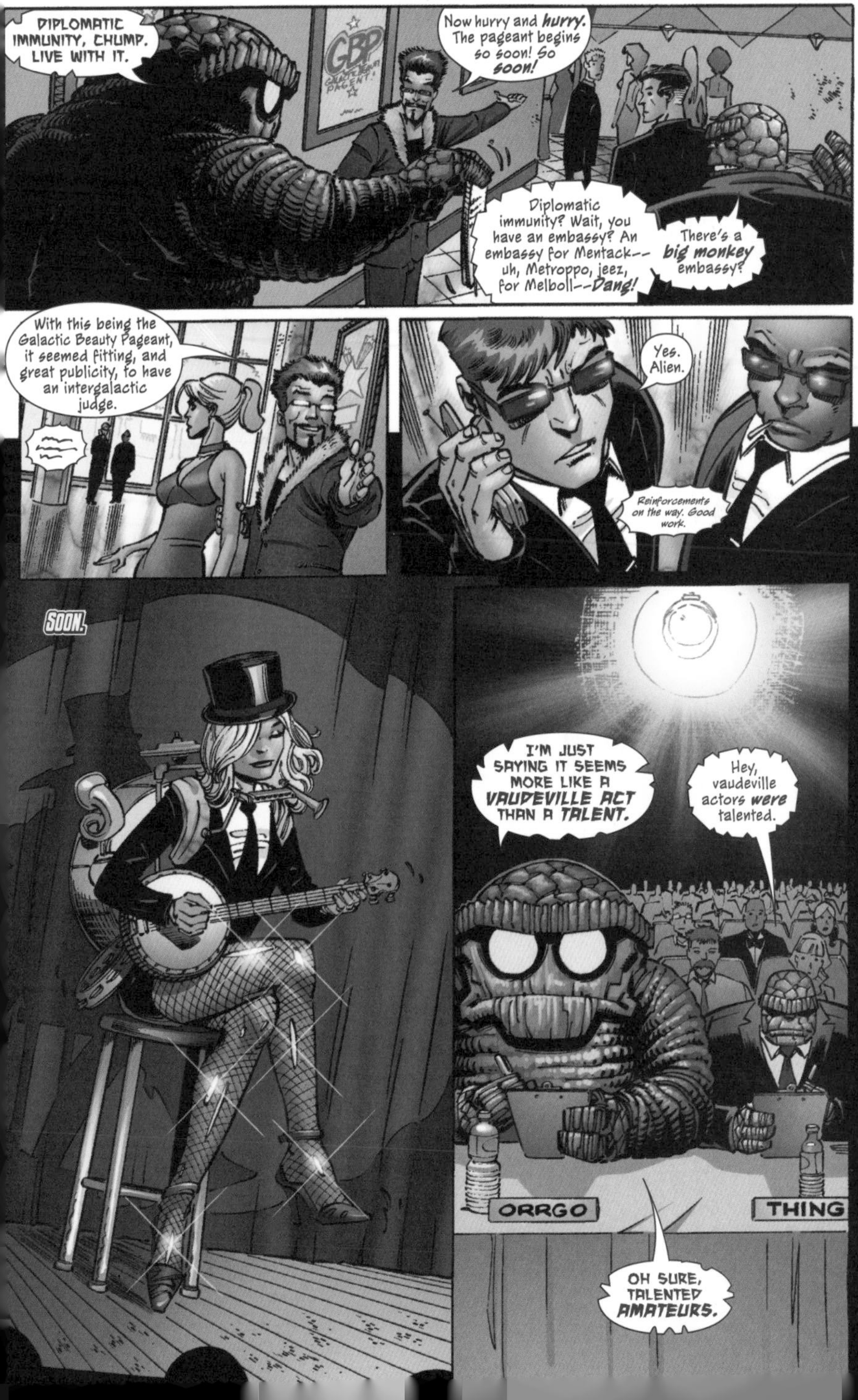
DIPLOMATIC IMMUNITY, CHUMP. LIVE WITH IT.
Now hurry and hurry. The pageant begins so soon! So soon!
GBP GALACTIC BEAUTY PAGENT!
Diplomatic immunity? Wait, you have an embassy? An embassy for Mentack--uh, Metroppo, jeez, for Melboll--Dang!
There's a big monkey embassy?
With this being the Galactic Beauty Pageant, it seemed fitting, and great publicity, to have an intergalactic judge.
Yes. Alien.
Reinforcements on the way. Good work.
SOON.
I'M JUST SAYING IT SEEMS MORE LIKE A VAUDEVILLE ACT THAN A TALENT.
Hey, vaudeville actors were talented.
ORRGO
THING
OH SURE, TALENTED AMATEURS.

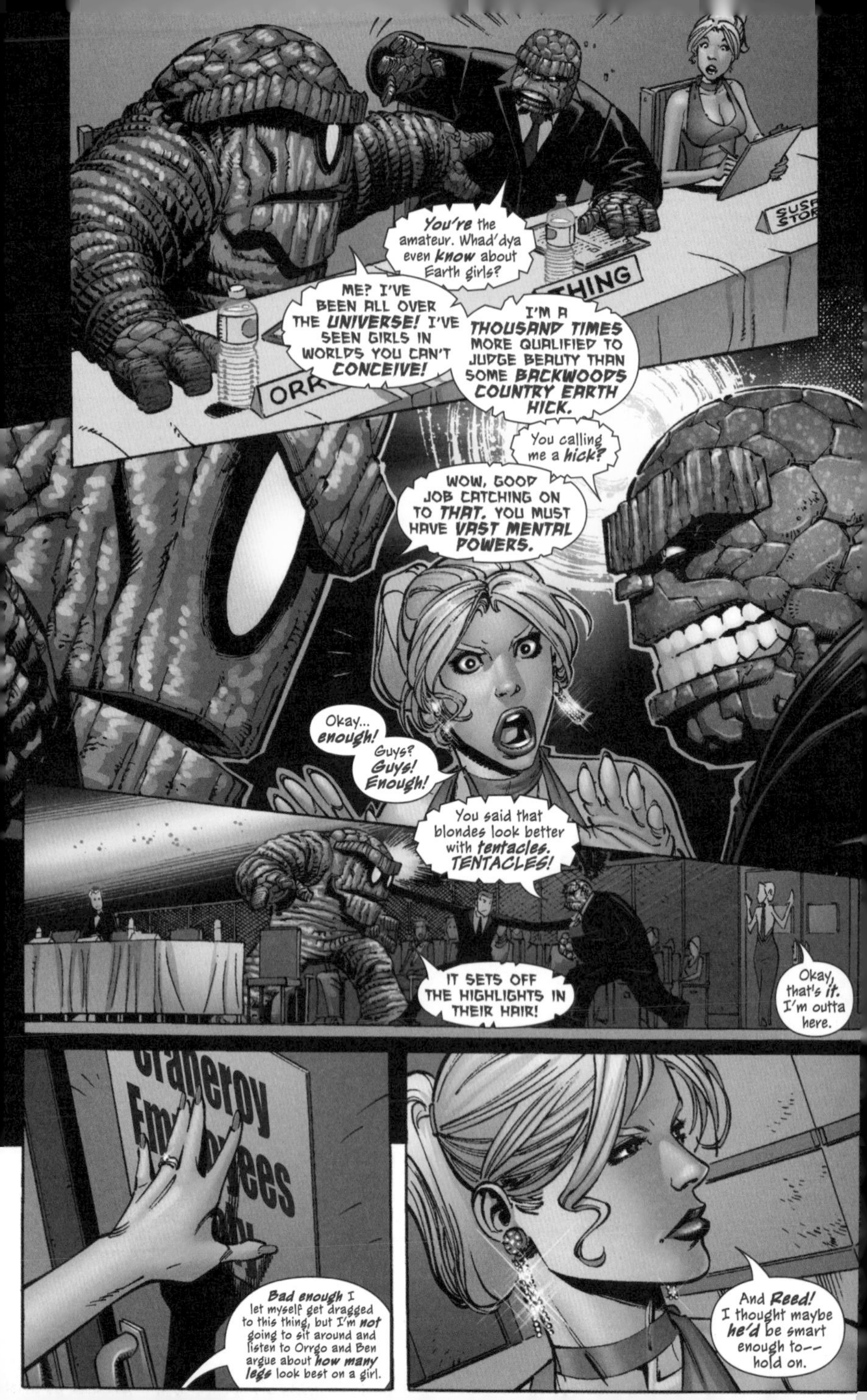
SUSAN STORM
THING
ORRGO
You're the amateur. Whad'dya even know about Earth girls?
ME? I'VE BEEN ALL OVER THE UNIVERSE! I'VE SEEN GIRLS IN WORLDS YOU CAN'T CONCEIVE!
I'M A THOUSAND TIMES MORE QUALIFIED TO JUDGE BEAUTY THAN SOME BACKWOODS COUNTRY EARTH HICK.
You calling me a hick?
WOW, GOOD JOB CATCHING ON TO THAT. YOU MUST HAVE VAST MENTAL POWERS.
Okay... enough!
Guys? Guys! Enough!
You said that blondes look better with tentacles. TENTACLES!
IT SETS OFF THE HIGHLIGHTS IN THEIR HAIR!
Okay, that's it. I'm outta here.
Bad enough I let myself get dragged to this thing, but I'm not going to sit around and listen to Orrgo and Ben argue about how many legs look best on a girl.
And Reed! I thought maybe he'd be smart enough to-- hold on.

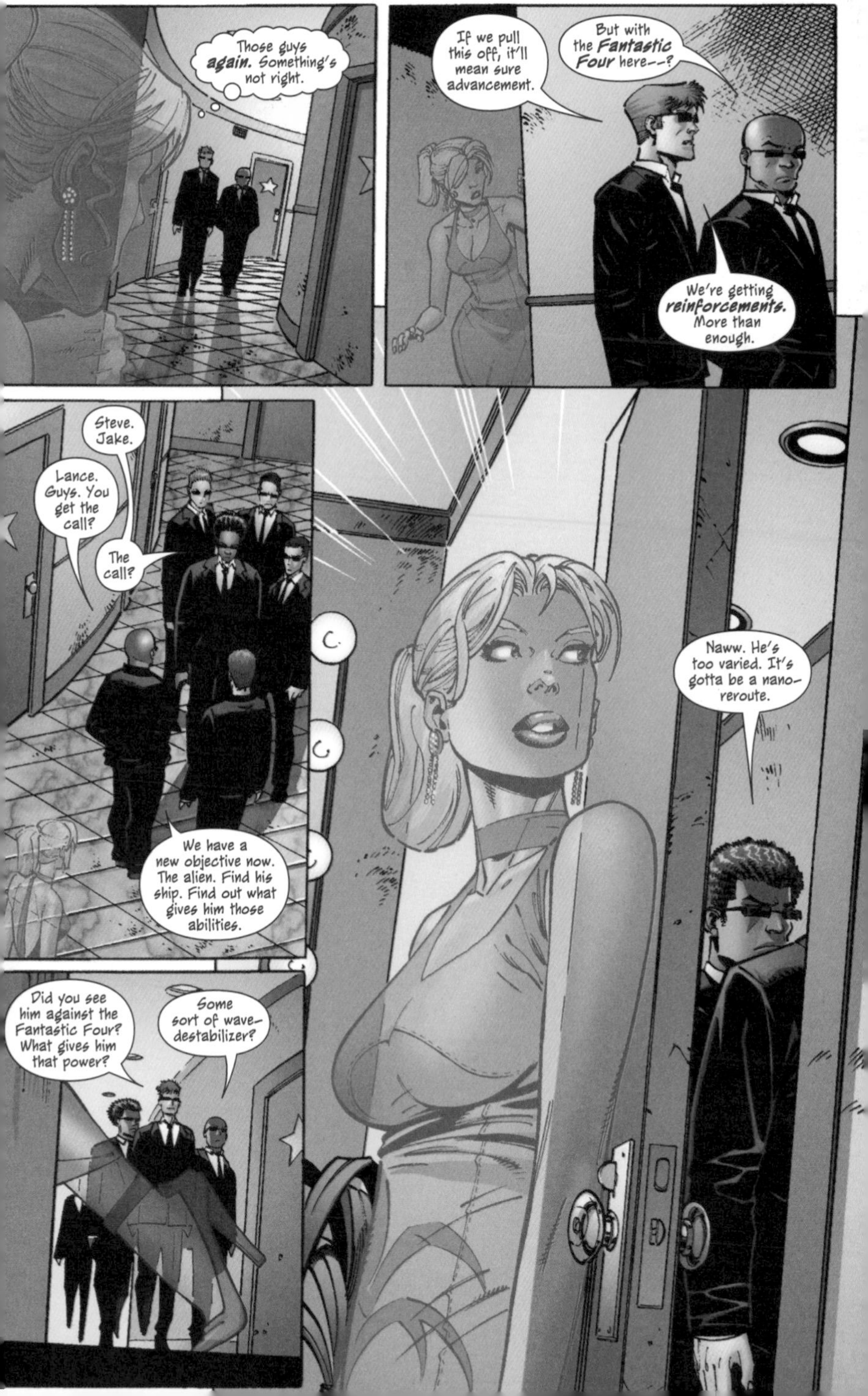

Those guys again. Something's not right.
If we pull this off, it'll mean sure advancement.
But with the Fantastic Four here--?
We're getting reinforcements. More than enough.
Steve. Jake.
Lance. Guys. You get the call?
The call?
We have a new objective now. The alien. Find his ship. Find out what gives him those abilities.
Did you see him against the Fantastic Four? What gives him that power?
Some sort of wave-destabilizer?
Naww. He's too varied. It's gotta be a nano-reroute.

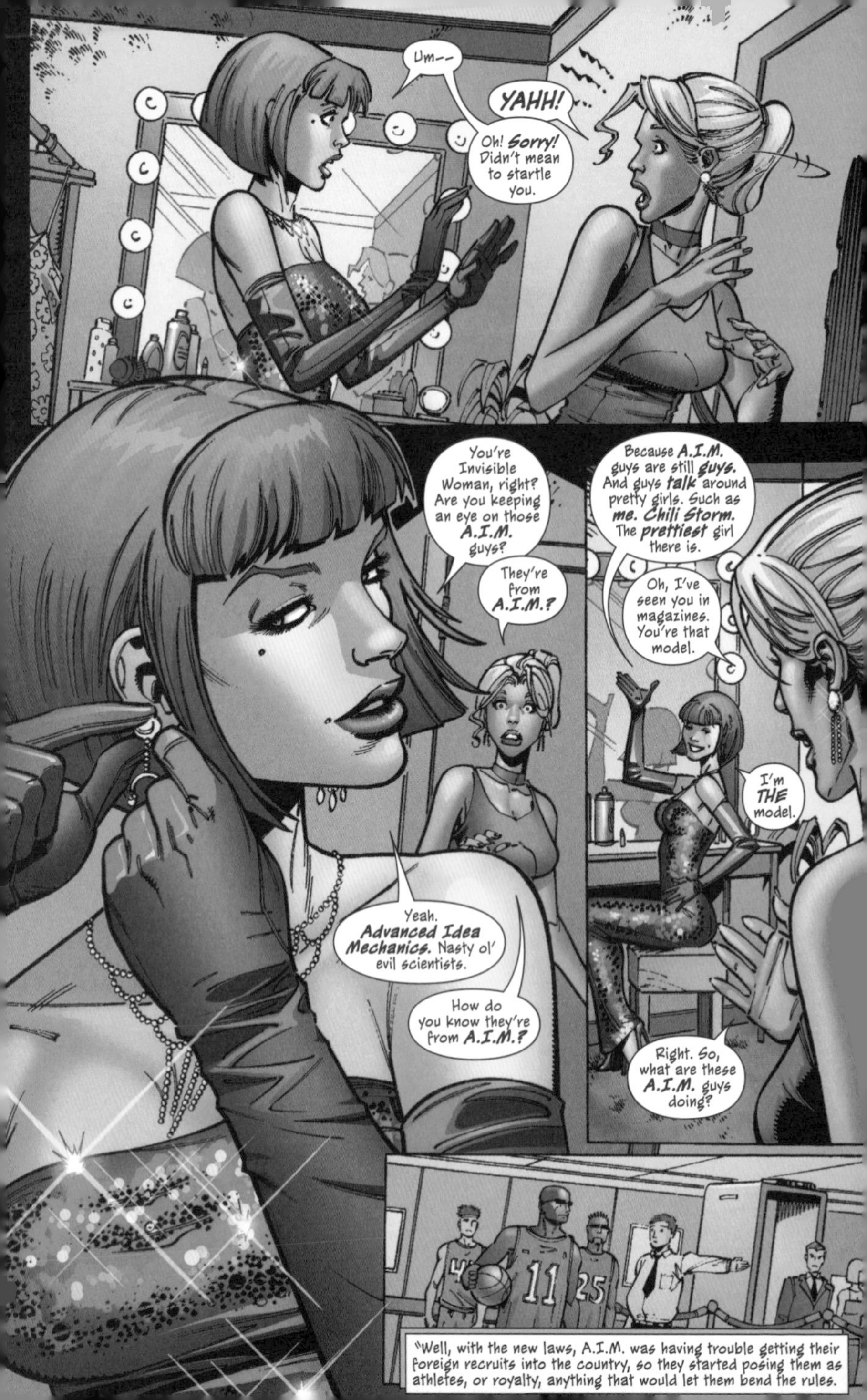

Um--
YAHH!
Oh! Sorry! Didn't mean to startle you.
You're Invisible Woman, right? Are you keeping an eye on those A.I.M. guys?
They're from A.I.M.?
Yeah. Advanced Idea Mechanics. Nasty ol' evil scientists.
How do you know they're from A.I.M.?
Because A.I.M. guys are still guys. And guys talk around pretty girls. Such as me. Chili Storm. The prettiest girl there is.
Oh, I've seen you in magazines. You're that model.
I'm THE model.
Right. So, what are these A.I.M. guys doing?
"Well, with the new laws, A.I.M. was having trouble getting their foreign recruits into the country, so they started posing them as athletes, or royalty, anything that would let them bend the rules.

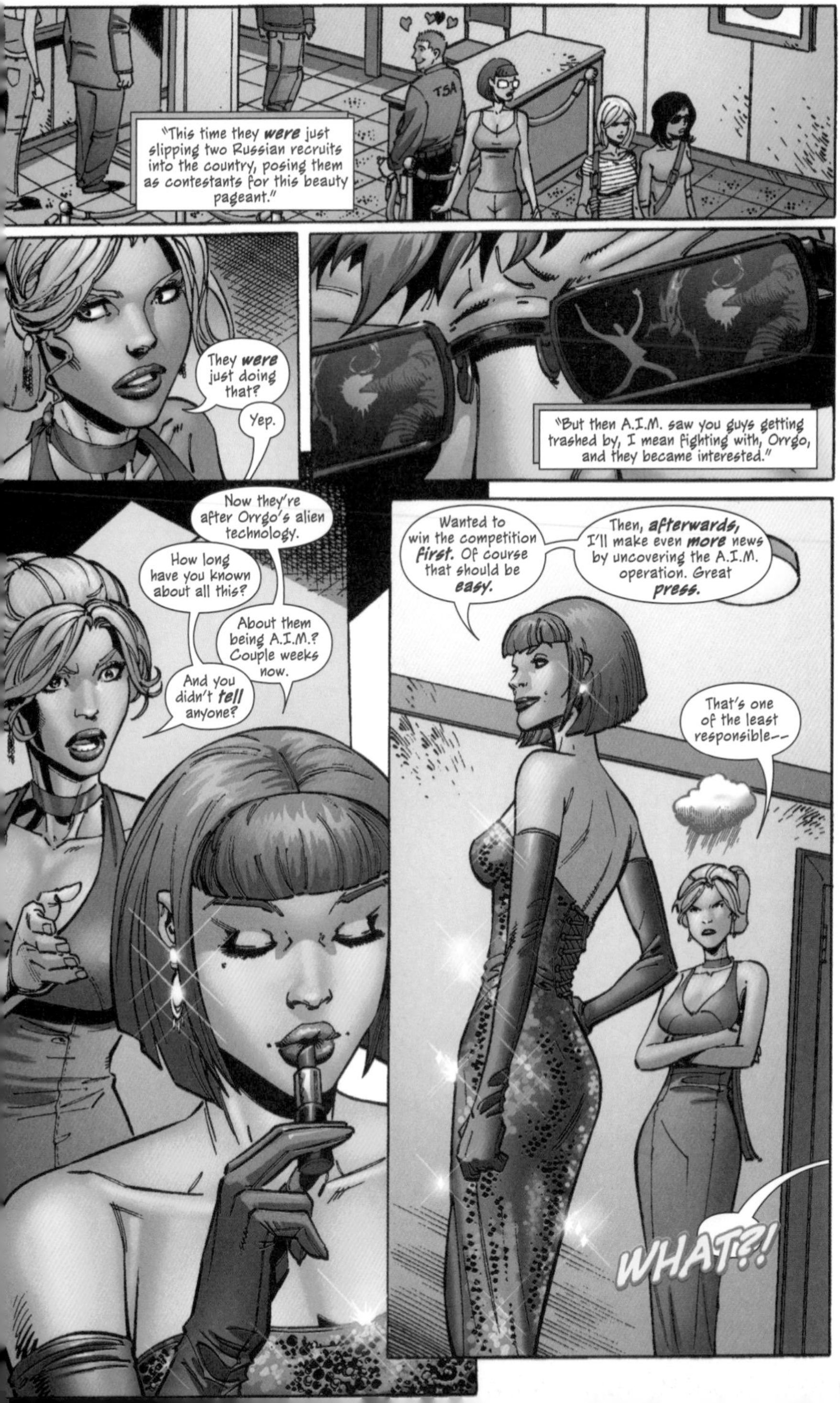
"This time they **were** just slipping two Russian recruits into the country, posing them as contestants for this beauty pageant."
They **were** just doing that?
Yep.
"But then A.I.M. saw you guys getting trashed by, I mean fighting with, Orrgo, and they became interested."
Now they're after Orrgo's alien technology.
How long have you known about all this?
About them being A.I.M.? Couple weeks now.
And you didn't **tell** anyone?
Wanted to win the competition **first**. Of course that should be **easy**.
Then, **afterwards**, I'll make even **more** news by uncovering the A.I.M. operation. Great **press**.
That's one of the least responsible--
WHAT?!

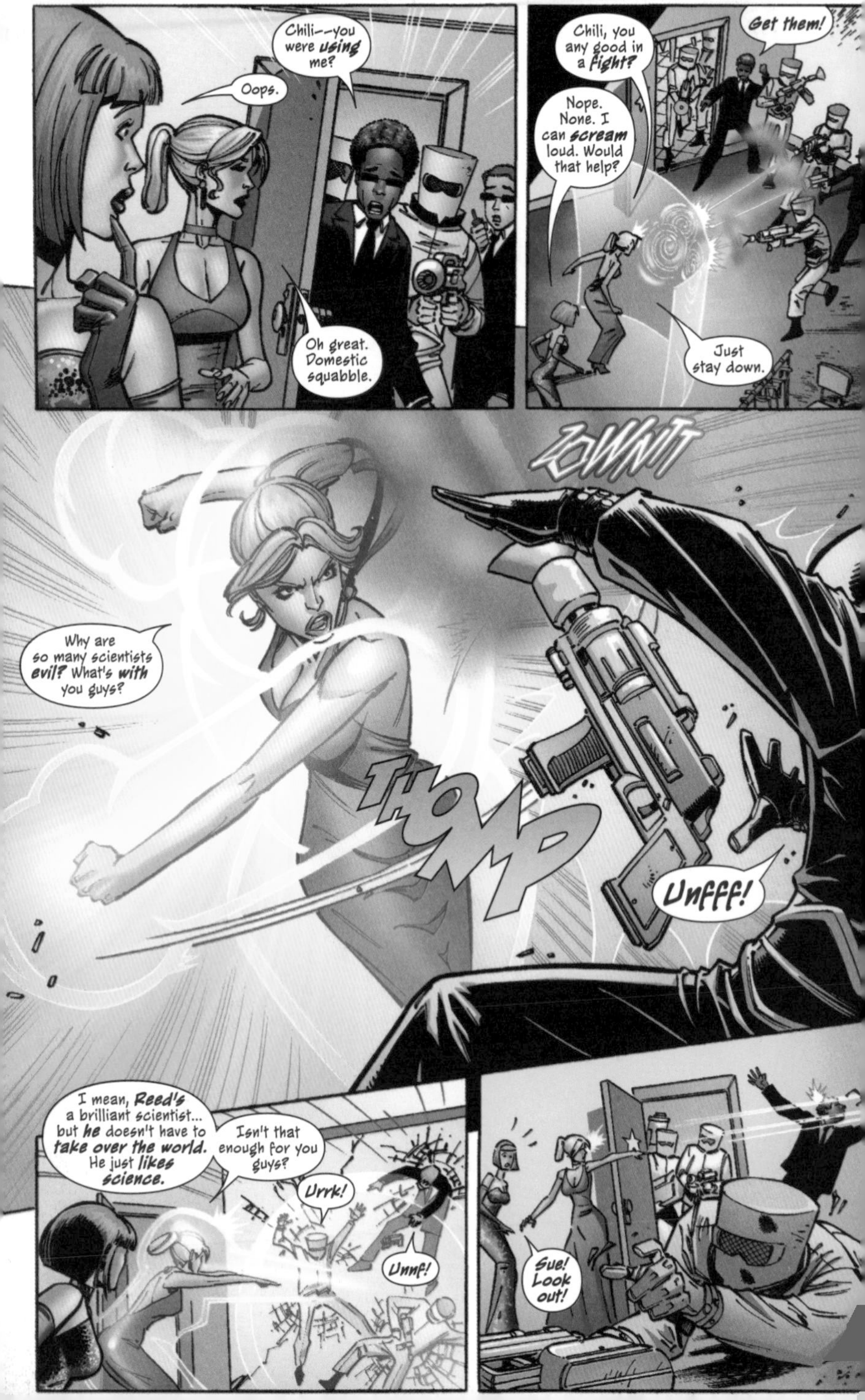
Chili--you were using me?
Oops.
Oh great. Domestic squabble.
Chili, you any good in a fight?
Get them!
Nope. None. I can scream loud. Would that help?
Just stay down.
ZOWNT
Why are so many scientists evil? What's with you guys?
THOMP
Unfff!
I mean, Reed's a brilliant scientist... but he doesn't have to take over the world. He just likes science.
Isn't that enough for you guys?
Urrk!
Unnf!
Sue! Look out!

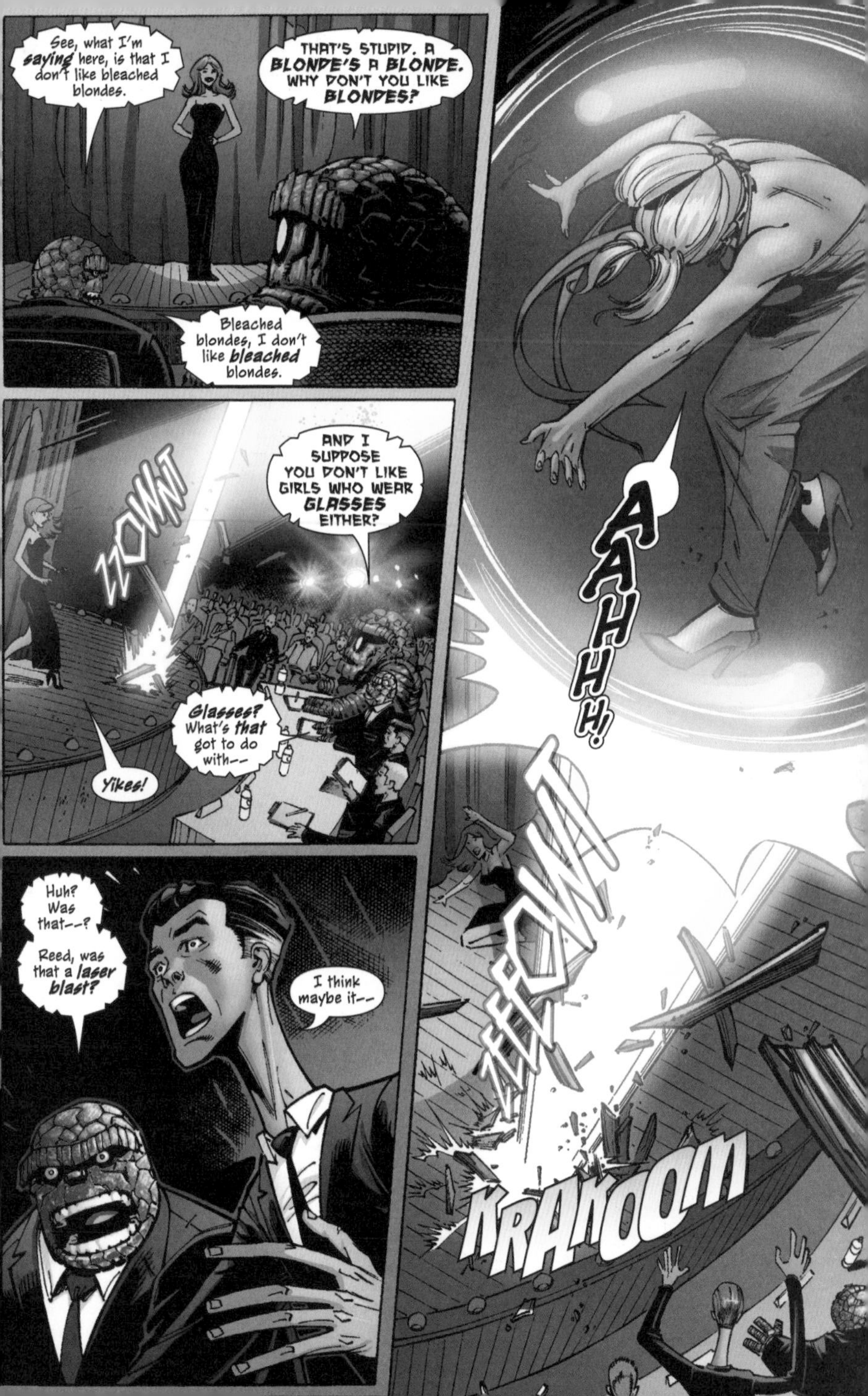
See, what I'm saying here, is that I don't like bleached blondes.
THAT'S STUPID. A BLONDE'S A BLONDE. WHY DON'T YOU LIKE BLONDES?
Bleached blondes, I don't like bleached blondes.
ZZOWNT
AND I SUPPOSE YOU DON'T LIKE GIRLS WHO WEAR GLASSES EITHER?
Glasses? What's that got to do with--
Yikes!
Huh? Was that--?
Reed, was that a laser blast?
I think maybe it--
AAHHHH!
ZZEEEOWNT
KRAKOOM

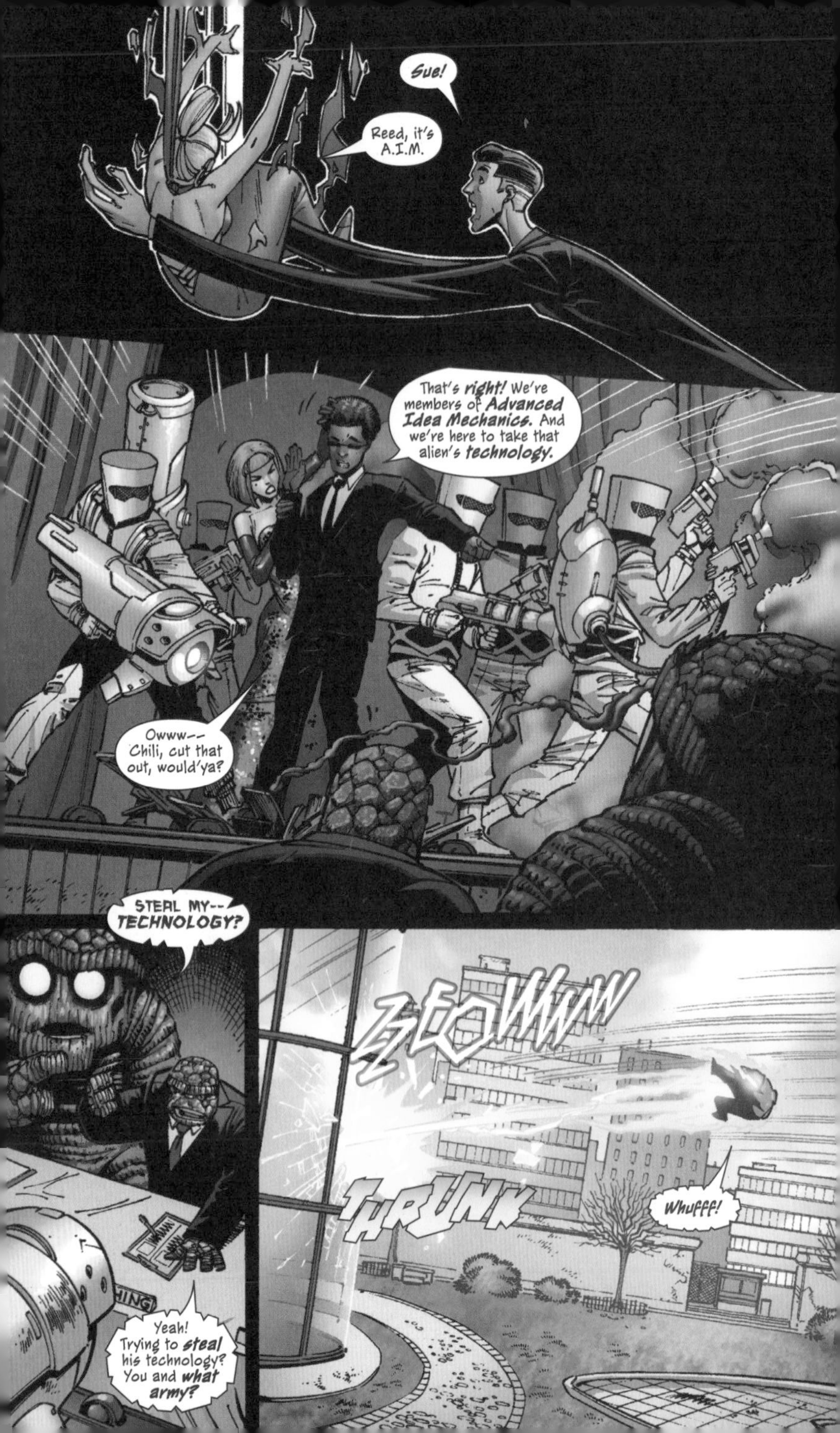

Sue!
Reed, it's A.I.M.
That's right! We're members of Advanced Idea Mechanics. And we're here to take that alien's technology.
Owww-- Chili, cut that out, would'ya?
STEAL MY-- TECHNOLOGY?
Yeah! Trying to steal his technology? You and what army?
ZEOWWW
THRUNK
Whufff!

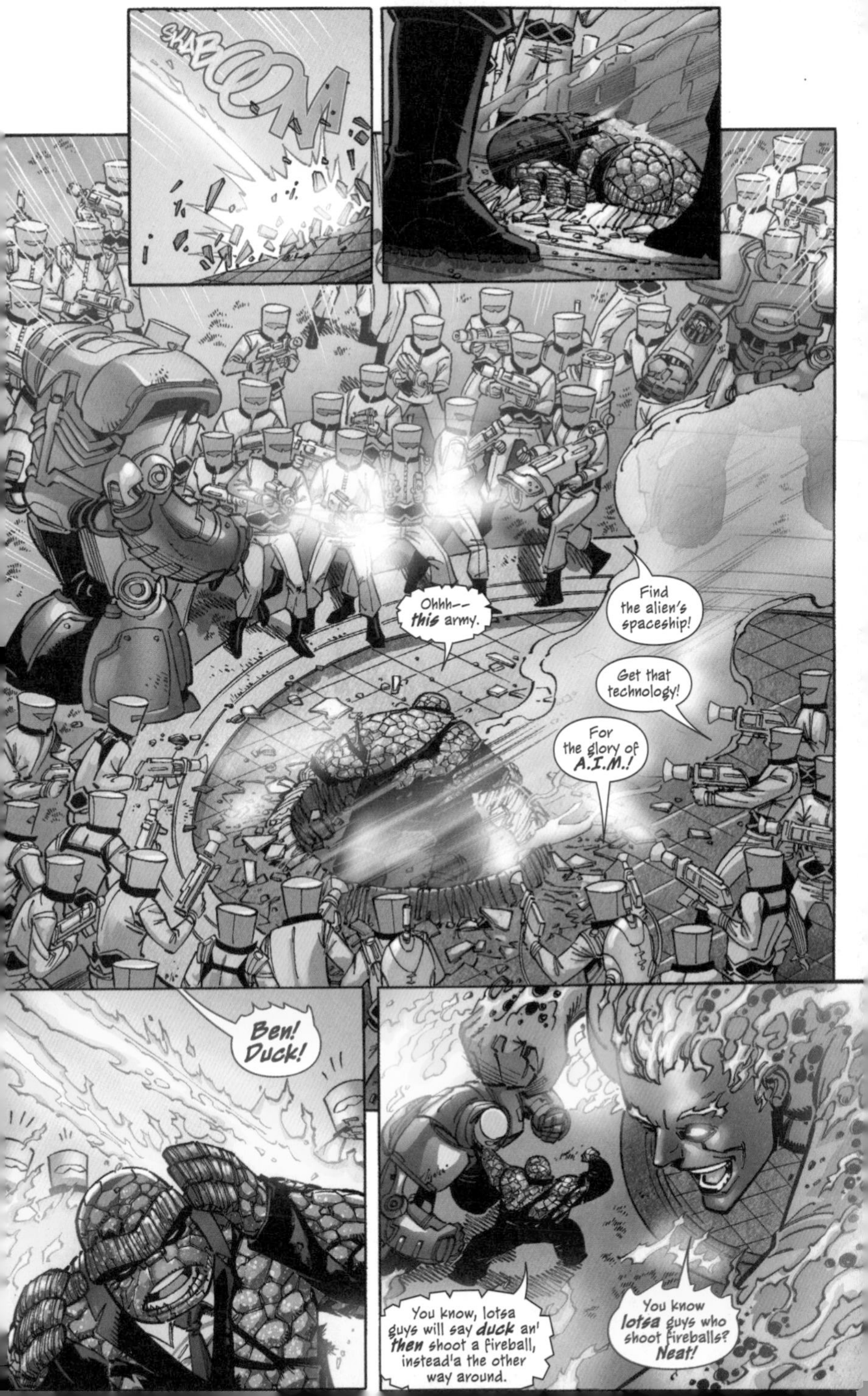
SKABOOM
Ohhh--
this army.
Find
the alien's
spaceship!
Get that
technology!
For
the glory of
A.I.M.!
Ben!
Duck!
You know, lotsa
guys will say duck an'
then shoot a fireball,
instead'a the other
way around.
You know
lotsa guys who
shoot fireballs?
Neat!

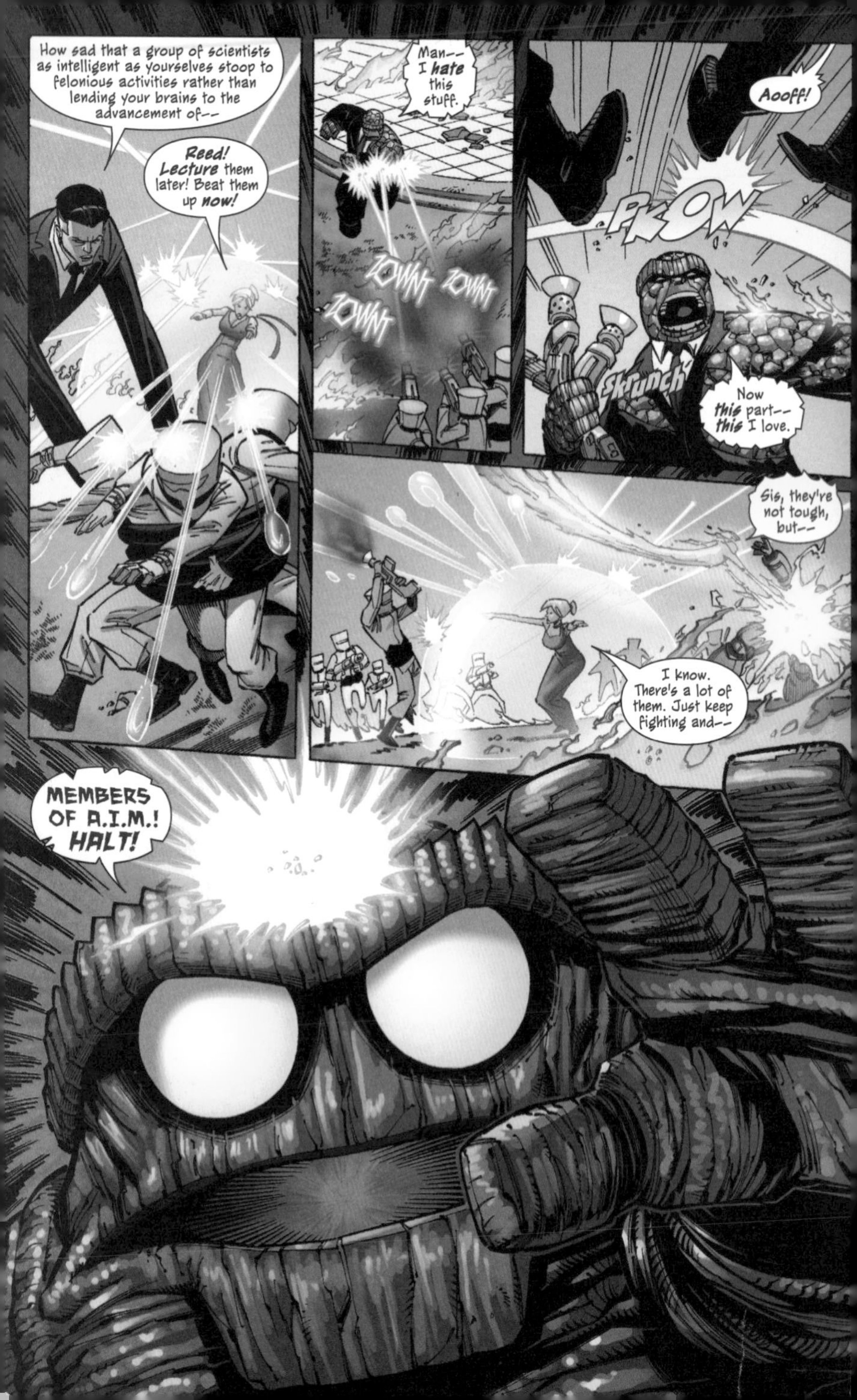
How sad that a group of scientists as intelligent as yourselves stoop to felonious activities rather than lending your brains to the advancement of--
Reed! Lecture them later! Beat them up now!
Man-- I hate this stuff.
ZOWNT ZOWNT ZOWNT
Aooff!
PKOW
SKRUNCH
Now this part-- this I love.
Sis, they're not tough, but--
I know. There's a lot of them. Just keep fighting and--
MEMBERS OF A.I.M.! HALT!

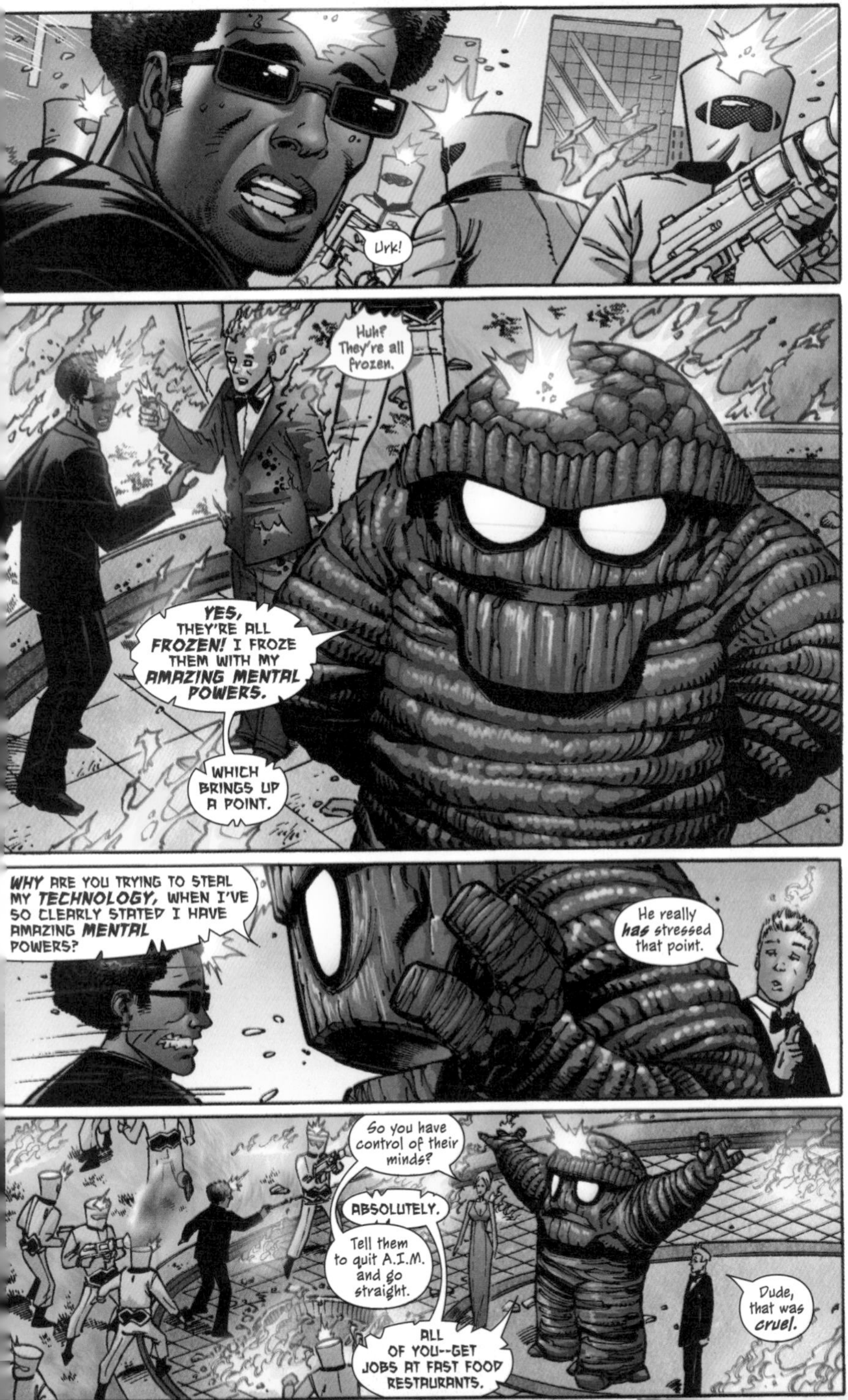
Urk!
Huh? They're all frozen.
YES, THEY'RE ALL FROZEN! I FROZE THEM WITH MY AMAZING MENTAL POWERS.
WHICH BRINGS UP A POINT.
WHY ARE YOU TRYING TO STEAL MY TECHNOLOGY, WHEN I'VE SO CLEARLY STATED I HAVE AMAZING MENTAL POWERS?
He really has stressed that point.
So you have control of their minds?
ABSOLUTELY.
Tell them to quit A.I.M. and go straight.
ALL OF YOU--GET JOBS AT FAST FOOD RESTAURANTS.
Dude, that was cruel.

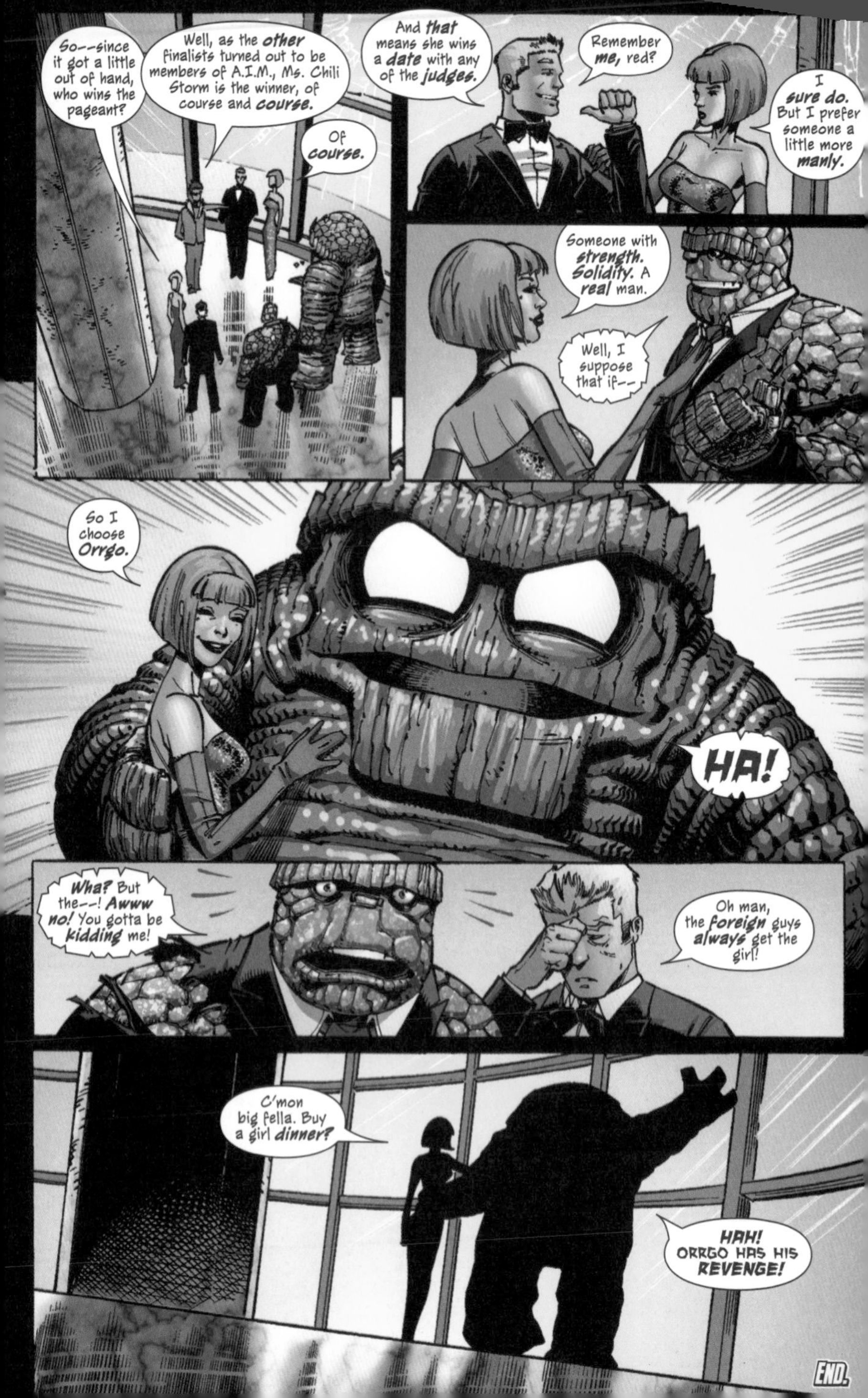
So--since it got a little out of hand, who wins the pageant?
Well, as the other finalists turned out to be members of A.I.M., Ms. Chili Storm is the winner, of course and course.
Of course.
And that means she wins a date with any of the judges.
Remember me, red?
I sure do. But I prefer someone a little more manly.
Someone with strength. Solidity. A real man.
Well, I suppose that if--
So I choose Orrgo.
HA!
Wha? But the--! Awww no! You gotta be kidding me!
Oh man, the foreign guys always get the girl!
C'mon big fella. Buy a girl dinner?
HAH! ORRGO HAS HIS REVENGE!
END.

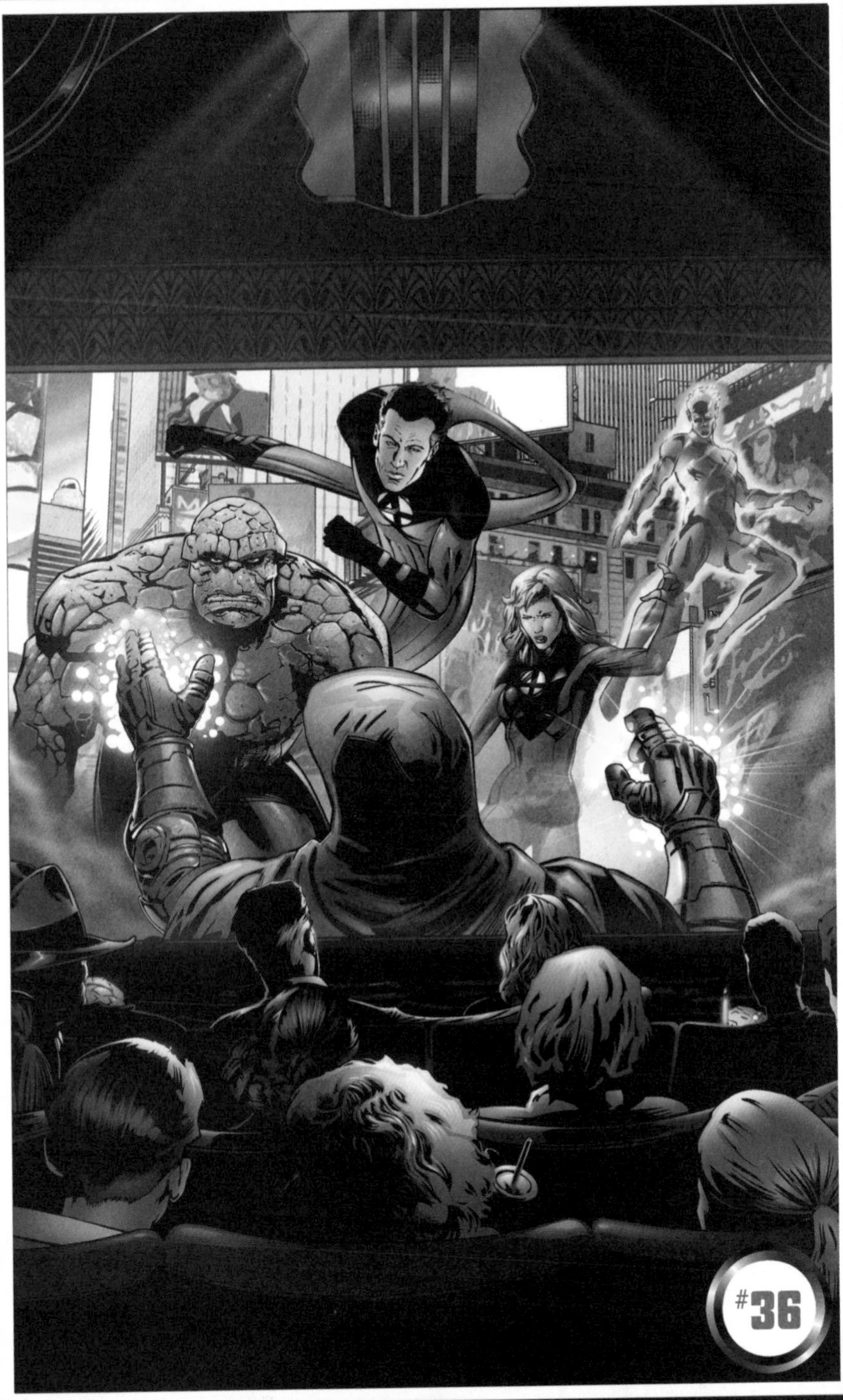
#36

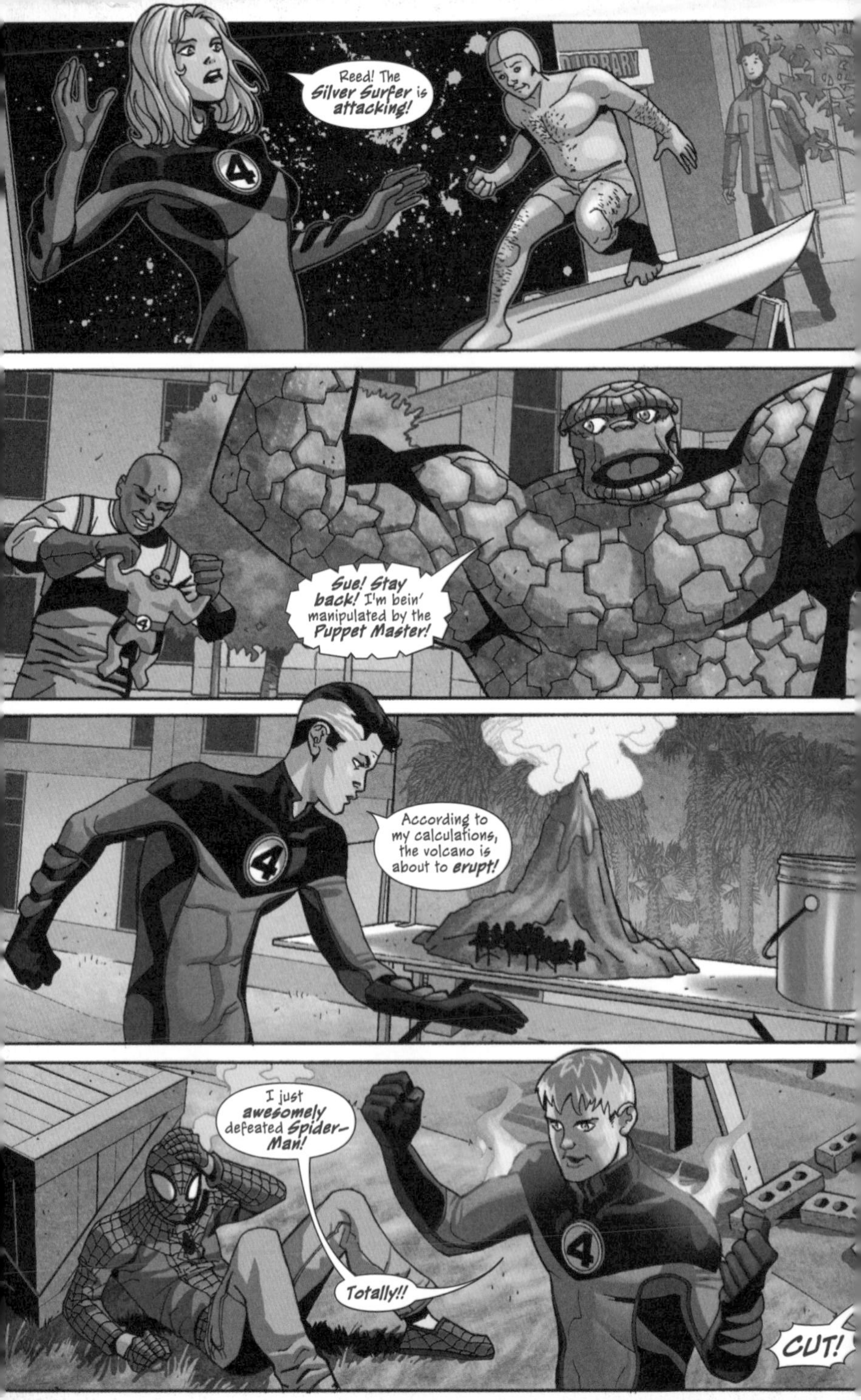
Reed! The Silver Surfer is attacking!
LIBRARY
Sue! Stay back! I'm bein' manipulated by the Puppet Master!
According to my calculations, the volcano is about to erupt!
I just awesomely defeated Spider-Man!
Totally!!
CUT!

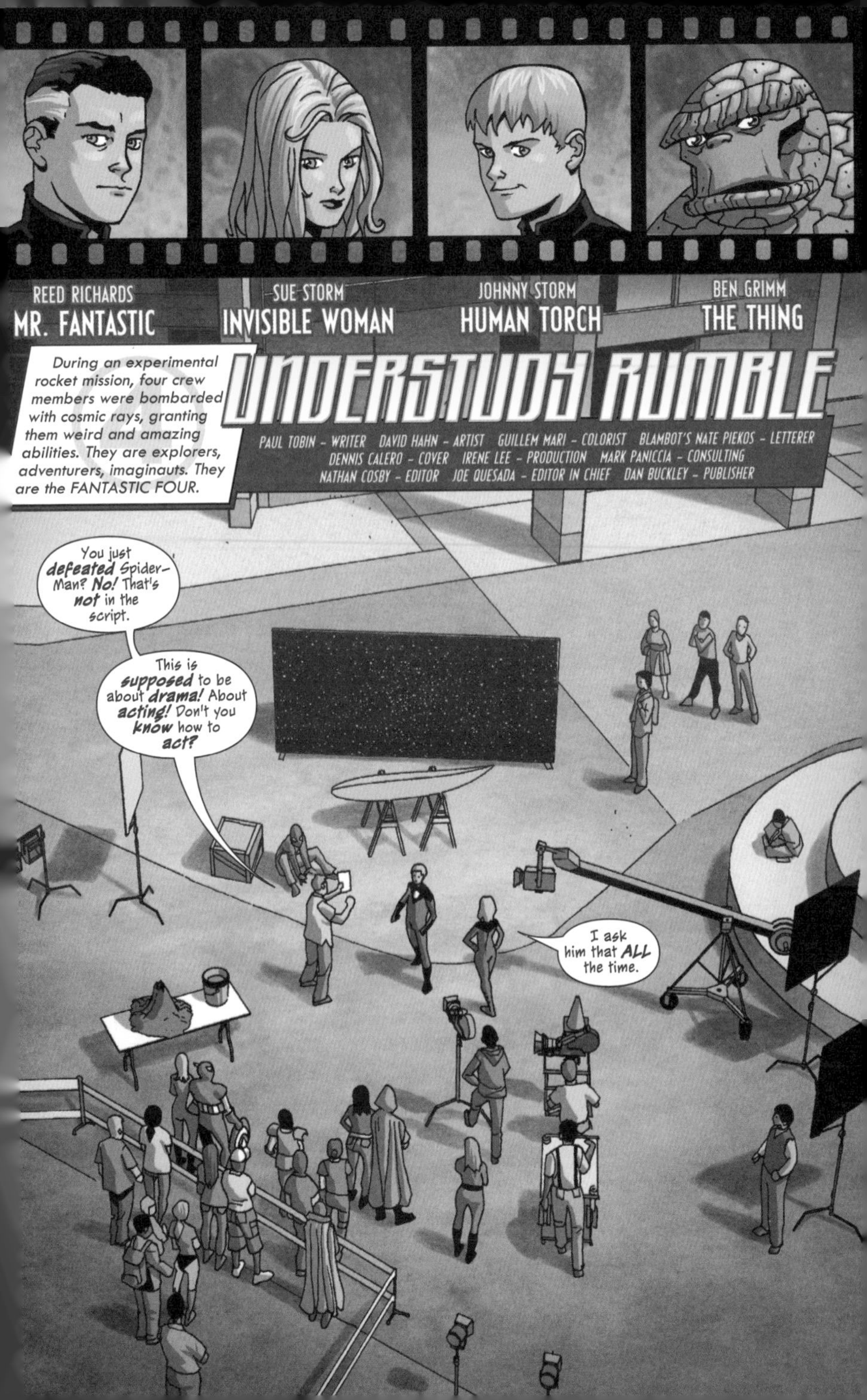
REED RICHARDS
MR. FANTASTIC
SUE STORM
INVISIBLE WOMAN
JOHNNY STORM
HUMAN TORCH
BEN GRIMM
THE THING
During an experimental rocket mission, four crew members were bombarded with cosmic rays, granting them weird and amazing abilities. They are explorers, adventurers, imaginauts. They are the FANTASTIC FOUR.
UNDERSTUDY RUMBLE
PAUL TOBIN - WRITER DAVID HAHN - ARTIST GUILLEM MARI - COLORIST BLAMBOT'S NATE PIEKOS - LETTERER
DENNIS CALERO - COVER IRENE LEE - PRODUCTION MARK PANICCIA - CONSULTING
NATHAN COSBY - EDITOR JOE QUESADA - EDITOR IN CHIEF DAN BUCKLEY - PUBLISHER
You just defeated Spider-Man? No! That's not in the script.
This is supposed to be about drama! About acting! Don't you know how to act?
I ask him that ALL the time.

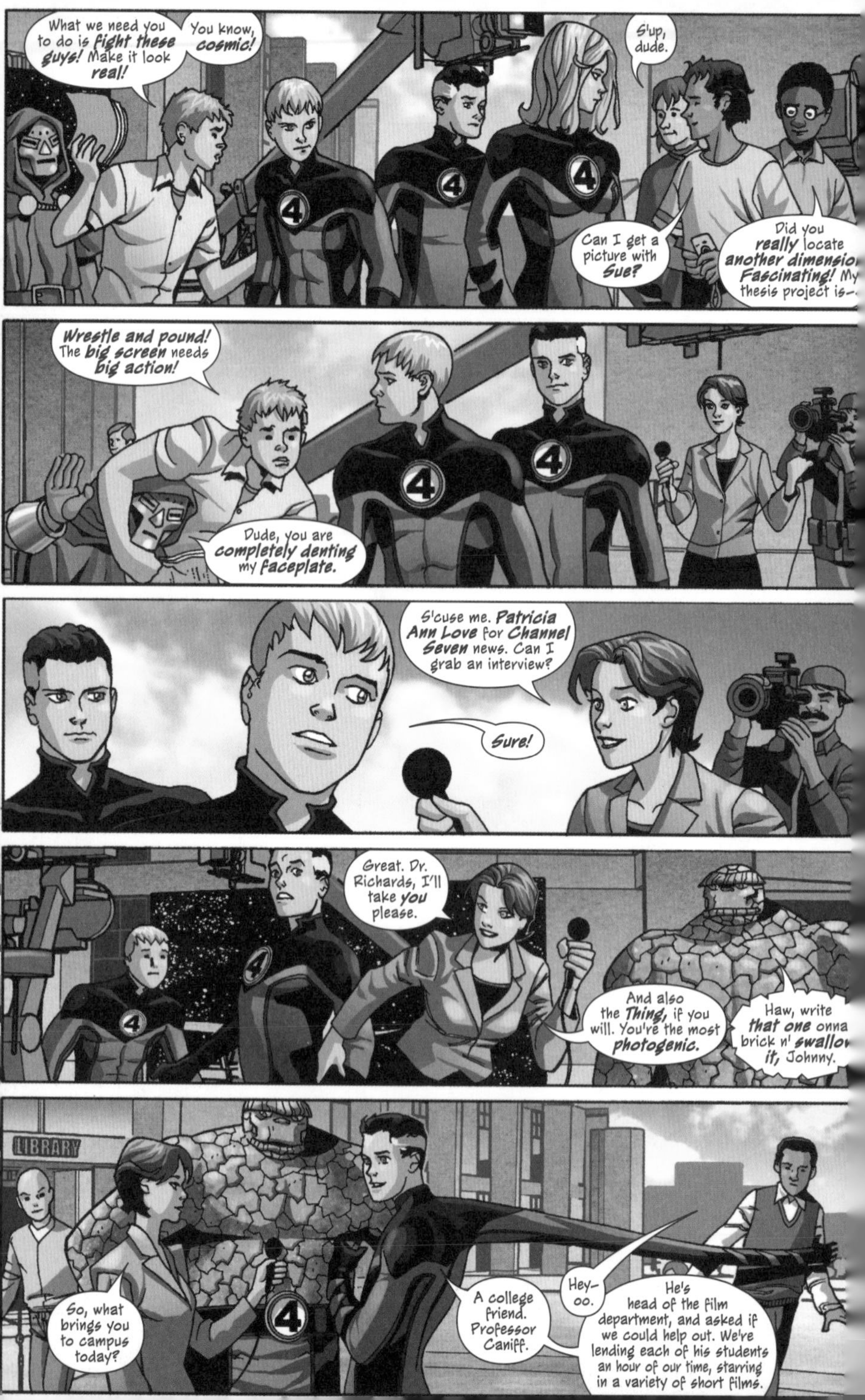

What we need you to do is fight these guys! Make it look real!
You know, cosmic!
S'up, dude.
Can I get a picture with Sue?
Did you really locate another dimension? Fascinating! My thesis project is--
Wrestle and pound! The big screen needs big action!
Dude, you are completely denting my faceplate.
S'cuse me. Patricia Ann Love for Channel Seven news. Can I grab an interview?
Sure!
Great. Dr. Richards, I'll take you please.
And also the Thing, if you will. You're the most photogenic.
Haw, write that one onna brick n' swallow it, Johnny.
LIBRARY
So, what brings you to campus today?
A college friend. Professor Caniff.
Hey-- oo.
He's head of the film department, and asked if we could help out. We're lending each of his students an hour of our time, starring in a variety of short films.

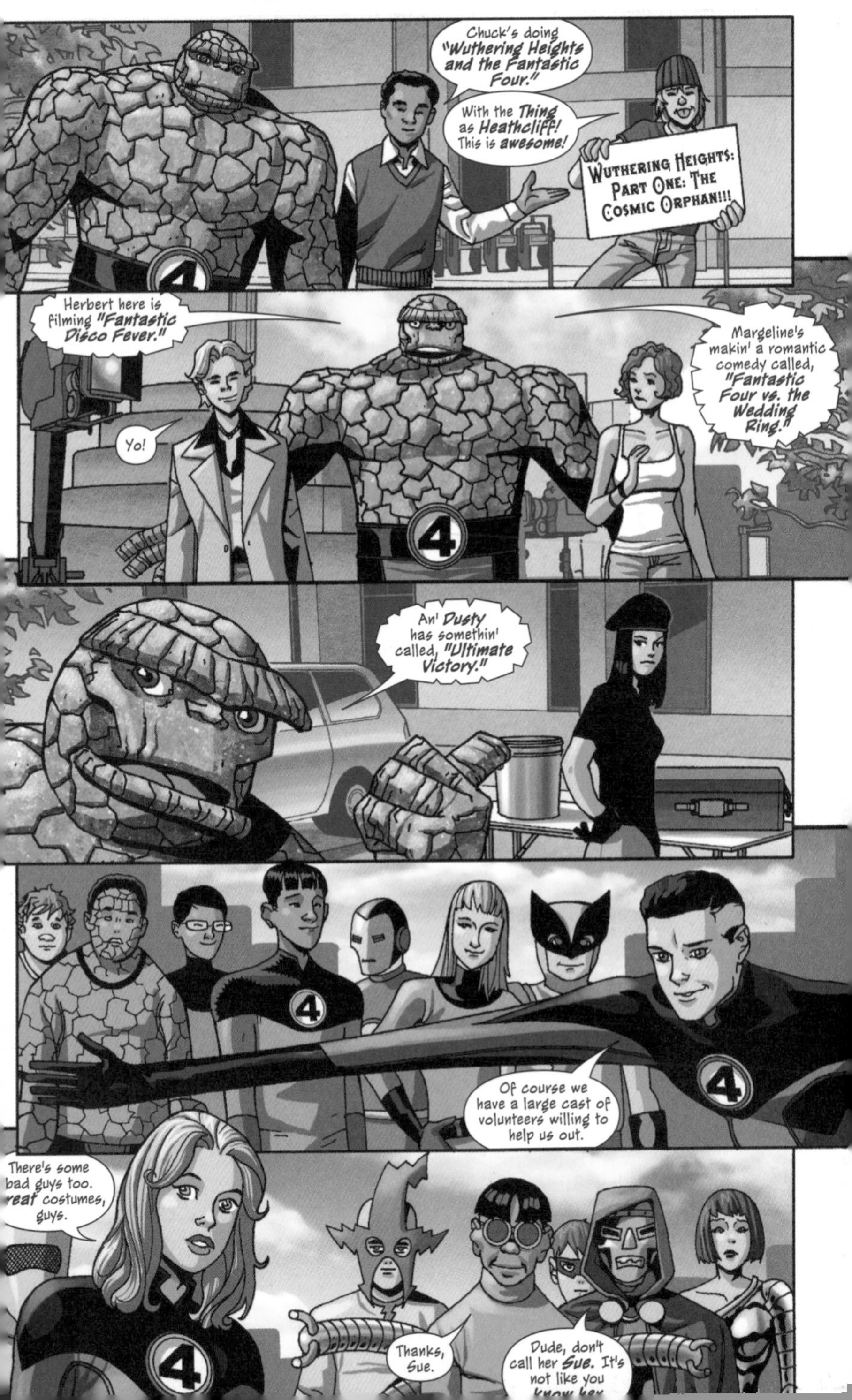

Chuck's doing "Wuthering Heights and the Fantastic Four."
With the Thing as Heathcliff! This is awesome!
WUTHERING HEIGHTS: PART ONE: THE COSMIC ORPHAN!!!
Herbert here is filming "Fantastic Disco Fever."
Yo!
Margeline's makin' a romantic comedy called, "Fantastic Four vs. the Wedding Ring."
An' Dusty has somethin' called, "Ultimate Victory."
Of course we have a large cast of volunteers willing to help us out.
There's some bad guys too. reat costumes, guys.
Thanks, Sue.
Dude, don't call her Sue. It's not like you

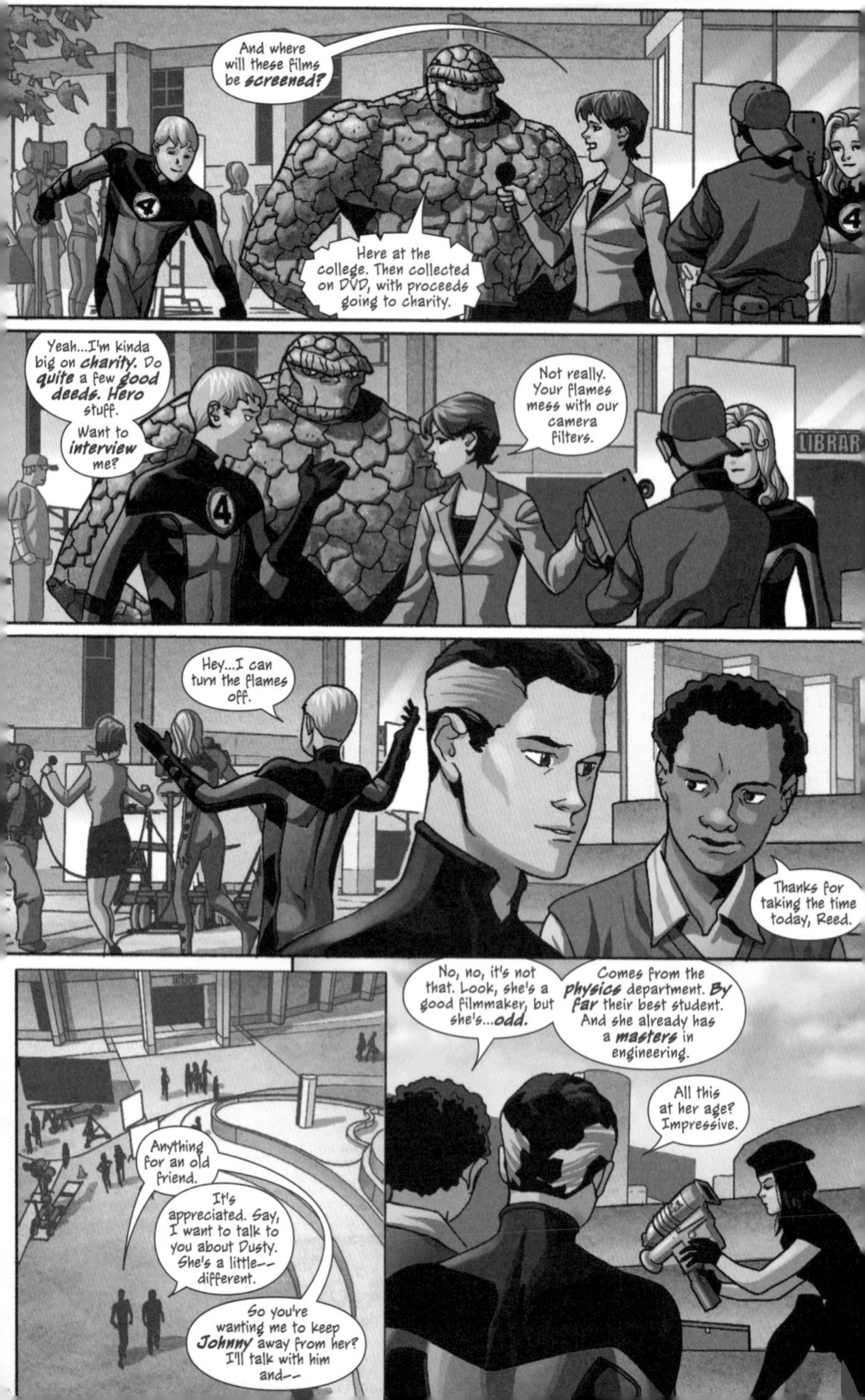
And where will these films be screened?
Here at the college. Then collected on DVD, with proceeds going to charity.
Yeah...I'm kinda big on charity. Do quite a few good deeds. Hero stuff.
Want to interview me?
Not really. Your flames mess with our camera filters.
LIBRAR
Hey...I can turn the flames off.
Thanks for taking the time today, Reed.
Anything for an old friend.
It's appreciated. Say, I want to talk to you about Dusty. She's a little--different.
So you're wanting me to keep Johnny away from her? I'll talk with him and--
No, no, it's not that. Look, she's a good filmmaker, but she's...odd.
Comes from the physics department. By far their best student. And she already has a masters in engineering.
All this at her age? Impressive.

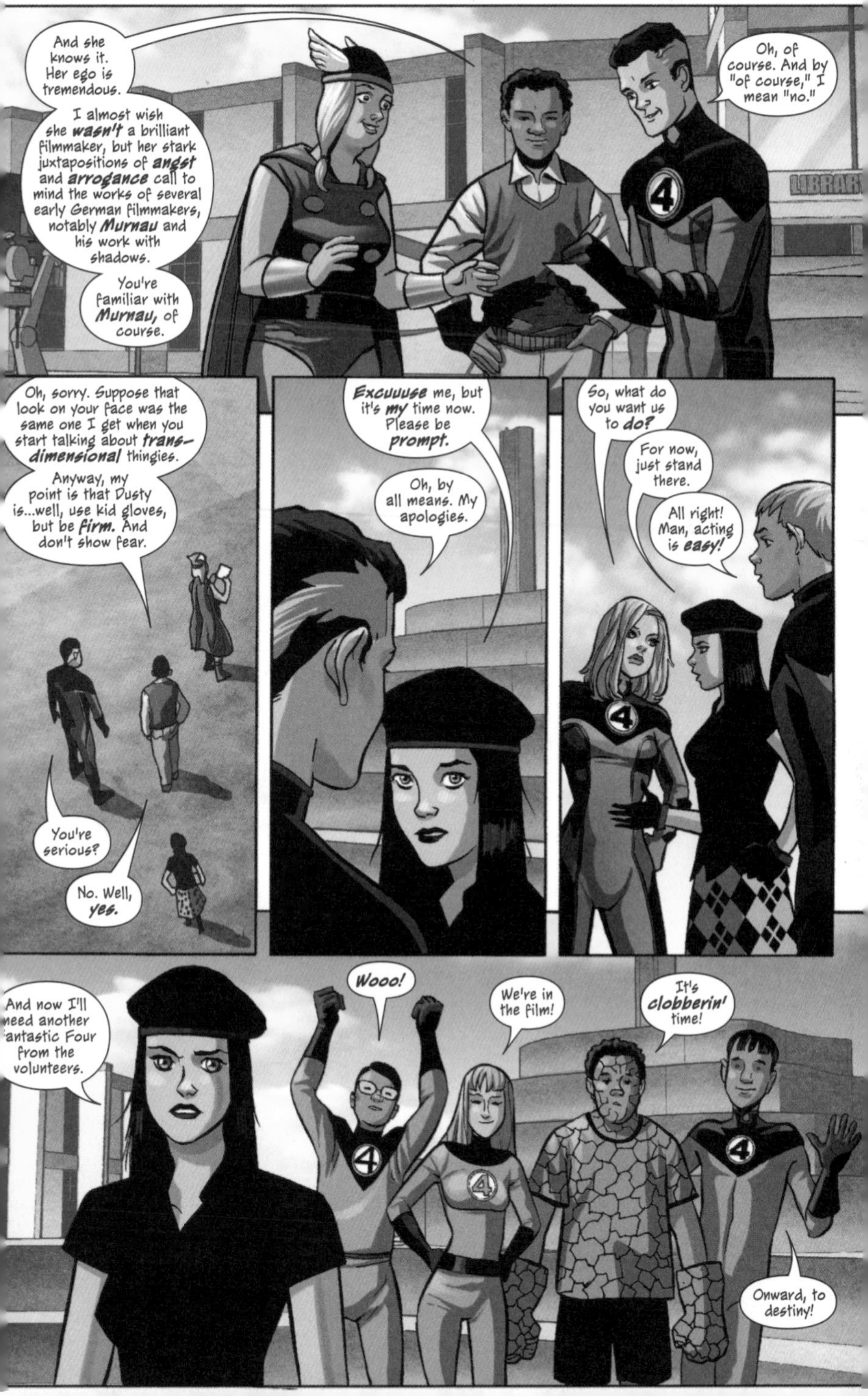

And she knows it. Her ego is tremendous.
I almost wish she wasn't a brilliant filmmaker, but her stark juxtapositions of angst and arrogance call to mind the works of several early German filmmakers, notably Murnau and his work with shadows.
You're familiar with Murnau, of course.
Oh, of course. And by "of course," I mean "no."
LIBRAR
Oh, sorry. Suppose that look on your face was the same one I get when you start talking about trans-dimensional thingies.
Anyway, my point is that Dusty is...well, use kid gloves, but be firm. And don't show fear.
You're serious?
No. Well, yes.
Excuuuse me, but it's my time now. Please be prompt.
Oh, by all means. My apologies.
So, what do you want us to do?
For now, just stand there.
All right! Man, acting is easy!
And now I'll need another Fantastic Four from the volunteers.
Wooo!
We're in the film!
It's clobberin' time!
Onward, to destiny!

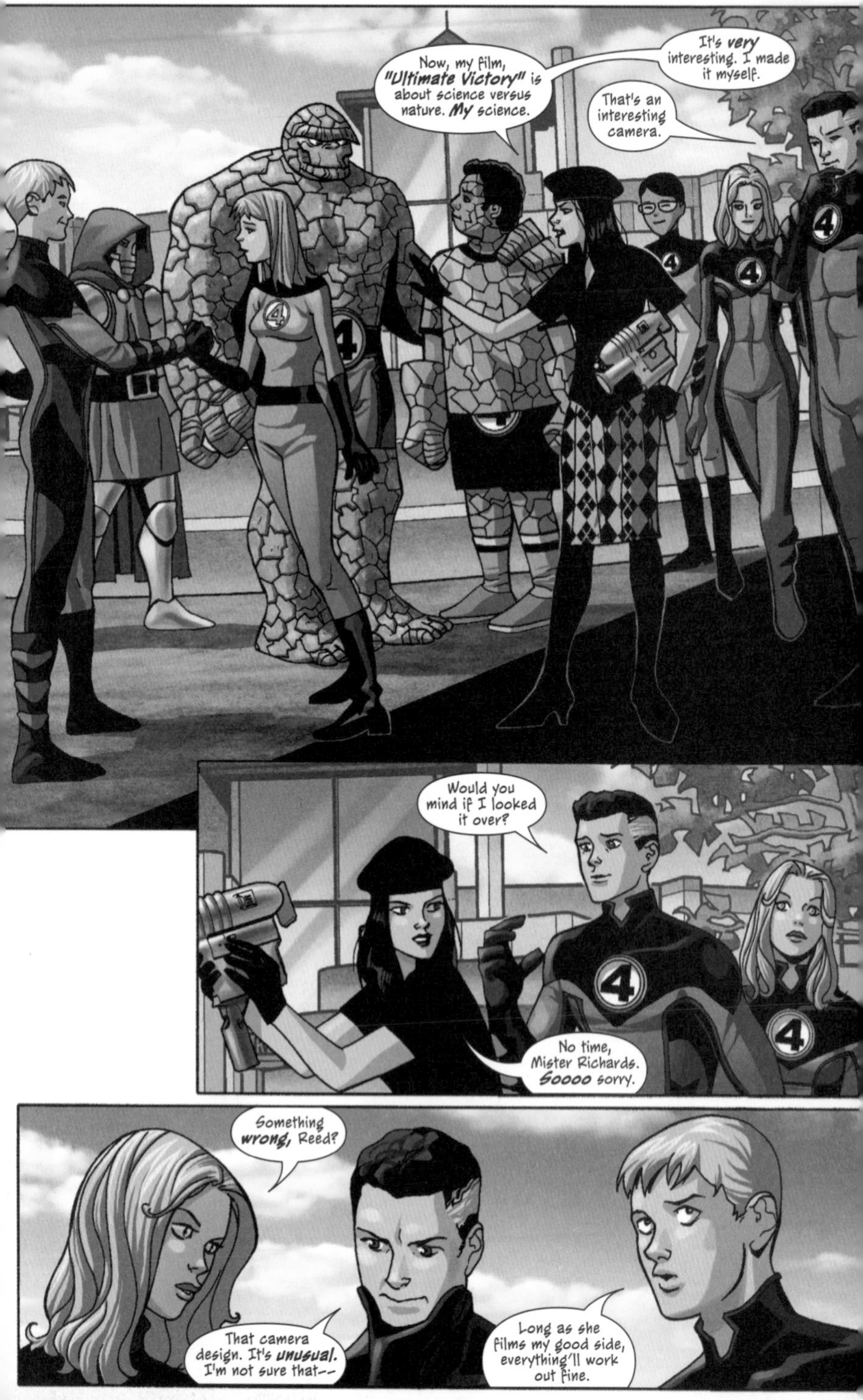
Now, my film, "Ultimate Victory" is about science versus nature. My science.
That's an interesting camera.
It's very interesting. I made it myself.
Would you mind if I looked it over?
No time, Mister Richards. Soooo sorry.
Something wrong, Reed?
That camera design. It's unusual. I'm not sure that--
Long as she films my good side, everything'll work out fine.

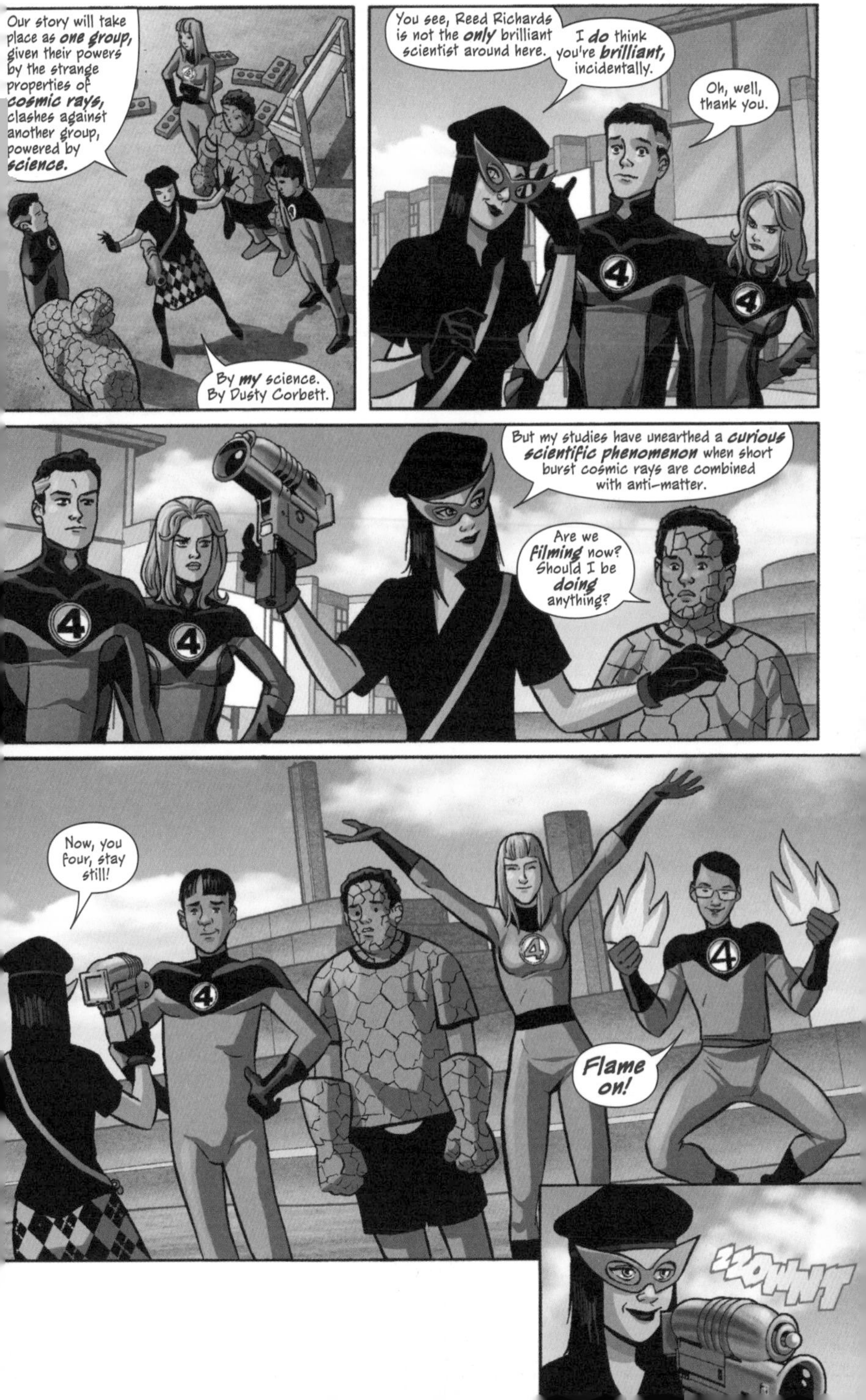
Our story will take place as one group, given their powers by the strange properties of cosmic rays, clashes against another group, powered by science.
By my science. By Dusty Corbett.
You see, Reed Richards is not the only brilliant scientist around here.
I do think you're brilliant, incidentally.
Oh, well, thank you.
But my studies have unearthed a curious scientific phenomenon when short burst cosmic rays are combined with anti-matter.
Are we filming now? Should I be doing anything?
Now, you four, stay still!
Flame on!
ZZOWWT

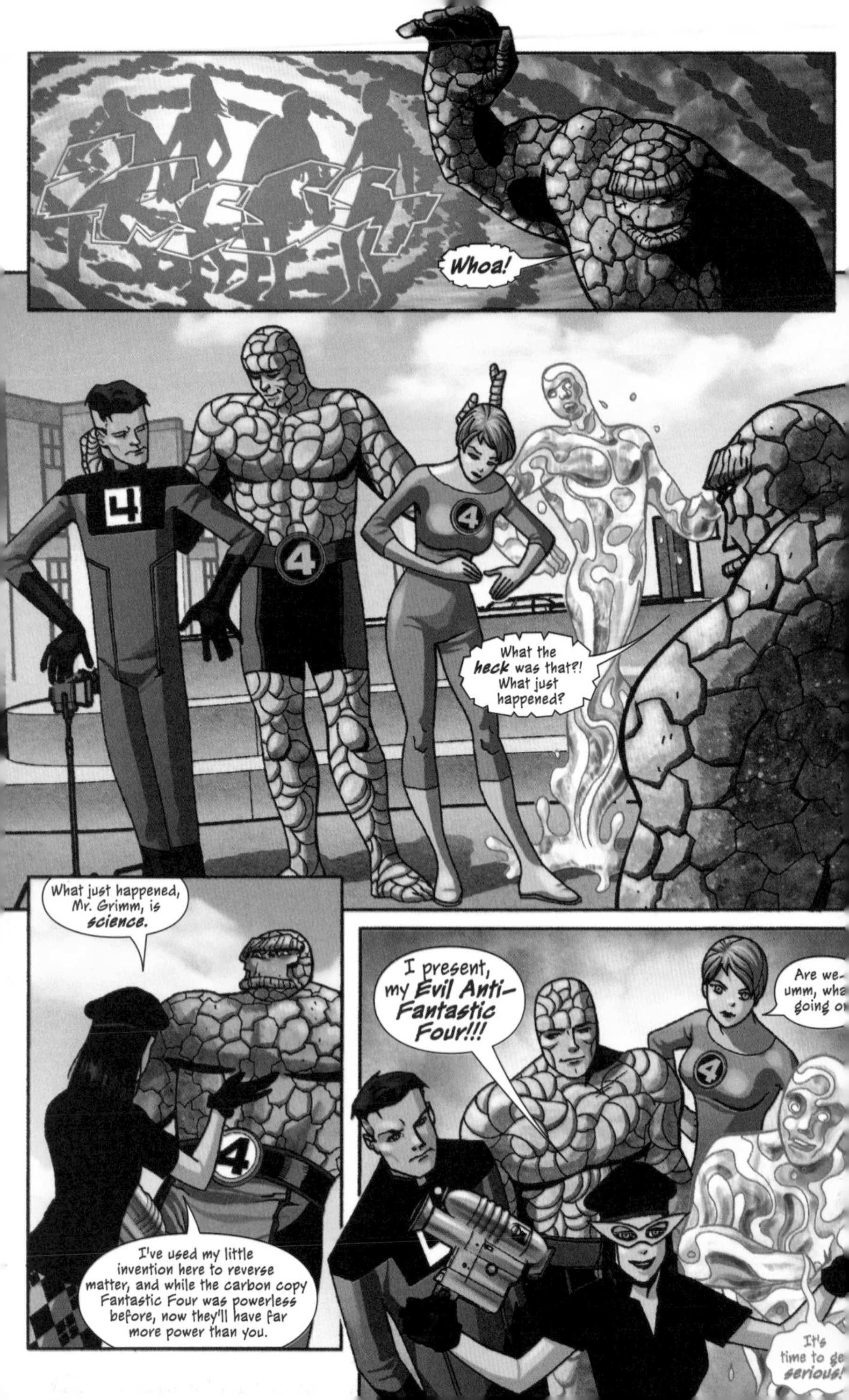
Whoa!
What the heck was that?! What just happened?
What just happened, Mr. Grimm, is science.
I've used my little invention here to reverse matter, and while the carbon copy Fantastic Four was powerless before, now they'll have far more power than you.
I present, my Evil Anti-Fantastic Four!!!
It's time to ge serious!

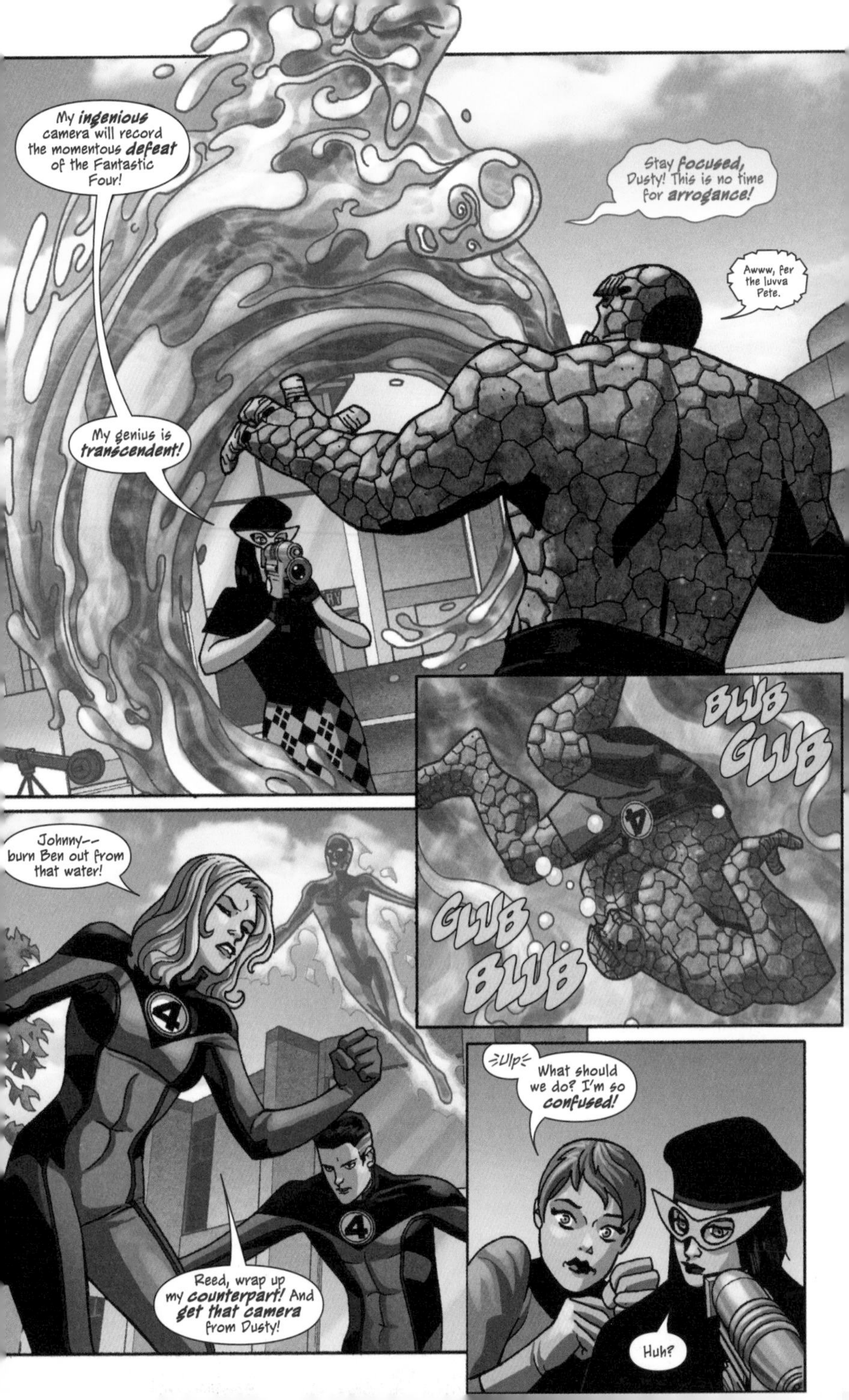
My ingenious camera will record the momentous defeat of the Fantastic Four!
My genius is transcendent!
Stay focused, Dusty! This is no time for arrogance!
Awww, fer the luvva Pete.
BLUB GLUB
GLUB BLUB
Johnny-- burn Ben out from that water!
Reed, wrap up my counterpart! And get that camera from Dusty!
Ulp
What should we do? I'm so confused!
Huh?

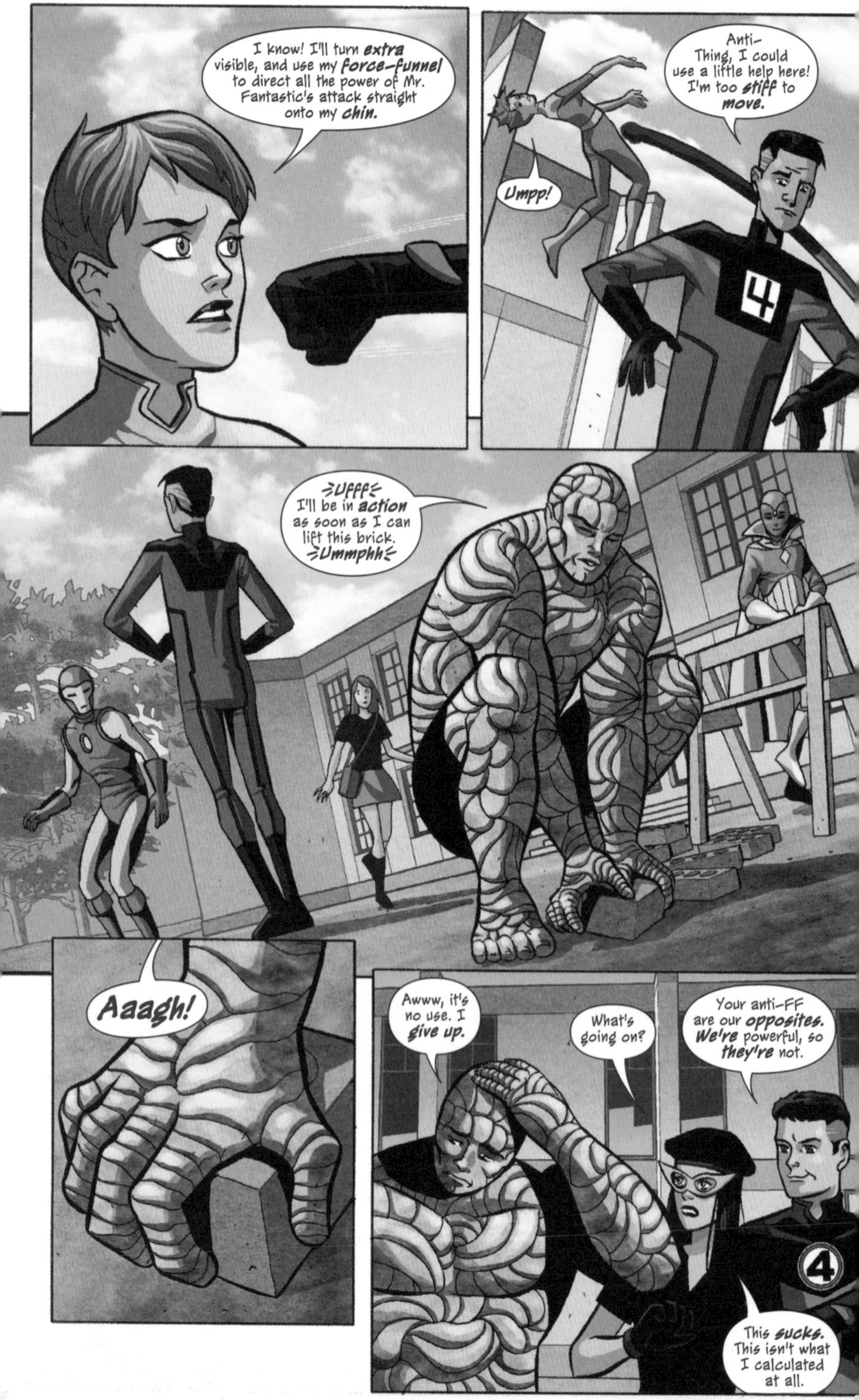

I know! I'll turn extra visible, and use my force-funnel to direct all the power of Mr. Fantastic's attack straight onto my chin.
Anti-Thing, I could use a little help here! I'm too stiff to move.
Umpp!
Ufff I'll be in action as soon as I can lift this brick. Ummphh
Aaagh!
Awww, it's no use. I give up.
What's going on?
Your anti-FF are our opposites. We're powerful, so they're not.
This sucks. This isn't what I calculated at all.

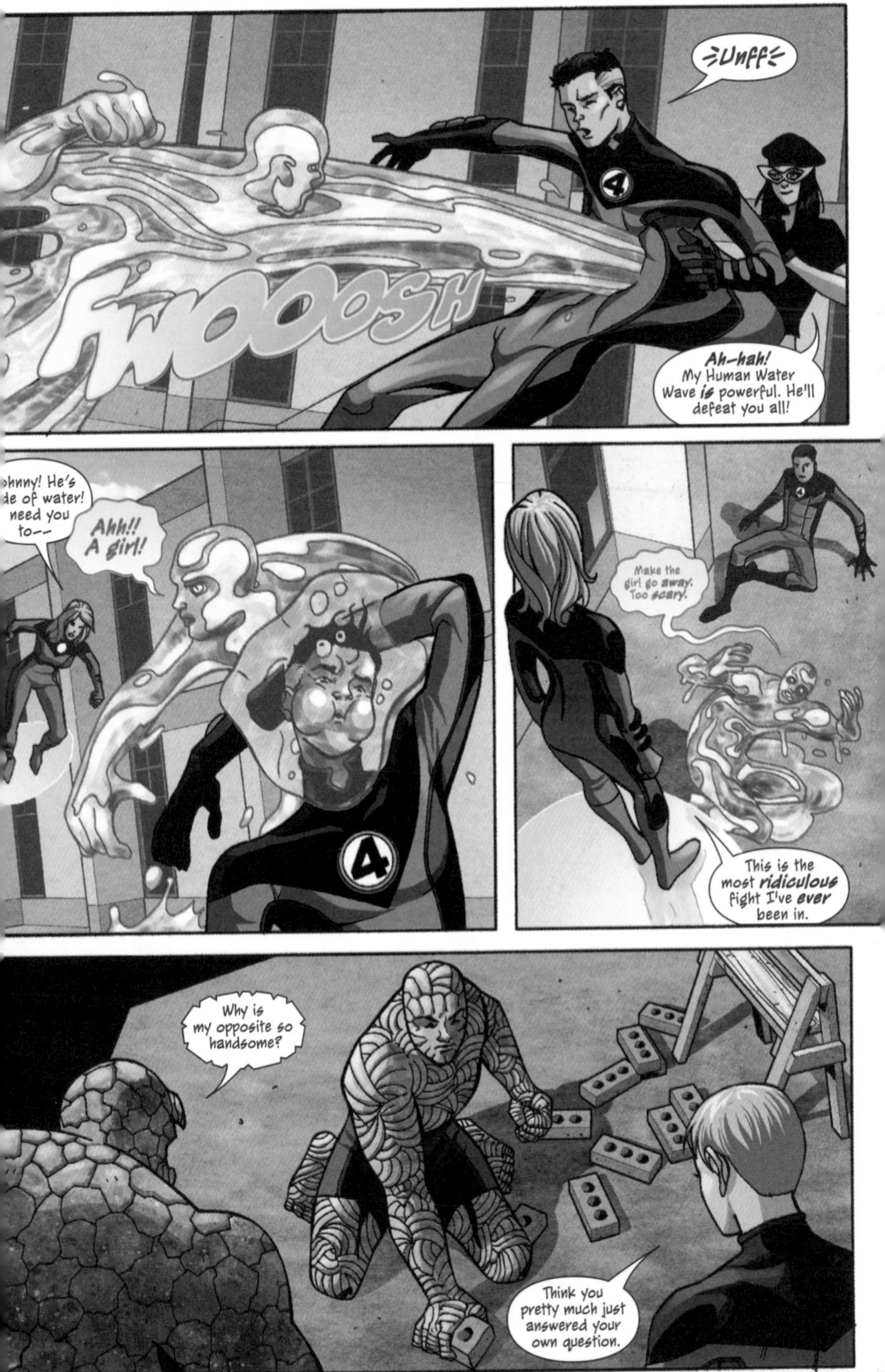

FWOOOSH
Unff
Ah-hah! My Human Water Wave is powerful. He'll defeat you all!
ohnny! He's de of water! need you to--
Ahh!! A girl!
Make the girl go away. Too scary.
This is the most ridiculous fight I've ever been in.
Why is my opposite so handsome?
Think you pretty much just answered your own question.

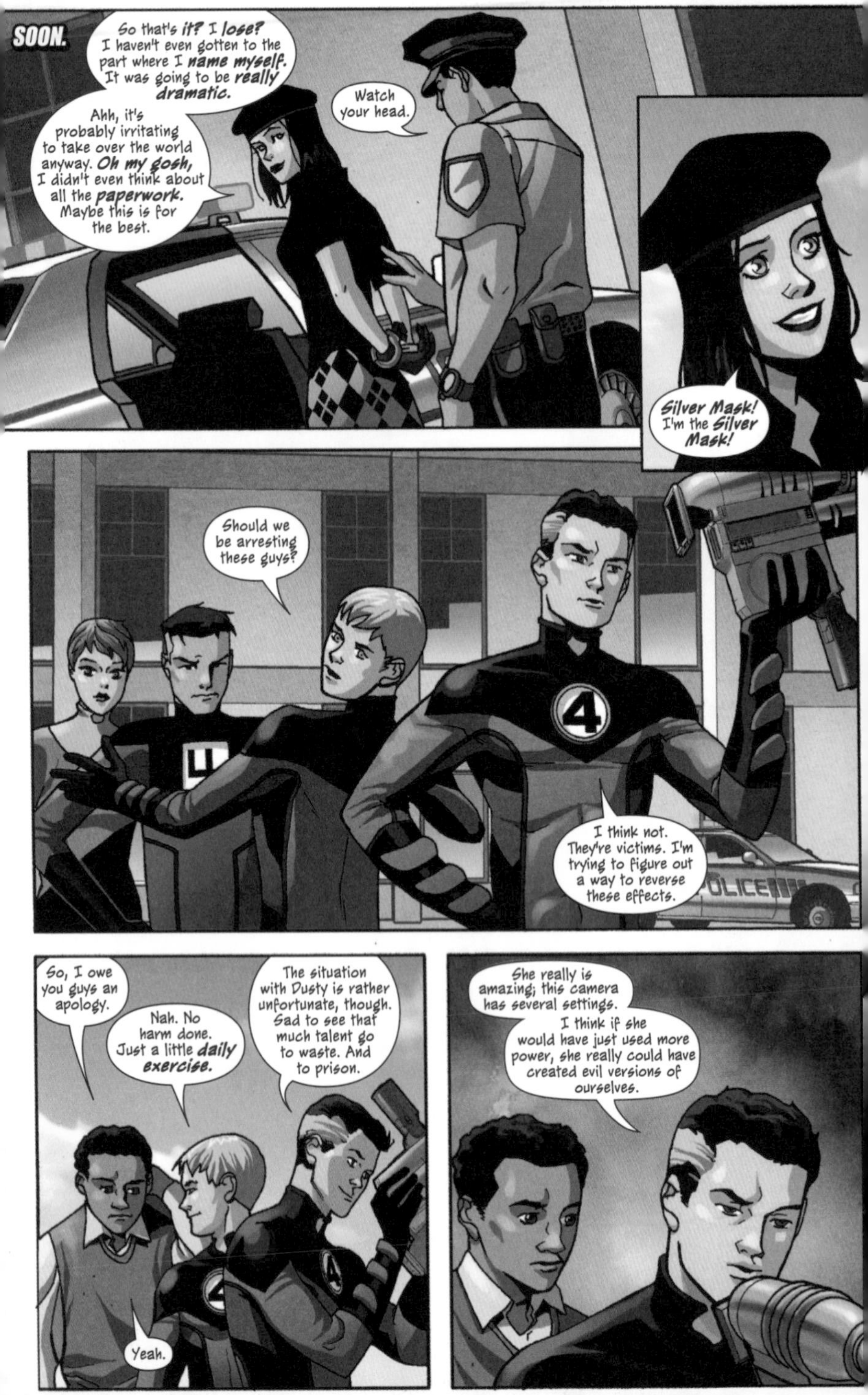
SOON.
So that's it? I lose? I haven't even gotten to the part where I name myself. It was going to be really dramatic.
Ahh, it's probably irritating to take over the world anyway. Oh my gosh, I didn't even think about all the paperwork. Maybe this is for the best.
Watch your head.
Silver Mask! I'm the Silver Mask!
Should we be arresting these guys?
I think not. They're victims. I'm trying to figure out a way to reverse these effects.
POLICE
So, I owe you guys an apology.
Nah. No harm done. Just a little daily exercise.
Yeah.
The situation with Dusty is rather unfortunate, though. Sad to see that much talent go to waste. And to prison.
She really is amazing; this camera has several settings.
I think if she would have just used more power, she really could have created evil versions of ourselves.

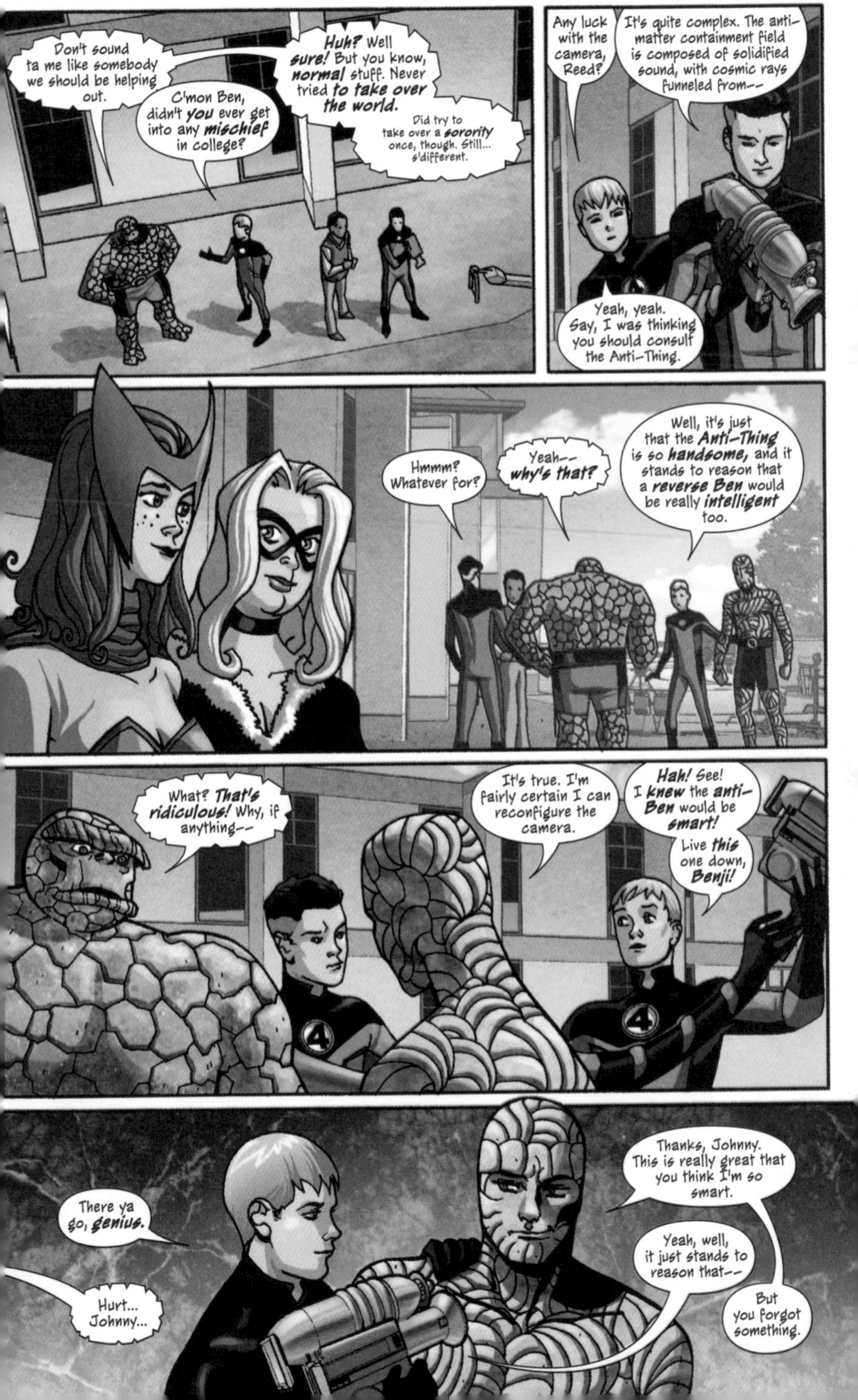

Don't sound ta me like somebody we should be helping out.
C'mon Ben, didn't you ever get into any mischief in college?
Huh? Well sure! But you know, normal stuff. Never tried to take over the world.
Did try to take over a sorority once, though. Still... s'different.
Any luck with the camera, Reed?
It's quite complex. The anti-matter containment field is composed of solidified sound, with cosmic rays funneled from--
Yeah, yeah. Say, I was thinking you should consult the Anti-Thing.
Hmmm? Whatever for?
Yeah-- why's that?
Well, it's just that the Anti-Thing is so handsome, and it stands to reason that a reverse Ben would be really intelligent too.
What? That's ridiculous! Why, if anything--
It's true. I'm fairly certain I can reconfigure the camera.
Hah! See! I knew the anti-Ben would be smart!
Live this one down, Benji!
There ya go, genius.
Thanks, Johnny. This is really great that you think I'm so smart.
Yeah, well, it just stands to reason that--
But you forgot something.
Hurt... Johnny...

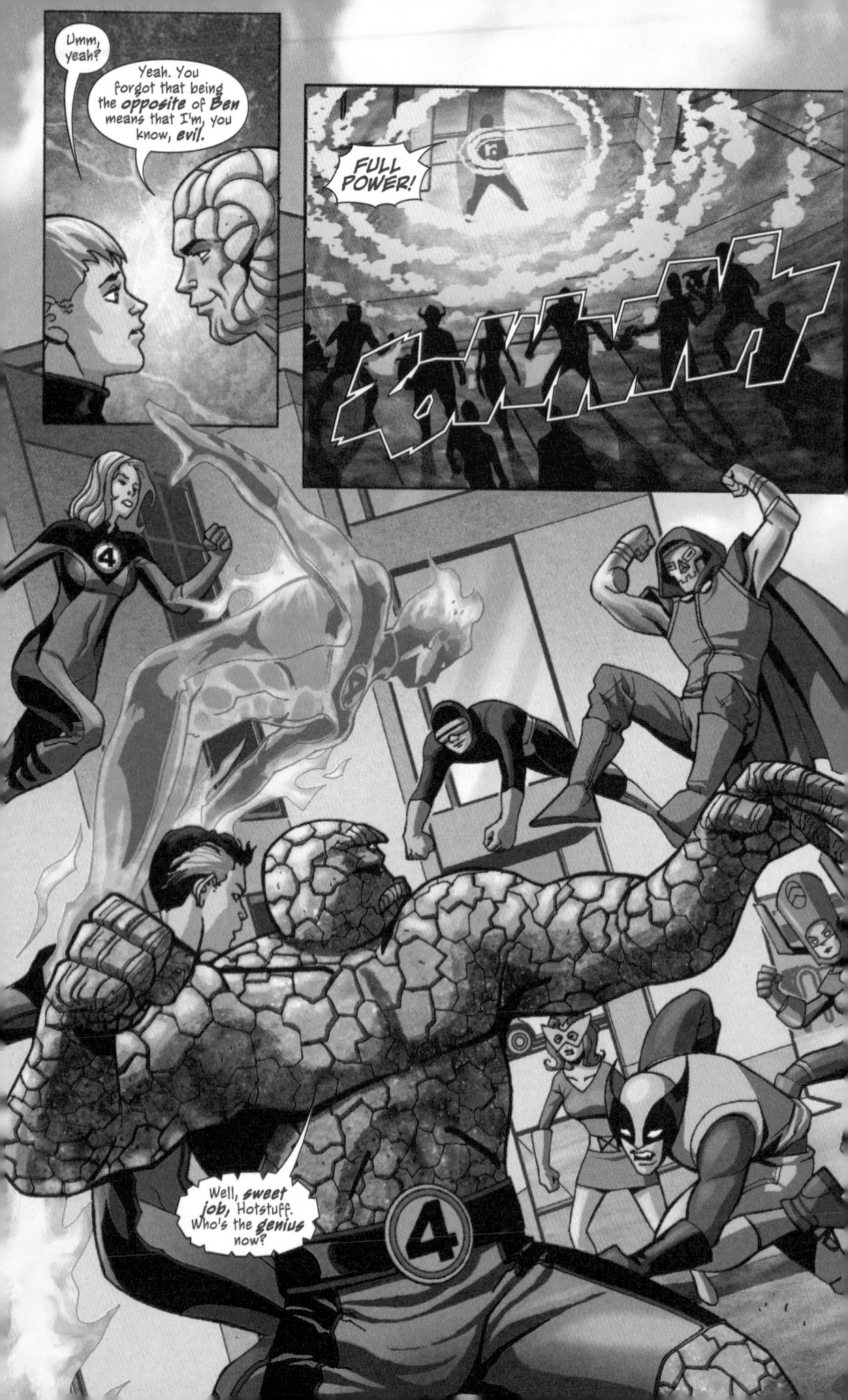
Umm, yeah?
Yeah. You forgot that being the opposite of Ben means that I'm, you know, evil.
FULL POWER!
Well, sweet job, Hotstuff. Who's the genius now?

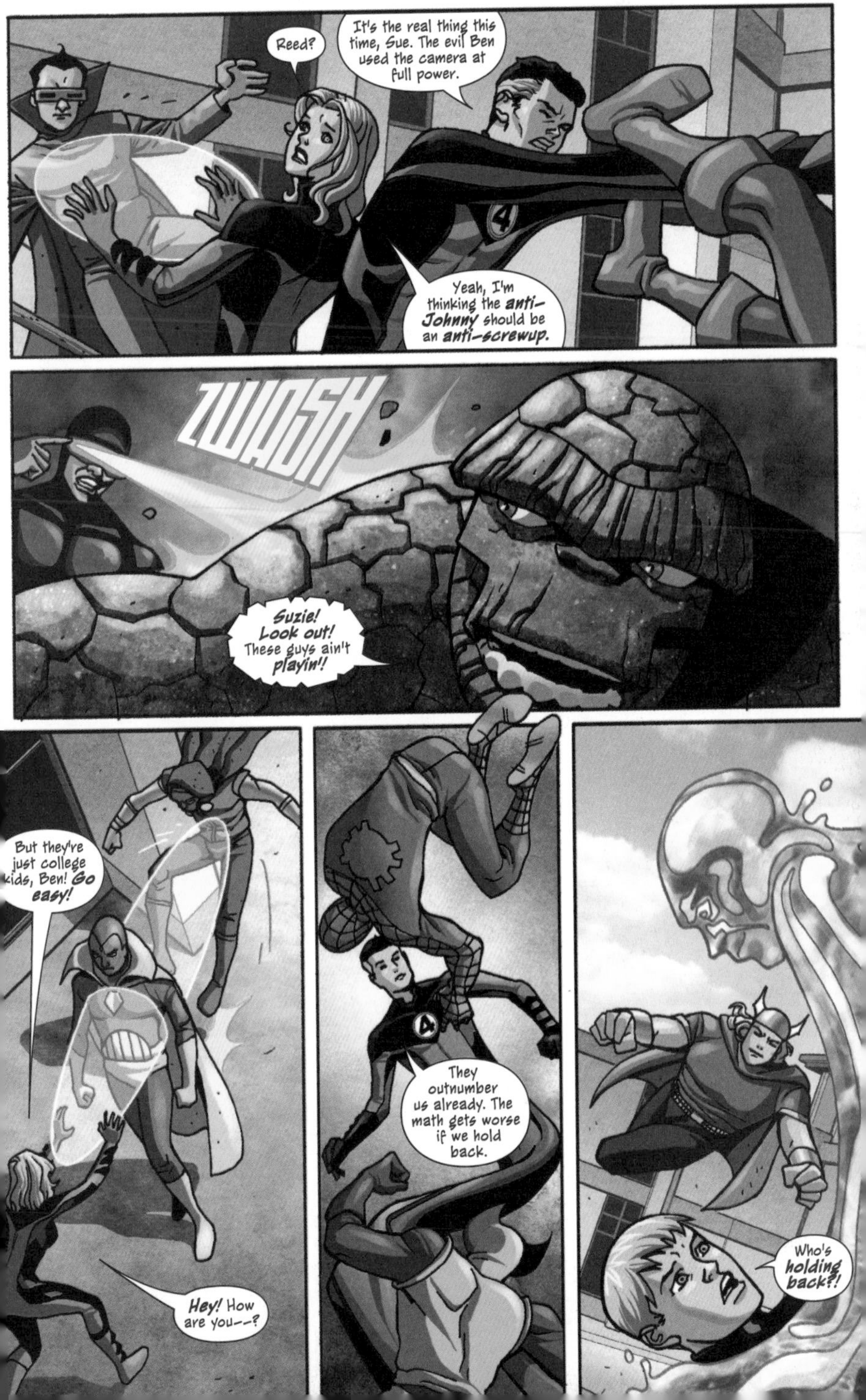
Reed?
It's the real thing this time, Sue. The evil Ben used the camera at full power.
Yeah, I'm thinking the anti-Johnny should be an anti-screwup.
ZWOSH
Suzie! Look out! These guys ain't playin'!
But they're just college kids, Ben! Go easy!
Hey! How are you--?
They outnumber us already. The math gets worse if we hold back.
Who's holding back?!

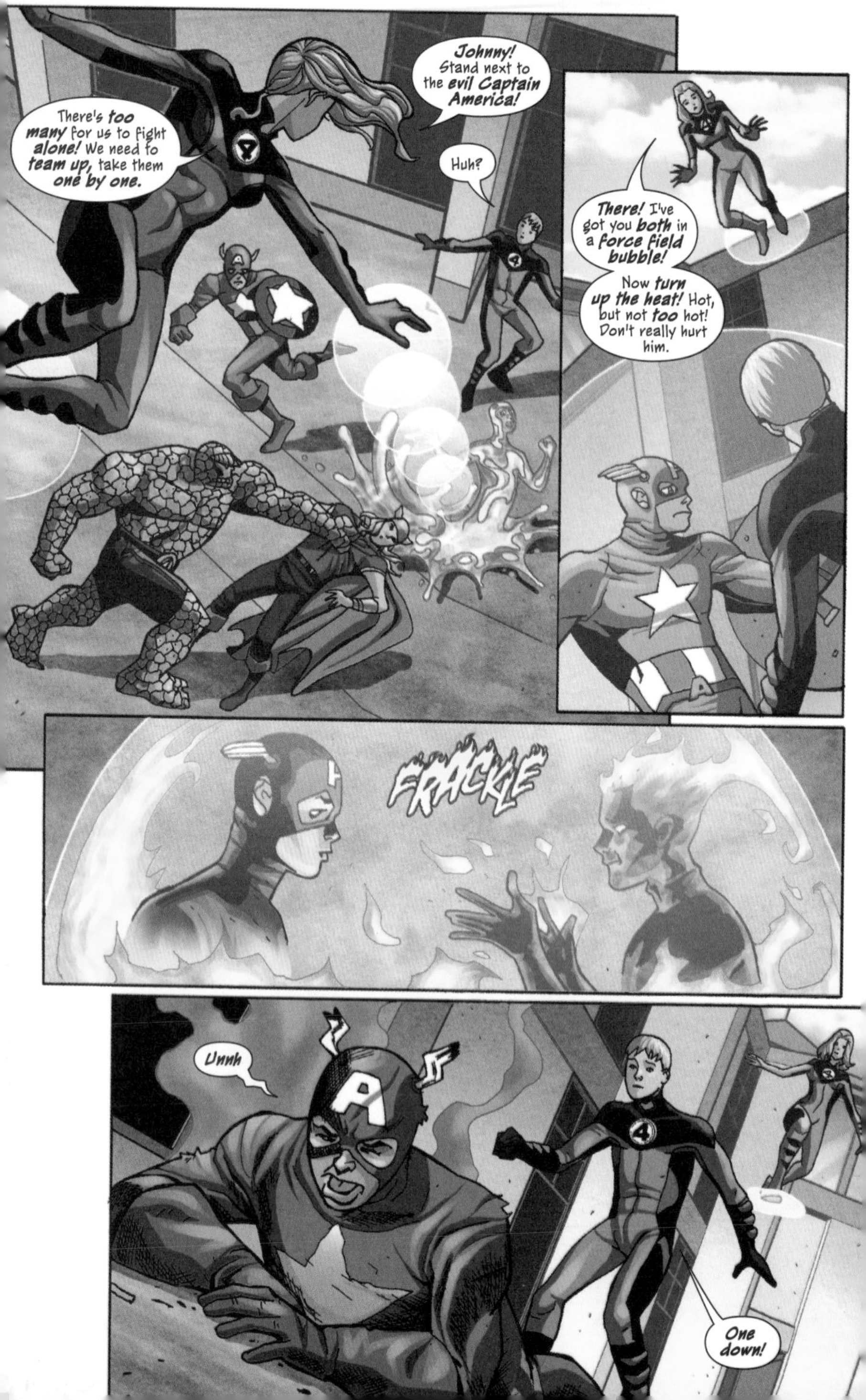
There's too many for us to fight alone! We need to team up, take them one by one.
Johnny! Stand next to the evil Captain America!
Huh?
There! I've got you both in a force field bubble!
Now turn up the heat! Hot, but not too hot! Don't really hurt him.
FRACKLE
Unnh
One down!

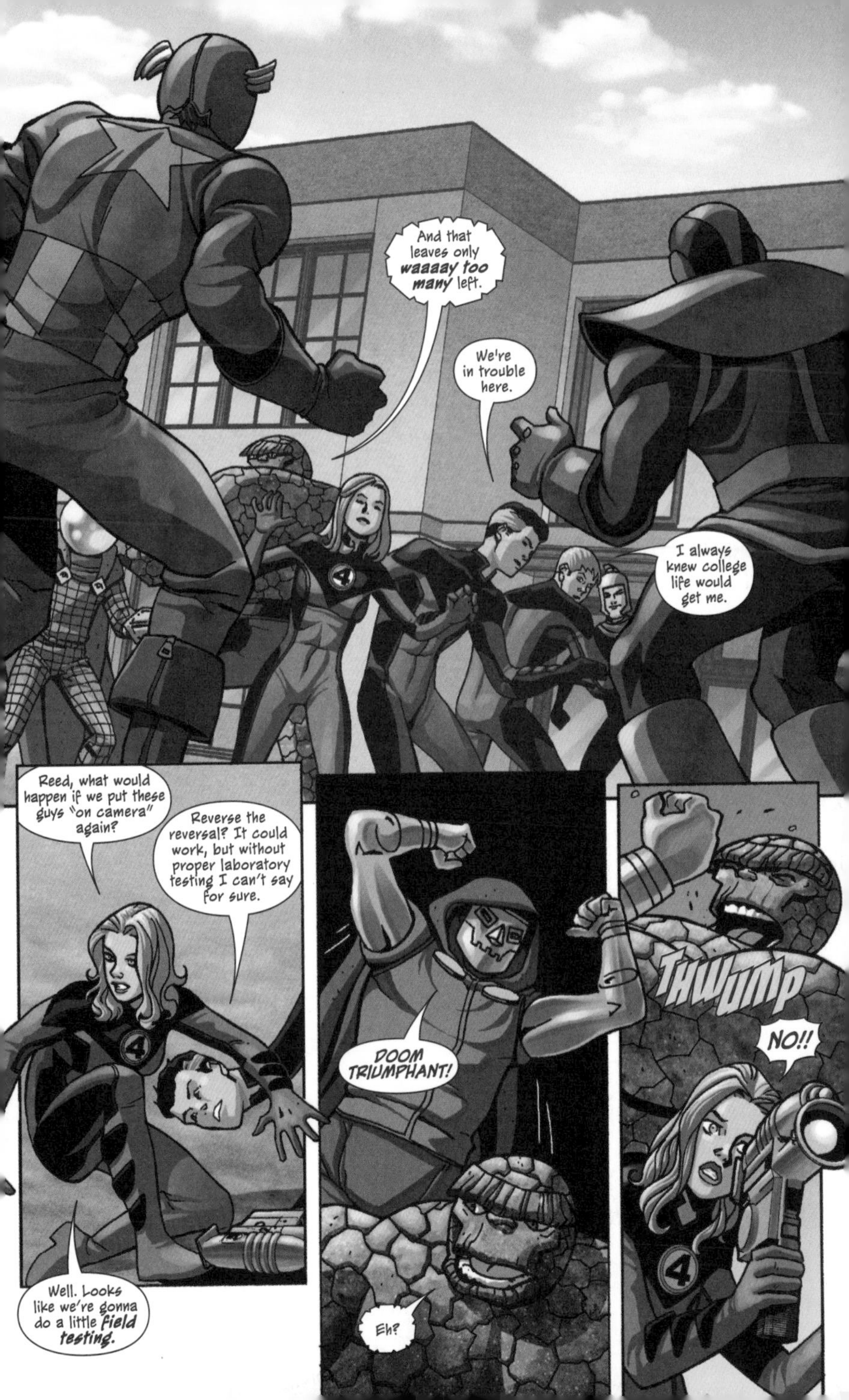

And that leaves only waaaay too many left.
We're in trouble here.
I always knew college life would get me.
Reed, what would happen if we put these guys "on camera" again?
Reverse the reversal? It could work, but without proper laboratory testing I can't say for sure.
Well. Looks like we're gonna do a little field testing.
DOOM TRIUMPHANT!
Eh?
THWUMP
NO!!

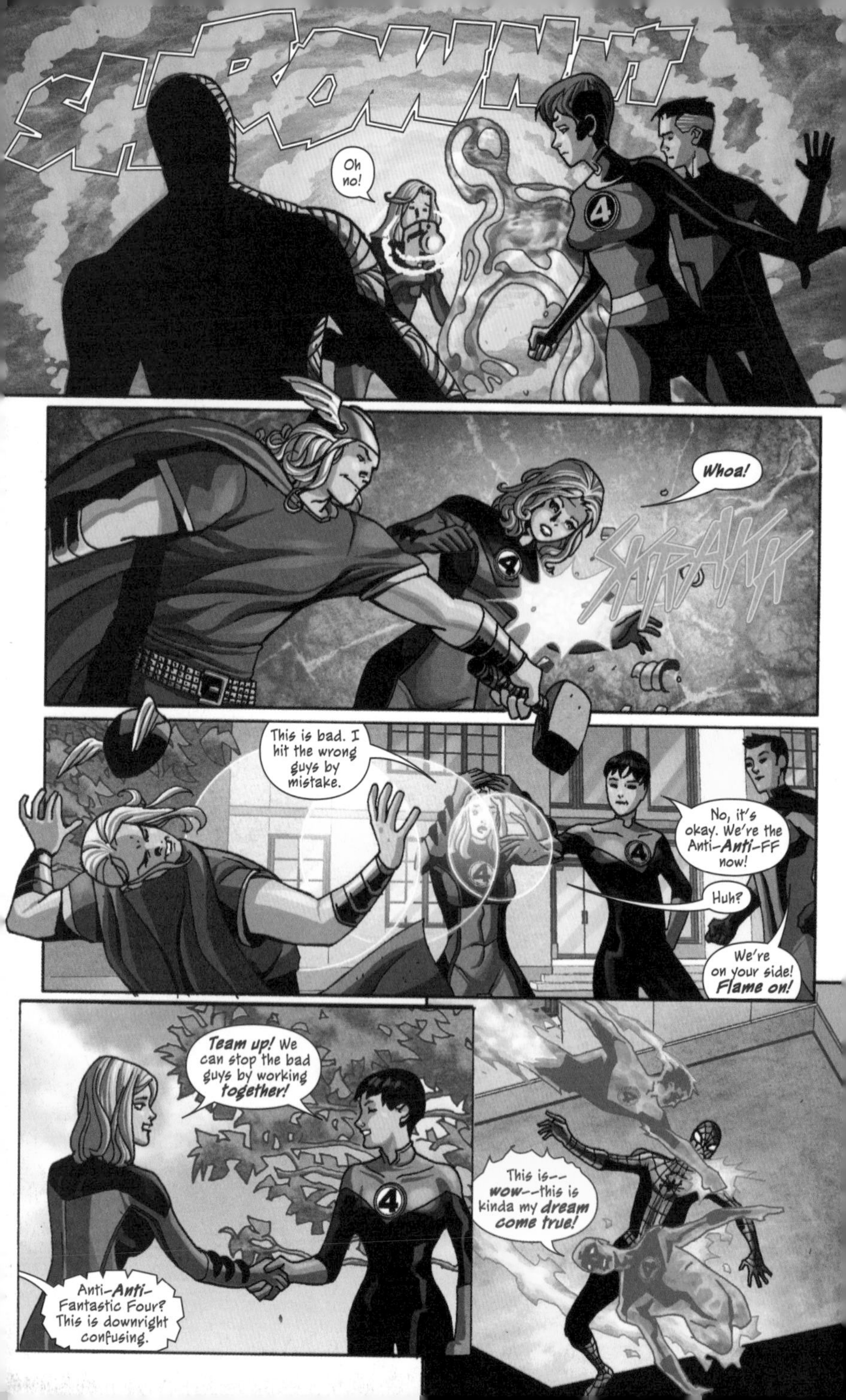
SHOOMM
Oh no!
Whoa!
SKRAKK
This is bad. I hit the wrong guys by mistake.
No, it's okay. We're the Anti-**Anti**-FF now!
Huh?
We're on your side! ***Flame on!***
Team up! We can stop the bad guys by working ***together!***
Anti-**Anti**-Fantastic Four? This is downright confusing.
This is-- ***wow***--this is kinda my ***dream come true!***

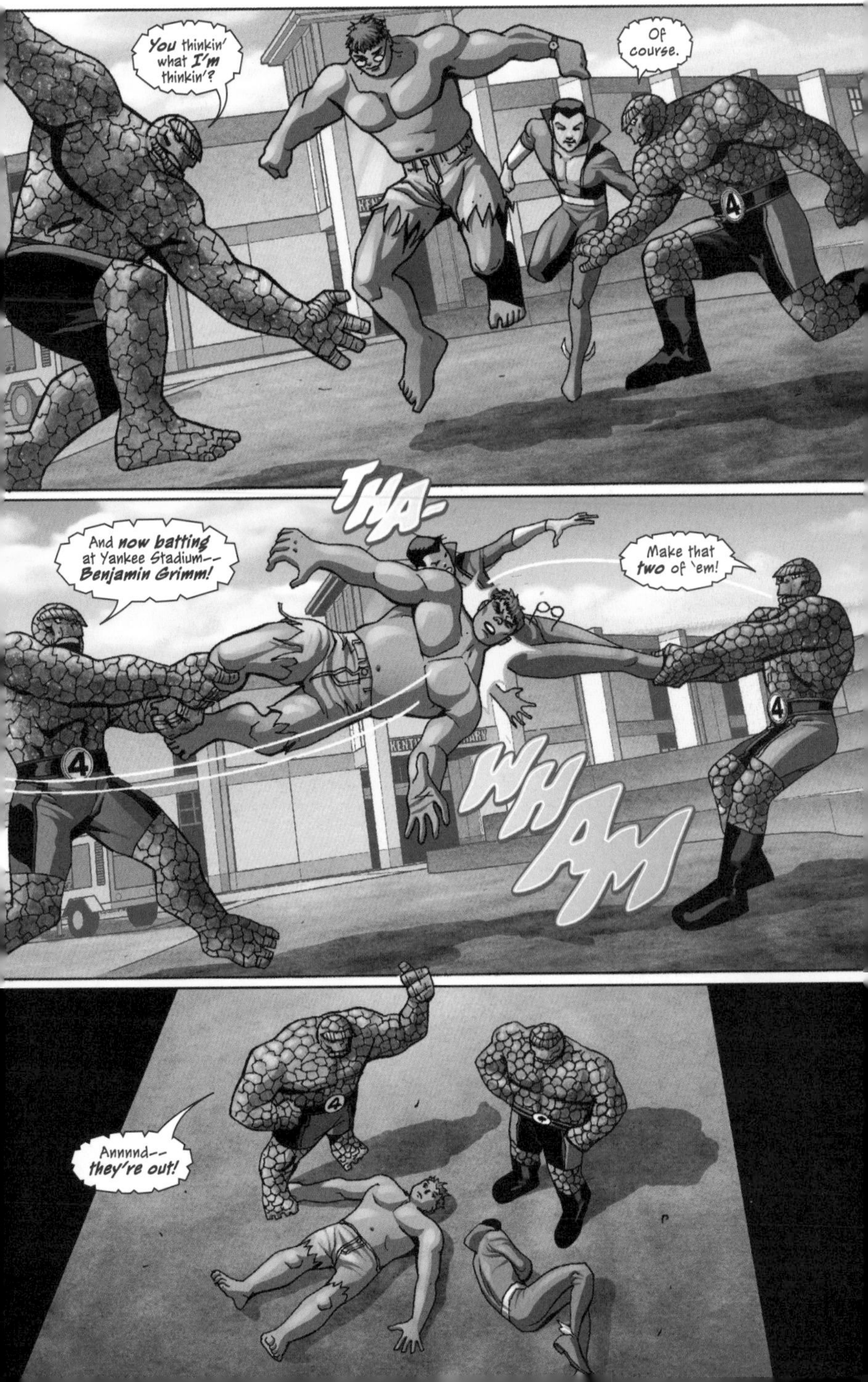
You thinkin' what I'm thinkin'?
Of course.
THA-
And now batting at Yankee Stadium-- Benjamin Grimm!
Make that two of 'em!
WHAM
Annnnd-- they're out!

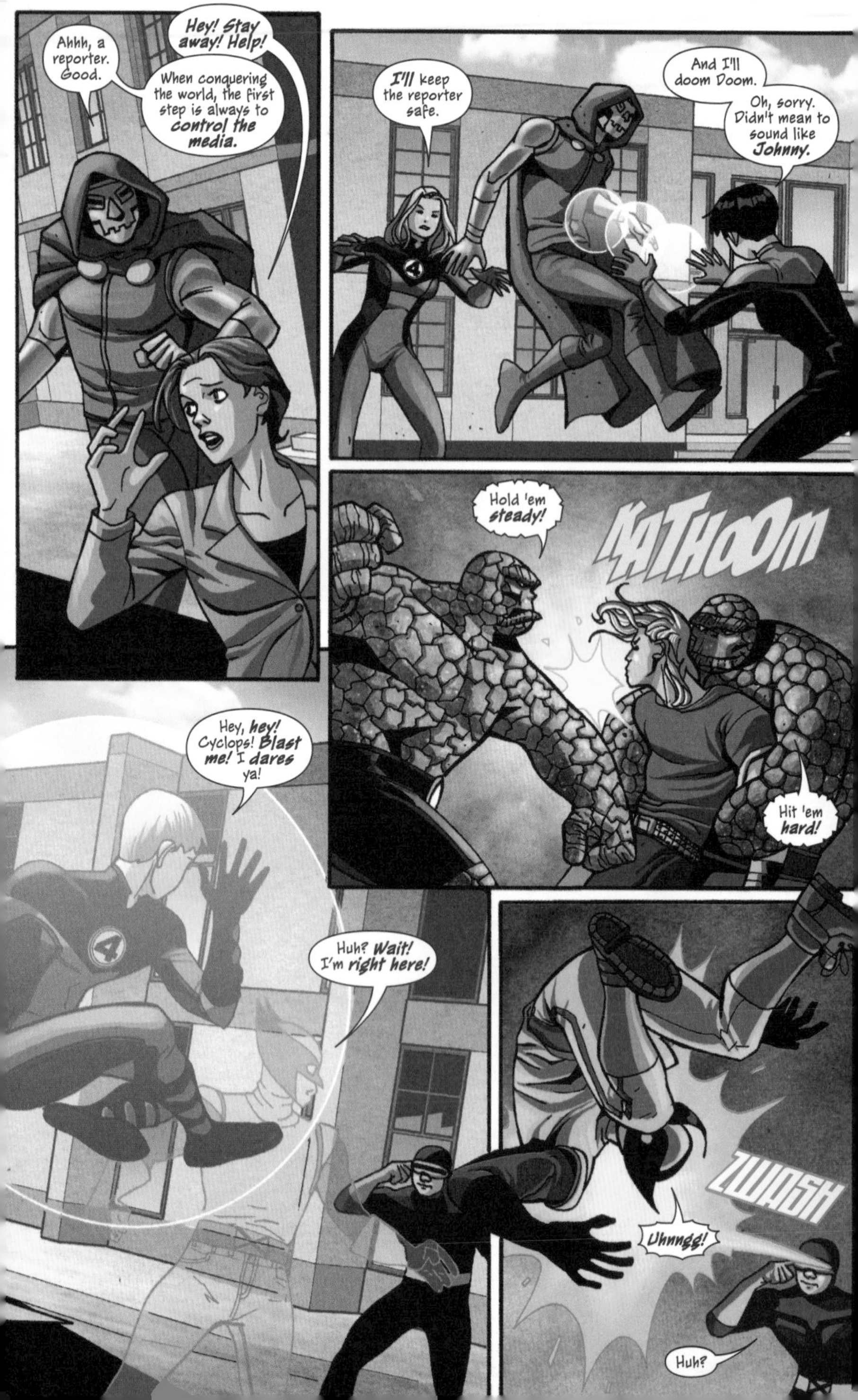
Ahhh, a reporter. Good.
Hey! Stay away! Help!
When conquering the world, the first step is always to control the media.
I'll keep the reporter safe.
And I'll doom Doom.
Oh, sorry. Didn't mean to sound like Johnny.
Hold 'em steady!
KATHOOM
Hit 'em hard!
Hey, hey! Cyclops! Blast me! I dares ya!
Huh? Wait! I'm right here!
ZWASH
Uhnngg!
Huh?

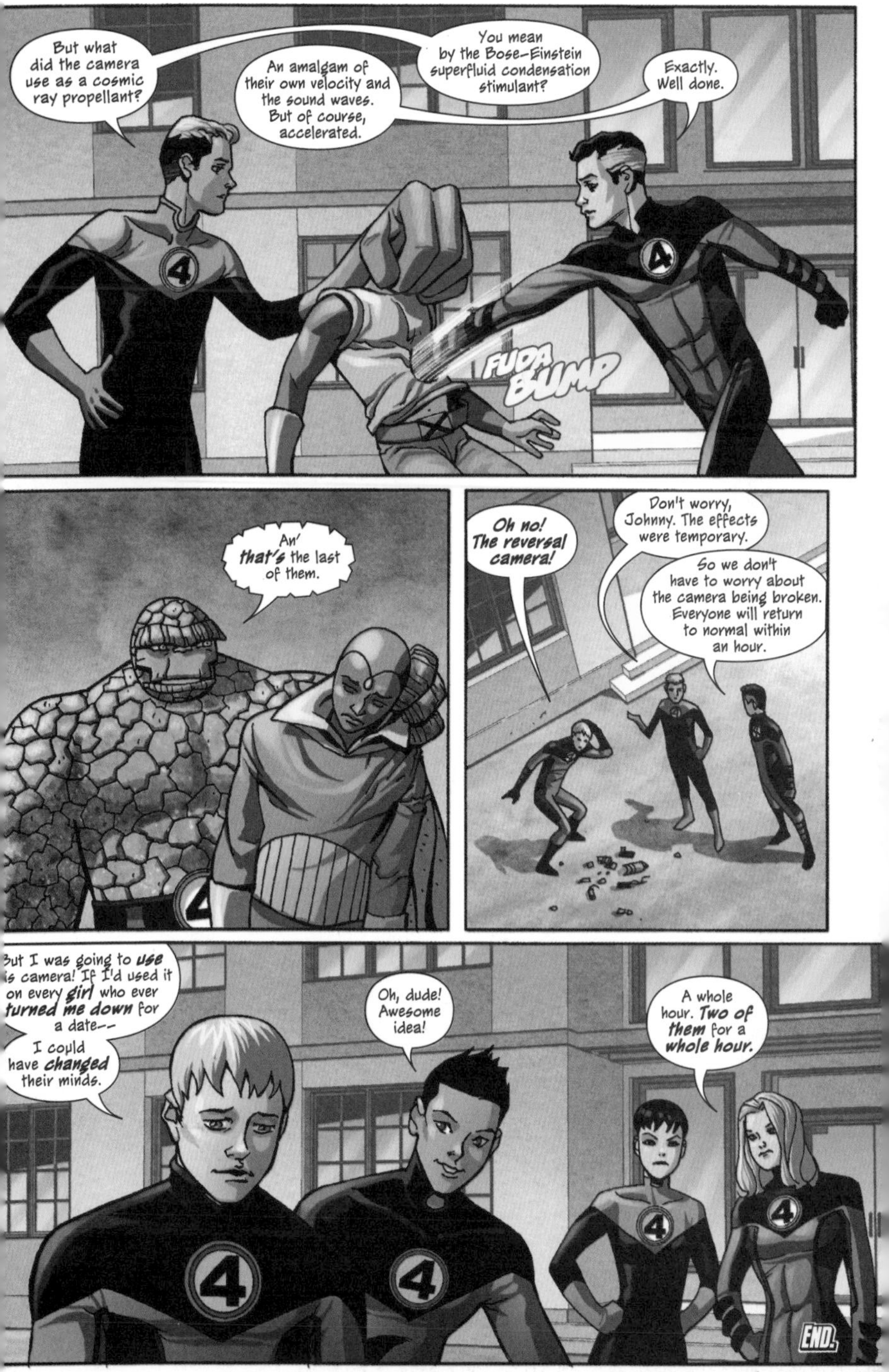

But what did the camera use as a cosmic ray propellant?
An amalgam of their own velocity and the sound waves. But of course, accelerated.
You mean by the Bose-Einstein superfluid condensation stimulant?
Exactly. Well done.
FUDA BUMP
An' that's the last of them.
Oh no! The reversal camera!
Don't worry, Johnny. The effects were temporary.
So we don't have to worry about the camera being broken. Everyone will return to normal within an hour.
But I was going to use is camera! If I'd used it on every girl who ever turned me down for a date--
I could have changed their minds.
Oh, dude! Awesome idea!
A whole hour. Two of them for a whole hour.
END.